Their Brazen Countess

LUSTFUL LORDS, BOOK SIX

SORCHA MOWBRAY

Published by Amour Press 2024, First Edition

Copyright © 2024 by Sorcha Mowbray

ISBN: 978-1-955615-22-8

Cover design from Fiona Jayde Media

Chapter Images from Illustration 13209099 / Victorian Vines © Freeskyblue | Dreamstime.com

A Note From Sorcha

Dear reader,

History is full of sex and joy, between people of all ages, all genders, all sexes—and just because they don't appear in the historical textbooks, that doesn't mean they didn't exist.

This story features people who understand love transcends society, and believe it or not, the laws of the time did not prevent the romance I've written in this story. If you're interested in details on the historical setting, make sure you stay until the end for my author's note!

And now, get ready for an incredible romance...

Chapter One

January 1862

Marion Thomas, Baron Lincolnshire, sucked in a sharp breath as he glanced down at the blonde woman prostrate between his splayed thighs.

His cock was currently lodged deep in the blonde's throat as her fingers delicately caressed his bollocks. Linc sank one hand into her perfectly coiffed blonde locks, dislodging more than a few hairpins, as his head lolled back against the chair. Pleasure pulsed through his body, rippling beneath his skin.

Across the room, Arthur Winterburn, Earl of Dunmere, was languidly prepping a woman's arse to take his cock. Linc watched eagerly as the man indolently stretched her with his fingers while using some salve to prepare for his passage.

Feeling his own arse clench with irrepressible need, Linc slipped the blonde woman off his cock and rose. "Grab your equipment, Jenny. I need you to fuck me tonight."

Jenny's eyes lit up as she rose to her feet and darted over to a cabinet in the Blue Room they currently occupied, the place draped in blues from ceiling to floor, from the two chaise longues to the extra-large ottoman and the canopied bed. After shedding his trousers, Linc crawled onto the resplendent bed on all fours and waited for Jenny to join him.

Matthew Derby, Marquess of Flintshire, and Grayson Powell, Viscount Wolfington, were busy entertaining a brunette, who appeared happily sandwiched between them. Flint was fucking her pussy as Wolf took her arse, the three of them moaning with no inhibitions.

Linc's gaze drifted toward Arthur and the redhead he was still preparing. He took in the man's mahogany hair and fair skin, which matched well with the woman who trembled beneath him. A rogue pang of jealousy speared through him as he watched Arthur breach her arse.

It had been months since he'd allowed a man to take him, and he missed the feel of masculine hands gripping his hips as someone thrust forcefully into him. Jenny was an enthusiastic lover, and always brought a great deal of energy when she fucked him—but it simply wasn't the same.

Linc watched Arthur for a few moments as he stroked his own cock: took in the way the man's arse and thighs clenched with each thrust into the redhead, relished the noises they made.

Arthur grunted and panted. "Take my cock deep, love." Then he slapped her backside. "God your arse turns a lovely red. It will look lovely with my seed dribbling from you. You want that, don't you?"

The woman moaned in response as he thrust once more.

Between the dirty talk and watching Arthur spank her, Linc felt a flush of warmth crawl up his neck and face.

"I've brought a friend with me. Now, on your hands and knees, my lord." Jenny's voice cut into Linc's observations. "She's a new girl at The Market, so she's a wee bit nervous about all this. Maggie, this is the lord we'll be servicing tonight."

He looked up to find she had brought a friend as stated. The girl stood with her gaze latched onto the floor and her hair hanging around her face, obscuring his view. While he often would prefer bedding a man, Linc still enjoyed women in the bedroom thoroughly. He liked the musky taste of a sweet pussy, the soft cries of their pleasure as they peaked, and of course, the tight clasp of their bodies.

Linc reached out and slid a finger under her chin, tipping her face up despite her slight resistance. "Let me see your face."

As she looked up at him, she seemed to wait for some harsh judgement, though she would get none from him. She wasn't what the Ton would call a Diamond of the First Water, but she was a pretty enough girl—and with a little coaching from some of the ladies of The Market, he was certain she would be a popular woman before long.

"Very nice. You've a pretty face. Don't hide it. Now if you'd let me, I'd like to lick your pussy while Jenny here takes care of me."

Maggie's eyes grew wide as she darted an uncertain glance at Jenny.

"If I thought you knew the first thing about shagging a man's arse, I'd trade places with you in a trice. The man's a god with his tongue," Jenny encouraged the woman as she shoved a salve covered finger in his arse the way she knew Linc preferred.

Linc groaned as he watched the new girl shed her shift and crawl onto the bed. By the time Jenny had three fingers stretching him out, he had Maggie's thighs spread and was leaning in for his first taste.

She was still shy and fairly new to servicing men, that much was clear. Despite his gentleness, she tensed up as Linc ran his tongue over her slit and gathered his first breath of her sweetness. He set about licking her in earnest as Jenny slid on the harness and dildo that would allow her to fuck him as he craved tonight. And Maggie? She was the icing on his cake.

Jenny pushed into him, sliding the leather covered false cock into his arse in slow measures as his tongue feasted on the new girl. The young woman whimpered as she sank her hands into his hair, pushing her hips up into his face.

The other woman was as deep as she could get inside of him before she slid out. Jenny worked in and out of him, pumping in long steady strokes as Linc concentrated on stroking his own cock with shaking fingers and pushing his tongue deep into Maggie. The woman moaned as she started to come as the sounds of the others finding their own peaks surrounded them.

He needed more.

Panting, Linc pulled the woman down his body, bringing her fully under him before sinking his cock into her still-convulsing quim. Jenny then allowed him to take over and set the rhythm as he pulled out of Maggie and impaled himself on her dildo, only to reverse course.

God, yes.

It was intense to the extreme to have his cock enveloped one moment and his arse filled the next, and yet something about it all was still...off.

His mind might be unsatisfied, but his body didn't know that. After a few strokes, Linc and Maggie both came. He was about to turn around and see to Jenny when he heard flesh slapping flesh.

"Fuck, that was amazingly dirty to watch." Arthur panted as he sank into Jenny's soaked cunny. "You three got me hard again after an amazing orgasm."

Linc's breath hitched in his chest as he greedily watched Arthur take Jenny. After all, their group was never shy about sharing partners. He tried not to imagine filling her from behind, feeling the other man's cock dragging over his. Arthur stroked into her, then bent over to suck on her breast as she moaned. Linc knew he was going to get hard again just watching Arthur take care of Jenny, and that didn't account for the little fantasy of his own.

"God, the way you fucked his arse...you filled him good, didn't you, Jenny?"

"Yes," she moaned. "He likes it hard. Rough."

"Mmmm. Likes the way you fuck him, does he—or will any cock do? Do you think he'd take my cock up his arse?"

Linc stilled as all the breath in his body left him. The thought of Arthur fucking him felt both very taboo and very, very tempting. The man seemed to have stamina for days, now that he was no longer attempting to drink the Thames dry.

But the man was Emily's brother. Lady Emmaline Brougham, who was married to his friend, Robert Cooper, the Earl of Brougham, asked them to look after him, keep an eye on him—not debauch him in completely fresh and illegal ways.

"Oh, I think he'd like it," Jenny moaned. "Don't—don't stop! Oh, God!"

She and Arthur exploded in a crescendo of sound that left Linc shaken, his mind unable to think of anything but having Arthur buried in his arse up to his sac...which was not a useful revelation, on the eve of them departing for Arthur's country house.

Sigh. It seemed he would be spending the holiday with his cock in hand trying to exorcise this new demon—because he absolutely would not be taking Arthur Winterburn, Earl of Dunmere, to his bed.

Chapter Two

A Week Later

A rthur Winterburn, Earl of Dunmere, inhaled the cold crisp air and focused on ignoring the very potent male standing next to him.

It was strange to think that he and Linc had been chummy for a few months now, even engaging in the Lustful Lords' usual activities at The Market fairly regularly. And then suddenly, in the midst of their most recent round of debauchery, his mouth had entirely gotten away from him.

"Do you think he'd take my cock up his arse?"

Now all he could think about was how Linc's mouth would feel wrapped around his cock. Who could blame him?

The unexpected thought had resulted in him walking around for the last week or so with a semi-erect cock. It was growing bloody awkward at times, especially now they were alone at Dunmere Manor, his country home in West Sussex.

"There, Arthur, across the way." Linc pointed then lifted his rifle. The sharp report of the rifle firing was followed by the loud squawking of birds and the flapping of wings as the birds took flight.

His own rifle sounded immediately after Linc's, adding to the kerfuffle as his matched retrievers bolted forward into the undergrowth.

"Good eye, old man." Arthur clapped Linc on the shoulder as they waited for the dogs. A frisson of awareness shot up his arm and had him jerking his hand back as he inhaled softly.

The pair reappeared each one carrying their prize. As they dropped the birds, the dogs were rewarded with treats and pats.

"Old man," Linc scoffed. "I'm but two years older than you! I'd take you in a fight, and handily."

Arthur laughed. "I'll take that challenge." He started to remove his outer coat, the anticipation of wrestling with Linc making his cock half hard before he'd even removed one arm from his sleeve.

"Put your coat back on, you great fool." Linc looked up at the sky across the meadow. "Can't you see the low clouds, feel the moisture in the air? It'll be snowing soon. We should head back to the manor before we get caught out here freezing our arses off."

"I thought you were supposed to be the jovial one," Arthur couldn't help but grumble as he pulled his coat back on. His disappointment was an unexpectedly sharp stab to the chest.

He couldn't avoid wondering what Linc would feel like beneath his fingertips. Would he be sinewy muscle? Or would he feel softer, more pliable? He'd seen the man naked more times than he could count, but seeing and touching were two entirely different things.

Linc grinned. "I am the jovial one, but I also have a healthy sense of self preservation, which is why Cooper trusts me to make sure you don't get yourself killed out here. Besides, Emily would never forgive him—or me."

"Bah." Arthur grumbled as they turned to head home to the warmth of a fire and a hot meal. "Emily worries far too much for a younger sister."

"A younger sister who managed to keep both you and your estate from penury, despite your best efforts." Linc had the gall to wink at him. The cheek!

"If you don't mind, I prefer not to be reminded of the lengths my little hellion of a sister went to all to accomplish just that. It's bloody embarrassing that I was too self-absorbed to notice what the blazes she was up to." Arthur wanted to cast up his accounts just thinking about how she'd prowled around London's ballrooms stealing jewelry to keep them out of hock. Good God! She could have been accosted. Or molested. Or discovered, which she very nearly was.

Thank heavens for Robert Cooper, Earl of Brougham's, timely intervention.

Linc stopped walking and examined him with a close eye. "Do you think yourself likely to repeat your mistakes?"

"Not at all. I should like to think I could never be so self-absorbed again." He hoped. No, he would never be that way.

His companion turned and resumed walking. "Then there you are. You've learned from the experience."

The dogs bounded ahead of them, periodically turning their heads back as though wondering what was taking so long. Despite the less than subtle prodding by the hounds, he and Linc continued at their leisurely pace.

As they arrived at the manor house, a gentle snow had begun to fall just as Linc had predicted. By the time they had cleaned up, donned clean clothes, and settled in by the fire, the snow was coming down in a thick snowstorm which promised to leave a blanket of white.

The flames of the fire danced in the grate as Arthur eased back into his seat and stretched his legs out. "Assuming we aren't snowed in, we can try stalking some pheasant along my eastern boundary. My neighbors along there have been there for decades and have no concerns if we crossover in our roamings."

Linc swirled a snifter of brandy. "That sounds excellent." The fire crackled, the only noise breaking the silence. "So. Tell me. How are you doing, with all the changes you've gone through recently?"

"Do you mean letting my old pals go?" Arthur asked, knowing that was what the blighter was asking, but stalling for time to sort out his thoughts.

"Certainly. You've given up your circle of friends, curtailed your past pursuits in a rather dramatic fashion, and in all honesty, sobered up significantly," Linc said carefully. "It's no small feat. Add to all of that the loss of your parents and the more recent marriage of your sister...much has changed for you. You've done well."

Arthur chuckled, his cheeks heating slightly at the praise. "I suppose it's not a few small changes. But once I understood what was happening with Emily it was all quite easy to change. I'm ashamed to say...well, I was so busy wallowing in my own despair and loss over my parents—not to mention my gambling problem—I quite forgot about my sister. In truth, I was overwhelmed by all of it. My father had tried to show me how to run the estate but he was no deft hand himself—as we discovered, he already had the family halfway to the poorhouse. What little advice he had bothered to gift me was entirely unsound, as you all saw."

Linc nodded. "I'm sure it was a lot to bear. I'm just glad Cooper found Emily, and by virtue of their connection, found you in time to save you both."

"I too. It has been an...enlightening journey in many ways." Arthur couldn't help but think back to their last night at The Market once again. His cock stirred, and once more he wondered about the feelings he found stirring within when it came to one particular Lustful Lord.

Feelings he absolutely had to ignore. His family had endured enough scandal already. The last thing Emily needed was for him to suddenly find other men attractive. Not to mention, such a thing would not aid his already sparse marriage prospects.

No, he could not afford to think of Linc in such a manner, not anymore. Well, not after tonight. Perhaps just a few more thoughts.

Chapter Three
The Next Day

Josephine Marie Fulton—or Jo, to her friends—drew in a deep breath, welcoming the sharp pain of the cold crisp air that came with the pristine blanket of snow that covered the ground. Hidden in the folds of her cloak she clutched a most titillating book she had discovered in her deceased husband's collection: Pleasant Polly and the One Thousand and One Naughty Nights. At first, she had thought it was simply a retelling of the familiar stories. When she started reading, she discovered the first story recounted how a serving woman was detained and pleasured orally by two men until the sun rose.

It was most definitely not the same book. This one was far more intriguing.

She had tucked it away safely as she doled out her husband's estate according to his wishes. The settlement he'd left Jo allowed her to return to her parents with a hefty bank account to live on...or so she'd thought. It appeared her father had very different ideas about her future. Ideas that included marriage—again.

She was thankfully now alone after another tedious breakfast featuring another lecture on why she must remarry. Jo was four and twenty, and a widow to boot! Certainly she was not of age yet, but it was dreadfully unfair that her father still had control over her finances.

Jo sighed and relished finding a quiet spot to devour another stirring story from her naughty book. As she tromped through the wooded countryside, she luxuriated in the solitude and peace that came with the fresh snow. Her father would never deign to follow her out into the frigid temperatures, so she was assured of plenty of uninterrupted reading time. But first she had to find the old gamekeeper's hut she had maintained diligently until her marriage to the now late Mr. Fulton, five years earlier. Hopefully it wasn't in too terrible a state.

In the distance she heard a rustling. A bird? A small animal?

No, it was too loud for that. Nerves jangling at what she might meet, she found a thicket of bushes to hide behind until she could assure herself it was nothing dangerous. Twigs snapped, snow crunched, and then—voices.

"Would you bloody well watch where you are going?" a man's voice snapped.

"It's not my fault you're so blasted tall. I didn't know that branch would snap back and hit you in the damn face," the shorter and darker of the two grumbled as he stepped forward. "Where is the fucking path? Or a deer trail? Anything to make this nightmare easier."

Jo snickered, unable to help herself—and the men stopped.

"Did you hear that?" the dark-haired one asked.

"Hear what?"

"I swore I heard someone laughing at us."

"Good God, Arthur. Are you hallucinating from the cold?" The taller one seemed truly concerned for a moment.

The dark-haired one, Arthur, growled and pushed his friend away. "Bugger off, you lob cock. I'm not bloody hallucinating, I tell you I heard someone snickering." He turned and faced the bushes where Jo still crouched. "Whoever you are, come out right now."

She did no such thing, staying where she was. She didn't know who these men were and had no intention of gaining that knowledge by exposing herself.

With her naughty book clutched to her chest, Jo squatted lower behind the bush, hoping her dull green cloak would blend in with the foliage and branches. Though...the men were very handsome. Her mind drifted to the scene in her book where two men kissed as Polly watched. Her breath hitched as she imagined these two men kissing.

Only then did she notice a little tickle on her nose.

Oh, no.

She wrinkled it and wriggled it, trying to make the sensation stop without moving her arm. Finally, it seemed to cease.

Then the tall one sighed. "Really, you can stop the charade. We're in the middle of nowhere. There isn't a soul here but us."

"Achoo!" The sneeze burst out of her, declared Jo's presence as assuredly as if she'd sprang up dancing from behind the bush. The force of her body's reaction caused her to topple over onto her backside, dropping her book, feet shooting forward, and making the bush shake.

"What was that?" the tall one blurted out.

"Bloody hell!" sounded Arthur at the same time.

Jo had just gotten to her knees and was struggling to get to her feet in the snow when two pairs of black boots appeared in her vision. Without looking up, she sighed. "I don't suppose you two would consider ignoring me and carrying on with whatever you were doing here?"

A rather large hand appeared in her field of vision.

"And leave a lady in obvious distress? I think not." The tall one waited patiently, waiting for her to take his proffered assistance.

Eventually good manners won out, and she took his hand.

The unnamed man appeared fashionably lean and trim, but he pulled her up with an ease belied by the superior cut of his winter coat. No reedy waif, she was the picture of the ideal Victorian woman with her ample breasts and full curves. Despite that, she had a tendency to shun a tightly cinched corset, and...well, she hadn't often heard herself described as attractive. At least, not by the men she'd been exposed to in her life, such as her deceased husband.

The man steadied her by holding her shoulders, and she couldn't deny the shiver of awareness that skated down her spine as she finally looked up. His pale blue eyes seemed to devour her as she stood there, caught in his thrall. Standing securely on her feet once more, he released her shoulders and took a step back.

Jo felt the loss of his touch immediately. It was strange; when her husband had touched her, all she could do was count the moments until he released her—yet this stranger's absence left her feeling almost bereft. *How odd.*

A throat cleared. "An interesting choice of reading material." The man called Arthur was gazing down at her book, clutched in his hands—and open!

Mortification swept over Jo like a warm wave of air in the Pellingham's cramped ball room at the last parish dance. She was certain her face had turned a hideous shade of red, but alas there was little she could do about it—with the exception of shoving her head into the nearest snow bank. "Do not be rude, sir, that is not your book."

"I was merely conveying the fascinating nature of your choice of reading materials." He looked up at her. "Particularly for someone such as yourself."

She let her head tip to the side a little. Curiosity had words bubbling from her lips. "Someone such as me? How so?"

The man's cheeks reddened, and she suspected it had little to do with the cold. He cleared his throat. "Um...well. Someone who looks so young and lovely. And obviously gently reared."

Her heart stalled in her chest at the word lovely, and then she laughed. Loud and long. When she finally caught her breath Jo managed to explain, "I'm afraid you have me confused with someone else. I am neither particularly young nor gently reared. Much to my parents' dismay I have struggled under the yoke of domestication my entire life. I appreciate the compliment, I do. But you, my good sir, are quite wrong about me."

The blonde man stepped forward and bowed. "My lady, please let me set this conversation back on course. I am Marion Thomas, Baron Lincolnshire, and this mutton head is my friend Arthur Winterburn, Earl of Dunmere."

She couldn't help the small gasp that escaped her. They were true nobility! And Dunmere—why, he was her neighbor. She'd known of him as a girl, had spied on him more than once when he was swimming. But they had never met since his family was so rarely in residence and even when they were, he was so much older than her. The boy she had once caught a glimpse of was now...all man.

"It's a pleasure to meet you both." She curtsied. "I am Mrs. Josephine Marie Fulton. My father owns Marshall House."

"A pleasure to meet you." Dunmere swept a bow at nearly the same time as Lincolnshire.

"But I feel we are all going to be the best of friends, so you must call me Linc, as all my friends do." The smile he flashed at her nearly stole her breath. His blue eyes sparkled with mischief which absolutely delighted her.

"Then you must call me Jo." She couldn't hide her smile, nor did she want to.

"Well, I refuse to be left out of this business. Call me Arthur. Dunmere is so drab."

She didn't quite agree with him, but was not one to ignore a request when it came to someone's name. "Very well then, Arthur it is."

"Excellent!" Linc plucked the open book from Arthur's hands and handed it to her. "I believe this is yours, Jo." He hesitated a moment. "Jo the Wood Sprite."

She laughed softly. "No, I'm not a mythical creature. Just a woman seeking a quiet place to...to read a book." She hated that her cheeks had heated once more.

"Well, please do not let us delay any longer." Arthur smiled at her. "Unless you'd enjoy the company."

She wrinkled her nose. "I dare say you two are trouble, but I think I would enjoy getting to know you both. Stay." Jo stopped and looked around. "Unless of course you have somewhere you need to be."

Both of their faces lit up with pleasure. "We are precisely where we need to be, I think." Arthur crooked an arm toward her. "Shall we find a place to sit and talk?"

"That would be lovely." Jo placed her hand on his arm and looked up to find Linc on her other side with his arm similarly crooked. Pleased by all the attention, she tucked her hand into his arm as well.

They found a log and the men cleared a spot for her to perch. Then they book ended her and the three of them chatted for what seemed like hours. The conversation was easy, their laughter light, and Jo realized she had not smiled like this in...well, in years.

Finally, Jo shivered and knew it was time for her to head home. It would be growing dark soon, and she could not remain out here forever, even if she might wish to. As diverting as it had been chatting with the handsome lords, she would be expected at home. There were chores to see to or she'd suffer an overly harsh punishment.

Jo stood and turned to face both of them. "It was lovely meeting you both."

They stood up, almost as one.

"We enjoyed meeting you, Jo." Arthur placed his hand over his heart and bowed.

Good heavens, these two must devastate the London debutants.

"When may we see you again?" Linc asked as he stepped forward. "I fear I shall suffer a deep despair if you do not say tomorrow." His jovial tone had her laughing at his dramatics.

Jo mock sighed as if so very put upon. "I suppose I could see you all tomorrow. I certainly wouldn't wish to be responsible for you to enter a decline of despair." She looked at Arthur. "Do you know where the old gamekeeper's hut is on our property?"

"I think I know well enough to find it," he nodded. "But why don't we simply call on you at home?"

She hesitated. Could she have them meet her there?

No, her father would force the issue of marriage immediately. It would be mortifying for them to come there and have her father sound them out immediately for marriage. Besides, it had been terribly hard not to imagine herself pressed between them in the most inappropriate manner. She supposed it served her right for her choice in reading materials.

"I think it's best if we steer clear of my parents for now. I'll see you at the hut around noon?" Jo looked from one man to the other, something she had never felt before bubbling inside her.

"Yes!" Linc grinned. "Noon tomorrow."

Jo leaned forward and pressed an impulsive kiss to Linc's cheek before turning to do the same to Arthur. "I'll see you both then." And then she fled before she did something truly inappropriate and asked them to kiss her...both of them.

Chapter Four

The Next Day

Arthur and Linc set out once again to go hunting, but not before asking Arthur's housekeeper to pack a picnic basket. She, of course, stuffed it with enough food to feed four, which was perfect as they could share their luncheon with their quarry.

It took Arthur a little longer than he liked to remember where the bloody gamekeeper hut was. But finally they found it, once they spotted the smoke piping up from the chimney.

With a knock on the door, they waited until Jo's voice called out, "Come in!"

They opened the door to find her bent over as she fiddled with the fire across the room. They looked at each other and grinned before Arthur said, "That is certainly a fine way to greet someone, Jo."

"Oh!" she shot straight up and spun around, her face beet red.

Arthur couldn't be sure if her coloring was from the heat of the fireplace, being bent over, or because she understood the innuendo of his remark. Perhaps all three?

"Hello there! I wasn't sure you two would come."

Linc let one eyebrow lift. "If you weren't sure who was at the door, why would you have called for them to enter?"

Jo chuckled. "I was certain it was you once you knocked. Who else would knock on that door in the middle of the forest? I just wasn't certain you two would come at all, after the way we met yesterday."

"Of course we were going to come. How often does one get an invitation to be friends with a Wood Sprite?" Linc smiled and winked at her.

"Oh, hush. You know very well I am just a woman and nothing more. Now come in and take your coats off, I've got a pleasant fire going to keep us warm."

"Excellent!" Arthur took off his coat, hung it on a peg by the door, and moved by the fire. "We brought luncheon." He set the basket down by his feet.

"How kind of you." Jo appeared pleased, but then looked around with a frown. "I'm afraid it will have to be something of a picnic. I had not realized there wasn't a stick of proper furniture left in this hut."

Linc walked over to the one trunk tucked into a corner of the hut and opened it. "Ah ha! I have found some old blankets in here. All is not lost."

"Well, at least we won't have to sit on your very fine coats," Jo quipped as she bustled over and reached into the trunk.

The first blanket she pulled out was so moth-eaten it barely qualified as a blanket, even in a bachelor's estimation. The next one was in a little better condition. By the fourth blanket, she'd found something they could spread out on the floor and sit on. Linc had taken the decent blanket and was spreading it on the floor before the fire.

Only then did Jo gasp.

"What is it?" Arthur asked, stepping swiftly to her side.

Though he was curious at her exclamation, he found himself distracted by the way her breasts moved under her bodice. Was she not wearing a corset as well as crinoline? The lack of crinoline had been hard to miss when they'd entered, but the missing corset only now caught his attention. Their little Wood Sprite was truly a free spirit.

"Look at this lovely quilt." Jo lifted the folded fabric from the trunk and smoothed a hand over the worn pieces. Something about it appeared to tug at Jo's heartstrings. She looked almost sad for a moment. "Someone must be heartbroken over having lost this. It looks to be a family heirloom. Perhaps it was their wedding quilt?"

"It does seem to be well taken care of, if well used." Arthur felt the softness of the cotton and the thickness of the filling. He looked at her, curious about the way she was reacting to the quilt. "It would add a bit of cushioning to the thin blanket we found—unless you would prefer to return it to the chest?"

"I suppose it's been left behind. We might as well put it to good use." Jo shrugged and carried it over to where Linc had spread out the blanket and followed suit with the quilt.

They settled down and began laying out their lunch, sitting in a little triangle so they could all see each other. As they nibbled on the cold meats, cheese, and bread, while sipping wine, they shared more stories of their lives. Conversation flowed so freely, so easily, Arthur wondered how he could feel so intimate with a woman he had not known four and twenty hours prior.

"I've always been something of a bookworm. My mother despaired of me until my father arranged a marriage for me. I was forever reading books on history, and of course I love the gothic novels." Jo shivered. "They always have a darkness to them that is exciting. If I was a heroine in a gothic novel I would be the most intrepid heroine, plunging into the darkness, candle raised high as I discovered what lurked." She grinned.

Arthur cocked his head. "Did you not play with other children? I wonder now why we never saw much of each other."

She smiled softly. "I played with my sister Becca when we were younger. But as we both grew up, our interests diverged. She began spending more time with mother learning about running a household, beauty regimens, that sort of thing. I have always been more the type to wander in the woods and explore once my chores were done. What were you two like as children?"

Arthur noted her deflection, but easily went along with the shift in focus. "I was a typical rascal—always in trouble, always picking on my younger sister Emily, and then I was sent off to school. That's where I fell in with a raucous crowd and developed...let us say, some bad habits. Gambling, drinking to excess." His cheeks heated as he brought up his past.

"But all of that is behind him now. He's keeping much better company these days." Linc cut in and clapped him on the shoulder.

"Indeed. Thanks to my sister falling in love with one of your lot." He grinned at Linc. "Linc and his friends took me in and helped me break from the bad influences in my life. They've been instrumental in helping me turn the tides of my life." He looked down at his hands, unable to look at either Linc or Jo. "I'll forever be grateful for them all."

"It's what we do for each other. You became one of us the moment Cooper set his sights on Emily." Linc laughed. "As for me, I was a quiet lad."

Arthur snorted. "That must be a bald-faced lie."

Linc feigned affront. "You wound me sir!"

Jo and Arthur laughed, their chuckles mingling in the increasingly warm air.

"Very well. I was a happy child. I laughed and I played outside a great deal of the time." A sadness passed over Linc so quickly Arthur wasn't sure he actually saw it. Was there more to his story than he revealed? But Linc pressed on. "When I was cooped up in the house, I got lost in history books. I've always been fascinated by the Greeks and Romans."

Arthur couldn't help but wonder if that was when Linc began to consider his interest in men, in addition to being attracted to women. Perhaps not a question he could ask…

"Not unlike your book about Polly, Jo, I discovered treaties that opened my eyes to all of the erotic possibilities in the world." He shrugged one shoulder as if perhaps a bit uncomfortable with his own path to self-discovery.

The turn in conversation gave Arthur the perfect excuse to ask Jo the question he'd wanted to ask yesterday. "Speaking of possibilities—I'm curious. Jo, have you ever been kissed?"

She slanted a look at him. "I was married, Arthur."

He smiled indulgently. Then he asked again, his voice growing rougher as he imagined what he wanted to do. "Yes, but have you ever been properly kissed?"

She hesitated, glanced from Linc to him. "Well, when you ask like that, it…it makes me think that perhaps I have not."

The fire crackled and popped in the silence as her face turned a delightful shade of pink.

Arthur wondered what she might be thinking. Had her thoughts strayed to the naughty book she'd been reading yesterday? Hope bloomed, but this was Victorian England, not Paris, France.

Jo swallowed as her chin tipped up ever so slightly as if in invitation. "Would you like to show me?"

Linc inhaled sharply next to him, but said nothing.

Arthur leaned forward and reached up, cupping her face in his hand. "I would very much like to do that. Would you like me to kiss you? Or perhaps you would prefer Linc to do it?" He felt the need to give her the choice, though he wanted to be the one to show her what a proper kiss could be like.

"I'd like you to kiss me."

He darted a worried glance at Linc, who sat there perfectly still but for a slight nod. This may not be The Market, but that did not mean they could not enjoy watching.

She shifted her gaze to Linc. "And...and then I'd like you to kiss me as well."

Arthur's cock throbbed in his wool trousers as her words sank in. *She wanted them both.* "I think we can accommodate that," he responded as he cast a confirming glance at Linc, who nodded.

No time to waste. Arthur leaned forward and slipped his hand from her cheek to the back of her neck to draw her closer. When he settled his lips on hers, she inhaled softly but did not tense and did not pull away. She was eager and willing, though beyond innocent even as a widow.

He slanted his lips along hers until she relaxed into him, then he slid his tongue along the seam of her lips. With a soft gasp of surprise, Jo opened wider, allowing him to slip inside to taste her sweetness. With a soft moan, her hands found his chest and latched onto his lapels. Following his lead, their tongues twined and tangled as he explored her mouth, and she responded in kind, his passion matched by her own.

Finally Arthur pulled back, allowing both of them to catch their breath.

"Oh, my." Jo nearly whispered the words. "Is it always like that?"

Arthur's heart pounded in his chest as his cock throbbed in unison. "No, not always. Only when it's special."

She angled to face Linc, eager anticipation shone in her eyes.

"Come here, my little Wood Sprite." Linc crooked his finger at her.

She moved toward him and unabashedly reached up to take hold of his jacket as she had Arthur's. Linc slipped an arm around her back and leaned down to sweep her into a kiss.

Arthur watched them, the sight deeply erotic. Linc had pulled Jo into his lap and angled her so she sat between them. Arthur leaned forward and pressed a kiss to the back of her neck as his hands eagerly spanned her waist. He couldn't help but enjoy the feel of her uncorseted curves in his hands.

Pressing up against her back, he brought his lips near her ear. "May we loosen your gown, Jo? We'd very much like to see your breasts."

Linc groaned as he pulled back from their kiss to let her respond.

"I don't know." She hesitated. "I-I want to, but I know I shouldn't. I only just met you both."

Arthur bit back his groan. "Widows take lovers all the time." He dropped a kiss on her neck.

Linc leaned back in and placed a kiss on her neck as he caressed her breast through her bodice. He murmured against her skin, "You've never known proper pleasure. Let us show you."

Jo seemed to melt against Linc. "Yes, please," she panted softly.

Linc turned her around to face Arthur and he promptly captured her lips with his once again. As he plunged into her warm depths, Linc worked on loosening her gown. Arthur sank his fingers into her hair and reveled in the fact that he had all her sweetness on his tongue, and a hint of spice from Linc. His head spun as their tongues dueled. She was learning quickly and becoming less shy with each passing moment. Then her gown dipped and a linen covered breast spilled into one of his hands. The other was cupped by Linc as he kissed and sucked on the flesh at her neck and shoulder.

Jo's nipple pebbled under his fingertips, growing hard as he plucked and twisted it. Her breathing grew more labored, the need to be inside her growing with each passing moment. But that was not where they were headed. He was certain, without having discussed it, that this would go no further than the two gentlemen giving her pleasure—doing only as they had promised.

Jo pulled back from him, ending their kiss as she whimpered with delight. Arthur leaned over and captured her nipple in his mouth and sucked through the thin linen. Linc's hands cupped both breasts, holding them up for Arthur as he moved from one to the other.

Then Jo pulled his face up and cupped each of their cheeks. "Will...will you two kiss? I-I read about it in my book and would very much like to see two men kiss." She bit her lip and waited.

Linc's gaze clashed with Arthur's as if he was seeking approval. The moment felt heavy, tense, as if they both knew that there was no coming back from this one moment. Everything would change.

Then slowly, wordlessly, they moved together until their lips pressed together in a tentative kiss, each keeping a hand on Jo while she watched.

Arthur's heart hammered in his chest as their tongues tangled in a passionate kiss that grew more and more intense with each heartbeat. He'd been dreaming of this for weeks, perhaps months, if he was honest.

When they finally broke apart, they both looked at Jo. She sat there, eyes wide and mouth in a small round O of surprise.

"That was incredibly erotic. I did not know two men kissing could be so arousing." Jo's pulse raced, her nipples ached for their touch again, and her core throbbed with need.

This was so much more than what she'd read in her book, and so much more than what she'd imagined.

Linc growled, "All of this is arousing—you are arousing. Now lay back, Jo. Let us show you what genuine pleasure comprises."

She did as directed and lay back on the quilt, heedless of the remnants of their lunch. The two handsome men moved to each side of her, where they leaned down and sucked one of her nipples into their mouths simultaneously. Her hands

flew to their heads, whether to push them away or hold them
closer, she wasn't sure, the pleasure was so intense. It grew
into a pulse of desire that raced through her body from the
heat of their mouths straight to her pussy.

As Jo lay there lost in sensation, she nearly missed the moment the cool air hit her thighs—but there was no missing
the brush of a finger over her slick flesh between her legs.
Then there was another touch, whirling over her opening.
The passion bombarded her from all directions as these two
men showed her what it was to be pleasured.

A feeling of restlessness coalesced in Jo's belly then lower,
growing as they continued to rub over her small bundle of
nerves. A finger slid deep inside her, long and thick. Then
a second finger joined it, filling her as another finger continued to circle over her nub. The fullness built until she
thought she was going to burst.

Only then Linc did bite down on her nipple as one of them
pinched her clit.

Jo's world exploded into a thousand points of light as she
arched up off the floor, nearly throwing them off her body.
"Yes! Oh God. Linc! Arthur!"

"Come for us, that's it, Jo." Arthur's baritone rumbled
through her, stroking her sensitive nerves and melding with
the aftershocks of her orgasm as they continued to stroke
her body.

Slowly the spasms gentled until the pair of them settled
down on the floor next to her, nuzzling and kissing her neck.
She wasn't sure what deity she had pleased to have these men
drop into her life, but she hoped they remained forever, or
at least for a while.

Nothing good in her life ever lasted forever, not when her father was plotting. For now, they were her little secret. Her respite in the storm of her life. The only thing she wanted to know now was, when could she see them again?

Chapter Five

L inc and Arthur sat in the gamekeeper's hut and waited. It had been two days since they'd first met Jo there and opened up a new host of possibilities for the three of them.

They had come to the hut each of the last two days both in hopes she would come again and to bring some much needed amenities. The first day, they used a dogcart to bring an old bed from storage. It wasn't fancy, but it would fit the three of them laying side-by-side. They were quite pleased once they'd moved it in the hut and settled near the fire. It dominated the space, but there was room for a small table and some chairs so they could sit and eat together.

Yet Jo had never appeared.

The next day, they had brought the table and chairs. Linc and Arthur worked together to bring the battered table into the room.

"I think the bed may need to move over a bit if we want the table to squeeze in near the fire." Linc pointed to a spot close to the fire but also close to the bed, gazing at the available space. Would it all fit?

"I don't know, perhaps we keep the bed closer and let the table be farther back." Arthur pointed to the space toward the back of the hut.

"But Jo will get cold when we aren't in the bed." Linc looked at the space again and considered how it could all fit comfortably. "What if we move the bed back a bit? Then we can fit the table in nearer the fire."

Arthur looked at it all and sighed. "Let's try it your way."

Linc nodded and together they shifted the bed back until the table was able to slide in. "See, now we can have the benefit of the fire when we are at the table and in the bed. And even better, we shouldn't be too warm in the bed." He grinned.

"You're right. I really should listen to you, I suppose." Arthur shoved a hand through his hair, causing the ends to stand up.

Linc resisted the urge to smooth the strands down. They hadn't discussed their kiss from the other day, and it seemed Arthur preferred to keep it that way.

Not that Linc could blame him. It would be awful if that one kiss ruined everything. With Arthur's sister, Emily, married to Robert Cooper, Earl of Brougham, Arthur wasn't going anywhere. Besides that, he had truly become one of their number. A Lustful Lord.

Linc's cock twitched, but he willed it to settle down. He needed to take his cues from Arthur.

With the chairs put in place, the pair sat and waited for most of the day, eventually eating the lunch Arthur's housekeeper had prepared for them. But again, Jo did not appear.

Worry trickled through Linc's mind. He was apprehensive about Jo's absence, and about Arthur who was ignoring the obvious attraction between them.

On the third day, they walked to the hut once again as Arthur looked at Linc. "Do you think she'll come?"

Linc considered all the reasons she might have stayed away. The possibilities ranged from her having regrets about

their interlude to far more nefarious options such as someone holding her against her will. After the way Stone and
Cooper had met their wives, it seemed possible there was
more at play than a simple case of feminine doubts.

But then, reading about being with two men and actually
doing something of that nature were two entirely different
things.

"I don't know. She seemed confident enough the other day,
but it is hard to say what influences may have taken hold
since then. I would suggest that if she does not appear today,
we consider paying a neighborly visit to her parents' home."

"It seems as though she would prefer to keep our existence
private at the moment," Arthur mused aloud. "And to be
honest, I don't know her family terribly well. My parents had
a cordial relationship with them and an agreement about the
boundaries. But, we so rarely came to Dunmere Manor that
Emily and I never met them, though I do hope she comes to
us."

Linc clapped Arthur on the shoulder, appreciating the
roundness of the packed muscle he found there. "As do I."

They arrived at the hut to find it devoid of their Wood
Sprite, which was not surprising since it was still morning.
The snow had grown thinner on the ground after melting
the last two days and the sun was shining once again.

Linc decided to take that as a good omen. "Arthur, why
don't you chop us more firewood? I assume you remember
how to do it. I'll see to things in here."

"Don't be ridiculous, of course I remember how. How do
you think I kept the house warm when things were tight for
Emily and me? Besides, the activity will help pass the time

until she arrives." Arthur shed his coat and jacket, then rolled up his shirt sleeves before heading outside.

Linc set about starting a fire, unpacking their food for the day, and attempted to make the bed with the fresh sheets they'd brought from the Manor. Sadly, his domestic skills were lacking, so it took more than one failed attempt to start a fire and make a bed, but in the end he was successful.

Perhaps an hour had passed when he finally stepped outside to check on Arthur. To his dismay, he found the man standing shirtless and glistening in the sunshine, ax raised. He let the blade fly as it sliced through the hunk of wood waiting to be split. It had grown harder and harder to ignore the changes in the man's physique since they'd rescued Arthur from his debauched ways. His body had grown leaner, losing the softness that came with a hedonistic yet sedentary lifestyle. Watching him split wood truly brought that home in a cock-hardening fashion.

Linc cleared his throat. "No sign of Jo yet?"

Arthur shook his head. "Nothing. But I do have quite a bit of wood stockpiled."

Linc cast a glance over at the hefty pile near the door. "Indeed. Perhaps you should come inside and clean up. We can eat lunch and then decide what to do next if she hasn't arrived by then."

"Very well. I'll be along in a moment." Arthur placed another piece of wood on the block, raised the ax, and let it fly.

Though he could have sat and watched all day, Linc somehow managed to tear himself away and walk inside.

Not long after, Arthur joined him, freshened up. "I found a barrel of water around the side of the hut. It was cold, but clean enough for a light bath."

Linc nodded. "I wasn't complaining about the sweat, but I appreciate the effort. I'm sure Jo will too, if she comes."

Arthur's gaze dropped to the floor. "I'm worried we scared her away."

"I thought that was a possibility as well at first, but then I realized that a woman who was reading Pleasant Polly and the One Thousand and One Nights isn't going to scare that easily. Something or someone is keeping her away. I think the question is, who or what is it?"

At that very moment, the door of the hut swung open and Jo walked in like a breath of sunshine. "Oh! I'm so glad you are here!" She slipped off her cloak and hung it on a peg, turning to face them where they stood, both somewhat frozen in shock at the suddenness of her arrival. "I am truly sorry I couldn't get here any sooner. I was tied up at the house helping my Mother with a few things."

Linc threw off the shock of seeing her first and stepped forward, taking her in his arms. "We were terribly worried about you."

"I'm very sorry, I did not mean to worry you. My mother insisted I help her clean and inventory the linen and silver closets. My father refuses to pay for enough staff to see to such things. My sister Becca often helps her with these things, but she is off visiting our cousins in London, shopping quite happily."

There were shadows in her gaze that suggested more was afoot than mere shopping, but Linc was unwilling to push her too quickly. For some, physical intimacy came much easier than emotional intimacy, and he dared not push a boundary she was not ready to let them cross. He refused to stop and consider how easily he had fallen into thinking of himself and Arthur as a unit. They were a *them*, no longer two separate entities.

"The important thing is that you are here now. Right Arthur?"

"Yes!" The other man finally seemed to shake his stupor off. "You're here, and you can finally see the improvements we've made in your absence."

"Indeed! I see you two have been very busy. It looks almost homely in here." She grinned at them both, even as she stepped out of Linc's arms and moved over to Arthur. "Hello."

He gathered her in his arms and hugged her as well. "Hello, sweetheart. We're very glad to see you."

"And I you." She stepped away from him. "So, besides setting up our cozy little love nest, what else have you two been up to?"

Linc looked at Arthur, momentarily at a loss for words, a first for him.

Arthur chuckled. "Well, we did quite a bit of eating and waiting around. But I also chopped wood, and we did a small bit of hunting here and there to distract ourselves."

"Oh my. If I could have, I would have sent a note. But that was impossible, not without revealing our...connection." She bit her lip, her eyes growing moist as she looked at them with pain-filled eyes.

Linc tutted, shaking his head. "Do not cry, Wood Sprite. It was clearly not your fault. Of course you couldn't send word. Do not worry about us old goats, we were fine. Are you hungry at all?"

She shook her head. "I had a rather big breakfast since I was going to walk here and I anticipated some other...well, strenuous activities."

Linc chortled. "And what might those activities be?"

Jo's cheeks grew rosy, but her full lips did not move. Instead, they pressed firmly together.

Oh, interesting. She had definitely been thinking about them. "Did you perhaps read another story you found intriguing?"

She nodded.

Arthur moved next to him and reached over, placing a finger under her chin to tip her face up to them. "Can you tell us about what you read?"

Jo's cheeks flamed even brighter.

Linc bit the inside of his lip to keep from laughing. She so clearly wanted to explore this, but was truly struggling with society's strictures. "You must find your words, Jo. We shall do nothing to you that you cannot ask for first."

A strangled sound escaped from her throat. "But...ah. I can't!"

Arthur smiled. "Oh yes, you can. You absolutely can ask for what you want. But we shall help you get started. Would you like one of us to kiss you?"

"Yes, please," Jo smiled.

"Which one?" Linc prompted.

"Either. Both." Her gaze darted back and forth, almost in a panic.

"Calm down. Nobody is going to be offended. Just tell us who you want to kiss first, then you can kiss the other one next," Linc said.

She took a deep breath. "I kissed Arthur first the other day, so it seems only fair that I kiss Linc first today."

Linc nodded solemnly, tugging her gently forward and into his arms. It was lovely having her soft curves pressed fully against him as their lips met. He relished the minty coolness of her mouth as their tongues twined. Jo moaned and leaned into his body, letting him take her full weight.

Arthur stepped in behind her and Linc relished that she had nowhere to retreat. Seizing the moment, he delved deeper into her mouth, exploring the various angles and textures. He wanted to know her inside and out. Finally, he drew back, shifting so that just his lips lingered on her lips and then nothing.

Before Jo could gather her wits, he turned her to face Arthur, who swooped in and ravaged her again in a similarly dominating kiss that clearly distracted her. As his friend plunged deep, Linc held Jo steady, bracing her by placing his hands on her hips and letting her lean against his chest.

When Arthur pulled away from the kiss, he and Jo were both panting. Need had Linc's cock growing long and thick even as he worked to slow things down. They all needed a moment to gather themselves.

Jo let her head tip forward until her forehead pressed against Arthur's chest, allowing their gazes to meet over her head. A long, silent moment of relief and joy passed between them. She was here and in their arms of her own volition—eagerly so.

"Perhaps a cup of wine wouldn't be amiss?" Linc let his hands fall from her hips as he stepped away.

"That sounds like an excellent notion." Jo slipped from Arthur's arms, turned, and smiled nervously at Linc.

Arthur grunted in agreement as he reached down and adjusted his very large and very hard cock with a wince that only Linc caught before he turned away. Once he'd poured them each a drink, they gathered on the bed since it was closest to the fire.

"Now Jo, why don't you tell us the latest story you read that interests you?" Arthur suggested as he sipped his drink.

Linc watched their little Wood Sprite's cheeks turn rosy, but she took a big gulp of wine, straightened up, and launched into her tale. Her bravery was intoxicating.

"It was about one of the early nights, when Polly had first brought Rupert and Martin to her bed. In the beginning she had only ever lain with one of them while the other watched, or perhaps helped a bit. Touching and wh-whatnot." She flapped her hands for a moment, before gathering herself. "But she was feeling bolder this night. So, she had them both get naked and then she allowed Martin to take her and then she rolled over and Rupert did so as well. She described being filled by them, used thoroughly and...and having their cum spilling from her in the most decadent fashion." She was turning beetroot red as she spoke, but her breathing had turned shallow and her eyes were glassy with desire.

Surreptitiously, Linc rubbed his own cock to ease the ache the woman had caused with her words. It was quite the image he now had in his head, and he was finding it hard to let go. "Is that something you wish to try? Having us fill you in such a way?"

"I would very much like to experience that with you two." Jo wouldn't look up as she answered him. Her gaze locked on the contents of her cup as though she could discern the secret of life within the wine. "While I am no maiden, I have yet to truly experience many—nay, all the things I've read about in Polly's tale. She makes it all sound so blissful, I find it hard to believe everyone is still managing procreation under the guise of it being for England. And in the dark."

She laughed nervously, which only made Linc admire her further. He was coming to appreciate her quirky blend of freshness and practicality.

"There are risks to such a proposition and we are still only getting to know you." Arthur stated the rather obvious point. "Normally we would take a precaution such as donning a French Letter to better protect you from getting with child."

Jo sniffed. "It seems to be an unlikely outcome since my late husband, who sired multiple children with his first wife, could never get a babe on me in the years we were wed. Despite that, I...I have taken the needed precautions to allow such activity to occur. I have placed a vinegar-soaked sponge to help prevent pregnancy."

Linc felt his eyebrows shoot up. There it was again. He shouldn't be surprised that Jo would know of such things, yet he couldn't help but think of her as innocent. She had a naivety about her that was endearing—charming, even—but it somehow seemed she was well versed in life and its hardships.

How did one do that? Experience life without becoming hardened or jaded by it?

He looked at Arthur for his thoughts and seemed to find similar surprise and respect for the woman they were getting to know. "Arthur?"

"I'm willing to do as the lady wishes based on what she's shared. I do not believe she has a deceitful bone in her body."

"Agreed." Linc looked back at Jo. "It seems your obedient footmen await your instructions, m'lady."

"Oh, but I...I wouldn't know what to tell you to do." She glanced back and forth between them.

"Of course you do, Lady Polly." Arthur winked at her.

"Use the story as your guide, but feel free to improvise as your natural curiosity shows itself," Linc suggested with a smile.

"Very well." She seemed to hesitate, as if considering what to do. "Then...then I shall need you two to strip."

Almost as one, the two gentlemen rose from the bed and began removing their clothes. As Linc shed his breeches and underwear, he looked up to find Arthur standing there entirely naked, watching him along with Jo. Stretching to his full height, Linc allowed them both to look their fill as he reached down and stroked his stiff cock. Arthur groaned softly even as Jo inhaled, her eyes widening in wonder. Then she looked over to Arthur, whose erection was admittedly even more impressive. The man was a few inches shorter than Linc's unusual height of six feet two inches, but his cock was longer and thicker by far. For a moment Linc got lost in the fantasy of feeling himself stuffed full of Arthur's cock from behind, and his length twitched in response.

Jo licked her lips as she let her gaze dart back and forth for a moment. As if she'd come to some decision, her gaze settled on Linc. "I'd like to taste you."

His knees nearly buckled at her request. Could he allow her to do that and not ruin the moment? Prevent himself from exploding like an untried boy? Did it matter? If Arthur was there to keep pleasuring their Wood Sprite, he'd have time to recover. "Very well, but we should give you some pleasure as well. Let us undress you first."

Jo nodded and licked her lips again, apparently unable to muster a response.

Arthur shifted onto the bed, crawling behind her, and began working her gown's laces loose. Linc moved closer and distracted her by raining kisses over her lips and then her cheeks before moving down the column of her neck. As he neared her lush, round breasts, the material gaped forward, allowing him access. He worked with Arthur to rid her of her upper garments, including her light corseting. She lifted her arms to cover herself as her top fell away, but Linc stopped her.

"So plump and beautiful. Do not hide your lovely curves from us."

Jo cast her gaze to the mattress. "My husband found my over-abundance of flesh off-putting. He suggested I should eat less, so I might cease to resemble a fishmonger's wife."

Arthur growled low and menacing behind her. "Were he not already dead, I'd be tempted to see to the deed myself. You are the embodiment of womanhood, lovely and lush." Then he untied her skirts, loosening those as well.

Link grinned. "Stand up, my Wood Sprite." He helped her off the bed, letting the material puddle on the floor at her feet. With his help, she stepped out of the material and turned back to the bed to find Arthur laying on the mattress.

"What is this?" she asked, clearly surprised.

Arthur smiled mischievously. "Do you remember how good we made you feel with our hands the other day?"

She nodded. "Yes."

"I'd like to do the same thing to you, but with my tongue."

Jo gasped, her areolas ruching around the hardened points of her nipples as his words hit her.

Linc leaned over and licked her nipple before looking over at Arthur. "I do believe she approves of that notion."

"I gathered as much," Arthur laughed. "Come, Jo. Straddle my face and lower yourself. We'll make sure you get a taste of Linc, too."

Pulse roaring, Linc helped her into position, leaving enough room for him to stand on the mattress and lean against the head of the bed so she could have access to his cock. As much as he would have enjoyed impaling himself on Arthur's cock while she sat on Arthur's face and sucked him off, it was probably too soon for such advanced arrangements. What he had suggested thus far was suitably paced.

For today.

As she lowered her pussy to Arthur's mouth, it was clear the moment contact was made. Arthur moaned loudly as Jo sucked in a huge gasp of surprise. Arthur's hands settled on her hips and helped her find a rhythm to riding his face while Linc bent down and kissed her long and deep. Jo eagerly met his tongue thrust for thrust, and moaned loudly when he added his hands to the mix by tweaking her pebbled nipples.

Only then did he draw back and straighten up. "Are you ready to taste me?"

"Yes, please—oh God, Arthur!"

Linc nearly spilled his load then and there, listening to the sounds of Arthur eagerly lapping at her juices as he was about to fill her mouth with his cock.

He took a moment to gather himself. One breath. Another. "Open up. Now watch your teeth, and no biting down."

Jo nodded and did as he bade, opening wide. Below her, Linc could see Arthur watching as he fed Jo his cock inch by slow inch. When he reached the back of her throat, he stopped and withdrew. Instantly, he missed the heat of her mouth. "Now this time I want you to try sucking on it like you would a sweet treat you were savoring, just no teeth."

His glorious Wood Sprite nodded, her eyes shining with an eagerness that was intoxicating. Linc pressed his cock's head against her lips, a dab of pre-come stretched from his tip to her lips as he pulled back slightly. She swept her tongue out to swipe it up and then immediately leaned forward to lick the tip for more. He moaned, unable to control the urge at such an overtly sensual act.

He pressed forward and pushed into her mouth—and quick study that she was, she sucked firmly, drawing him in and engulfing him. Once in her mouth, he stayed for a moment and then drew back a bit before pumping forward. In and out in quick strokes, Linc pumped into her willing mouth as Arthur continued to lap at her pussy. Jo was moaning and wiggling, her body flushing the most delightful pink as she neared her peak.

Linc's balls tightened. "Jo, I'm going to come. Let me go."

She whimpered and latched a hand on his backside, keeping him from pulling back. Linc's knees nearly buckled, but somehow he kept going.

Below them Arthur moaned and seemed to redouble his efforts as Linc came, shooting his load into her mouth. Jo couldn't capture all of it, despite her best efforts, particularly because her own crisis hit her in the middle of his own. Jo ended up pulling away from him as she quivered in ecstasy, the last of his cum landing on her chest. Some even dribbled down her chin. But she'd hardly noticed as she thrashed about on Arthur's face, lost in her own release.

Linc was no barbarian but there was something primal about seeing his seed on her flesh. He resisted the urge to rub it in and mark her as his—just barely.

Arthur slid up her body as he sat up, running his tongue over the splatters of Linc's cum on her breasts before he leveled Jo with a deep kiss.

Well, he should not have been worried about getting hard again. Watching Arthur lap at his cum and then kiss her with his taste mingled with hers on his lips was more than enough to get Linc's blood pumping again.

It would not be long before he was ready for round two.

Chapter Six

Jo's head spun. Perhaps it was from lack of air—after all, Arthur had just kissed her as though his life depended on it.

But it could also have been the fact that she had just participated in—not one, but—two acts that before that day, she had only read about. And there was more to come.

So she allowed herself the moment of disorientation as the pleasure lingered.

Jo was not prepared for Arthur to press her to the mattress with his decidedly muscular physique and rain kisses all over her face and breasts. Goosebumps rippled over her skin despite the warmth of the fire as the flame of desire rekindled. Then Linc was there, touching and kissing her as well. It seemed no place on her body was left unexplored.

Arthur slipped between her thighs and spread them wide to make room for his hips. "Jo, look at me." He loomed there, his dark hair falling over his forehead and dark brown eyes gazing at her intently. She wanted to look away, but something in his gaze would not allow it. "Are you certain this is what you want? To be taken, by each of us in turn? To be left filled with our seed until it runs down your thighs?"

His graphic words which echoed those of the story sent a shudder of need rippling down her spine until it lodged deep in her quim.

"Yes. Please, yes." Jo heard the pleading tone in her husky response and could feel no shame in it.

Without further discussion Arthur pressed into her, the head of his cock stretching her wide. She quickly realized that while he would undoubtedly fit, it would be a tight squeeze compared to her late husband. She focused on breathing and relaxing to accept him, coming to relish his invasion until he had completely seated himself inside her. Once there, he remained still for a few long moments as Linc watched the two of them.

"Are you well?" Arthur finally asked her.

Jo considered for a moment, then wiggled. "I would be better if you would move."

Linc chuckled as Arthur grumbled about smart mouthed wenches while he withdrew. In and out, in and out he pumped, creating a lovely friction. Her body grew warm and slippery where they were joined. Before Jo could acclimatize to the sensations, Arthur lifted one of her legs over his shoulder.

Jo's heart pounded as Arthur slid deeper than before. It was as if she could feel every inch of him invading her body and...she bit her lip. Dare she say, her heart? No, it was too soon. Far too soon for such musings. She was clearly overwrought from all the sensations.

As Arthur continued to slide in and out of her sheath, Linc started licking and sucking on her breasts, biting and tugging on her nipples. Jo shivered, wanting Linc to never stop such delicious torture—especially because it distracted her from her silly thoughts.

At some point Linc moved down her torso with his kisses, while Arthur thrust into her quim, over and over. She was getting close to coming, but couldn't quite find that same release as before. Only when Linc leaned down and slid his tongue over her nub and licked around Arthur's cock as he fucked her did she feel the precipice approaching.

Arthur moaned. "Oh, fuck Linc. Bloody do that again!"

Jo sank her hand into Linc's golden hair, loving how it felt to have Arthur filling her as Linc licked at that bundle of nerves. He kept lapping at them as Arthur pounded into her, harder and harder. She was so close, right on that edge.

Linc pinched her nipple as he licked her clit and Arthur sank into her.

Jo screamed as her body seized up and contracted, only to expand into a million little bits. Arthur continued to thrust into her and Linc lapped at her clit, pushing her over crest after crest. She screamed long and loud until she heard Arthur join her in his release, pouring himself into her.

As they both remained there, catching their breaths, Linc came up and kissed her. She could sense herself and a trace of Arthur as he gently lapped at her mouth as though tasting her.

When Arthur withdrew Jo moved to sit up, but Linc pressed her back down. "Stay, we're only half finished with your request. I want to feel all of his load in there as I fill you with mine."

"Yes," Jo whispered, shaken by how badly she wanted that and how much she appreciated their willingness to not only fulfill her request, but to do so with such thoroughness.

"Fuck, you are a dirty, erotic bastard," Arthur said. "If you keep saying things like that we may never leave this hut."

Jo giggled, delighted at the thought of staying there forever to fuck, chat, and read books. It sounded like the perfect existence. But before she could process any other thoughts, Linc was between her legs and sinking into her still quivering pussy, and she gasped at the sensitivity that lingered from her orgasm.

"Are you too sore?" Linc hesitated.

"Probably, but I refuse to stop." And Jo meant it. Her marriage had been typical in that her husband had never looked at her and only performed in the most basic and perfunctory manor in the bedroom. It was about getting a child on her, though why she wasn't certain since he'd had two sons and a daughter from his first wife.

Linc hesitated.

"Please, don't stop." She waited to see what he would do.

The gorgeous man hesitated until, mind made up, he pressed on. As Linc sank into her, she realized he was thicker, though possibly not as long as Arthur, but still filled her well. With all the lubrication from her earlier lovemaking, he slipped in and out of her quite easily. Arthur had not forgotten her, sucking on her nipples as Linc had done before him.

"God Arthur, she's so wet. So full of your cum," he panted as he pumped in and out of her.

Arthur groaned. "You like it, Linc? Having your cock in her sliding around in my seed? You've always been dirty like that, haven't you?"

Jo loved hearing their banter, loved the filthy words. They added to the pleasure and the need pulsing through her.

Had they been lovers before they all came together?

She would have guessed previously that they were not but now, she wondered. They certainly seemed to have found a connection. Had they kissed again since she had asked them to?

"Fuck yes, I love feeling your seed around my cock. The only thing better would be to have your cum in my arse," Linc said on a groan. He stopped and looked up at them, surprised by his admission.

So Jo had been right, this was all new to them as well. It pleased her to think she had helped them connect. Before she could think any more, Linc slid inside her and hit a particularly sensitive spot, causing any rational thought to flit away on a tide of pleasure.

Arthur grinned. "Perhaps next round I'll do just that while you take Jo's for the first time."

They all groaned at the thought as Linc pounded into her and spewed more coarse words that painted vivid pictures of what they could do to her and each other, helping Jo to climb toward the precipice of bliss.

"So damn slippery, Sprite. You're going to have our cum dripping down your legs when we're done." More thrusts. "I'm going to dip my fingers in your pussy and paint your nipples with our seed before I lick it off."

Arthur lay there, sucking her nipples and stroking his own erection, groaned with each utterance, until he reached down and stroked over her clit. "Can you come, love?"

Jo thrashed her head side to side, need burning through her, but seemingly unable to find its way free. "I don't know. I need...I need..."

"Don't worry Sprite, I know what you need." Arthur leaned down and just as Linc had done, lapped at her pussy as the other man slid in and out of her.

She was so wet down there, Linc had been right, but Arthur seemed undeterred. He lapped at the sensitive nub and pinched her nipple.

"Oh fuck, Arthur. You're right, that feels so good." Linc's moaned words spurred her need higher.

Finally Jo could feel her orgasm crest, just as Arthur smacked her thigh and licked her clit. She exploded once more. Her entire being seeming to disintegrate into tiny pieces that scattered on the wind. Then she heard a shout and Linc stiffened as he came as well, filling her for a second time.

As she lay there, replete with their seed leaking from her body as requested, Linc followed through on his earlier promises. He withdrew from her body and ran two fingers through her cum soaked pussy. Jo quivered at his touch, her body strung tight from her multiple orgasms. Ignoring the wet spot she lay in, she watched rapt as Linc painted each nipple with the mixture. Instead of just him licking her clean, he and Arthur each took one tip in their mouths.

Her body shuddered with each caress and touch, and she reveled in the complete way they had used her, had filled her, and had cared for her. Some time later she lay there and heard the men whispering as they knelt between her thighs together.

"Look at her pussy. She's stuffed full of us," Linc murmured.

"She is. I had no idea it could be like this, sharing a woman."

Linc snorted. "It's never like this. She is unique. Special. She is as wanton and hedonistic as we are, but somehow has retained her innocence. It is a heady combination. I'm not sure I can let her go."

Jo's heart skipped a beat. Had she heard that correctly? Or had her own heart heard what it wanted?

"I know. But we can work that all out in due time. For now, we simply need to calculate how to spend more time with her. How to spend more time together...the three of us?" Arthur looked over at Linc to ensure he had heard him.

Linc stared back. "Agreed, the three of us." Then the pair of them settled on either side of her and snuggled close.

Their whispered words made something warm and wonderful swell in her chest until Jo drifted off to sleep. She was exhausted, yet ready for whatever they had planned next.

Perhaps an hour later, Arthur awoke up from their nap to find Jo and Linc sucking his cock. Together.

It really was the most delightful way to awaken.

Arthur moaned and reached down with both hands to sink one into each head of hair nestled into his groin. Linc had his cock down his throat and Jo was avidly working on his sac as they worked in tandem.

He growled in warning. "If you two don't stop, I shall be rendered useless."

Linc released him and then tapped on Jo's head to get her to stop as well. "So nice of you to join us, sleepy-head." Linc grinned.

Arthur pulled Jo up and kissed her soundly. He loved how their tastes had mingled into a unique flavor that was *them*.

Swept up in the moment, he grabbed Linc and pulled him in for a kiss as well. The man hesitated for a heartbeat before shoving his tongue deep in Arthur's mouth. The kiss was long and powerful, as each of them fought for dominance. In the end Arthur won out, to his own surprise, and he couldn't deny that he enjoyed wielding the power Linc yielded to him. It reminded him he was a new, stronger person—not the same weak-minded follower who nearly ran his family into the poor-house.

When he let Linc up, he looked at him with fresh eyes. "Kiss Jo."

Linc nodded. He turned to their woman and kissed her as thoroughly as he had him. It was damned arousing to watch.

Arthur decided to see how far the pair would let him take things when it came to leading their merry band. "Nicely done. Now, spread her legs and tell me how wet she is. Has she cleaned up the mess we made?"

Linc grinned and reached over to where Jo sat on the bed with her legs tucked under her and to the side so that she wasn't exactly on the mattress. He nudged her legs open and slid two fingers between her legs. He pulled them out, glistening with moisture. "I'd venture to guess she hasn't cleaned up. She still has an extremely wet quim. And I will note that she woke me up as she explored me with her fingertips. Running her hands everywhere."

Arthur looked at her and wanted—no, needed to hear her admit she still had their cum inside her. Dripping down her thighs. "Tell us the truth, Jo. Did you clean while we napped?"

She bit her lip as though trying to decide if she should tell him the truth. Her dark head tipped forward so the curtain of her now disheveled hair fell forward to hide her pretty face. "I have not cleaned up." Silence hung for a few moments. "I-I liked the slippery feel of your cum on my thighs."

"We like it too, Sprite." Arthur reached over and placed a finger under her chin, tipping her face up. "There is no shame in something we all enjoy together."

She smiled shyly.

"My shaft seems to be good and hard, but I think you and I need to help Linc out a bit. Keep that arse tipped up so you don't lose too much of our cum."

She moaned as she bent over and did as he bade, trying to swallow Linc's half-hard cock.

Arthur had watched Linc at The Market for so long, had fantasized about doing these things with him—to him. But he'd never imagined it would be as good in real life as it was. He coached Jo a little then decided to experience sucking Linc's cock for himself.

As he swallowed his cock tentatively, the man moaned. "Fuck, Arthur. Yes. Suck it hard. Suck me down."

Arthur couldn't believe he was really doing it for a few moments, but swiftly lost himself, relishing the intimacy. He did as the man demanded, sucking harder and taking his thick length deeper. Finally he let go and had Jo lick the length with him, their tongues tangling around Linc's shaft over and over until he pleaded with them to stop.

"Now I need you to stay on your hands and knees, Jo." Arthur grabbed each globe of her arse in a hand and squeezed as he pressed her upper body into the mattress. "Do you remember what I suggested earlier? That Linc would take your arse for the first time while I took his?"

She moaned. "Yes. I remember."

"Linc?" Arthur moved to the side so he could get behind her as well.

Linc gripped her arse with both hands and squeezed as he heaved in a breath before looking over at Arthur. "Are you sure? You really want this?"

Arthur paused for a moment. *Did he want this?* "Fuck yes. I've thought about taking your arse so many times." And he'd thought about giving up his arse for the first time to a man—no not just any man, to Linc—almost as much.

Eagerness lit up Linc's gaze. "Here's the jar of salve we brought." he set it on the mattress after removing the top, scooping two fingers of the thick concoction and dropping it on Jo's rear pucker. With an expert finesse, Linc slipped the first part of a finger past her tight opening. "That's it, Jo. Now I want you to just relax for a moment. Get used to the feel of my finger back there."

"That's just your finger?"

Arthur could hear the wry humor in her tone.

Linc grinned. "It's not even my whole finger. Now breathe out and push as if you were releasing the hounds."

"Linc! I can't believe you said that." Jo's words came out muffled by the mattress since her face was currently buried in it.

"Just do as I suggested, push," Linc urged as Arthur watched his finger slide deeper inside her backside.

Jo moaned.

Linc slid in and out a few times before he added a second finger. She squirmed and moaned louder, but pushed back against his fingers with each thrust. Then he scissored his fingers, spreading them wide to ensure she was stretched a bit more.

Linc looked at him and nodded. "I think she's ready."

She panted as she shook. "Yes. Please."

"Very well. Are you hard enough?" Arthur couldn't resist reaching over and stroking Linc's cock, partly to ensure he was hard enough to enter Jo, but also for his own needs. He loved the feel of Linc's shaft in his hand, how different it felt from his own cock.

"Any harder and you could use my cock instead of an ax to split wood," Linc said as he dropped a glob of salve on his shaft before he returned to working his fingers in and out of Jo. "Spread that around for me, will you?"

Arthur bit back a moan as he stroked the salve over Linc's erection, almost wishing he was the one to be filled by it. But soon he'd be content, as he fucked Linc's very fine arse. "You're ready."

Linc pulled out of his hand and pressed his tip to Jo's entrance, pushing against her tight ring of muscle. "Push out again, Sprite. I am going to stretch you even more."

Arthur held her cheeks apart to allow them both a better view as Linc sank inside her. All three of them were panting by the time Linc had fully seated his cock in her anal passage.

As they sat still with Jo catching her breath, Arthur leaned down and kissed her. "You look so lovely with Linc balls deep in your backside. Just hold still for a little longer and then we shall fuck you good."

With his words, Arthur shifted behind Linc and used the salve to cover his own rock hard cock. He slipped two fingers inside of Linc who took them easily. Pressing against his back with his fingers buried inside him, he murmured, "Are you ready to take my cock in your arse?"

SORCHA MOWBRAY

Linc groaned. "Fuck yes. You can't know how long I've been waiting to have your cock inside me."

"Bloody hell." Arthur's hands shook as he pulled his fingers out and pressed the head of his cock against Linc's sphincter for the first time.

Christ, it was the first time he'd ever fucked a man. His stomach rolled in a confusing mix of excitement and trepidation. This would unequivocally change things between them. Using both hands to spread his cheeks, he pushed inside and relished the fact he could feel Linc stretching to accommodate him.

"Christ, how big is that shaft of yours?" Linc growled as he continued pressing deeper.

Arthur chuckled. "Big enough to make you notice. Fuck, you're tight and hot." Slowly, slowly, he finally sank all the way in. "God, you feel good."

"So good," Linc echoed with a groan.

"Is everyone ready?" Arthur withdrew from Linc until just his tip remained lodged inside him.

"Yes, please." Jo's voice came out soft and breathy.

"Fuck, yes." Linc tensed, as though he didn't want to let Arthur leave his body.

"Then Linc, you should set the pace." Arthur smacked him on the arse. "Fuck us."

Linc pulled back, sliding out of Jo and impaling himself on Arthur's cock.

And bloody hell, it was amazing.

Linc's head spun, the pleasure was damn near overwhelming as he slid forward, sinking into Jo's tight arse. Then he withdrew and stuffed his own arse full of Arthur's gloriously thick cock. There was no escape from the bliss shooting through his body.

Below him Jo had started panting, and Arthur was groaning as he met him part way.

"Jo, rub your clit, sweetheart." Arthur directed from behind him. "I know Linc wants to feel you come around his cock before he explodes deep in your arse. And I won't be far behind, filling him up too."

Linc's cock throbbed at Arthur's words. The thought of Arthur coming inside him was nearly too much. "Fuck!"

"Oh God. Yes. I want to feel him come inside me." Jo's voice was still muffled as she panted into the mattress, overcome by the sensations, but Linc caught her words that echoed his own thoughts.

He felt her shift her weight so she could do as Arthur commanded. The feel of her fingers working furiously between her legs as he continued to fuck her bottom pushed him closer to the edge he danced along.

Arthur continued to meet him thrust for thrust, filling his arse each time, starting a low litany of dirty talk just for him. "That's it Linc. Take my cock. Take it nice and deep in your arse, just like you wanted." *Thrust. Thrust.* "I'm going to pump my load deep inside you. Coat your arse in my seed."

Linc's balls drew up. It was too much! His words, the feel of him filling his arse, and the grip of Jo's arse around his cock. These two undid him. *They bloody owned him.* "Fuck, I'm going to come soon."

"Oh! Oh! Yes!" Jo started slamming her backside against him as her body clamped down on his cock. "I'm—"

Her words were lost as she screamed her pleasure and came hard around him. As her body clamped down on his cock, Linc lost his own battle and bellowed his release as he shot his load deep into her backside. Once he sank inside her and held still, Arthur took over, pumping into him from behind. With each stroke, the man hit a pleasure spot that seemed to make his orgasm continue on and on until stars danced in his vision and he collapsed forward, unable to fully hold himself up.

He was at Arthur's mercy.

Arthur seemed to find a new burst of energy and pounded into him with total abandon. Linc relished it, loved the well-used feeling he would be left with for days after a fucking like this.

"God, I love your arse, so fucking tight, Linc. So good wrapped around me."

Linc smirked and tipped his hips up slightly, giving Arthur a better angle. "That's it, Arthur. Fuck me good. Fuck me as rough as you need. I can take it. I want to take it as much as I want your cum filling my arse."

And just like that, Arthur cursed and jammed himself deep inside one last time. "Fuck!"

He came long and deep inside Linc, just as he had as promised.

Chapter Seven

A Week Later

J o woke up to sunshine, which suited her mood.

How could it not? She'd found two men who made her deliriously happy. When they weren't making love to her, they discussed books and history, their hopes and their dreams. They hadn't spoken of their future, but it seemed a matter of time before they ventured into such topics.

She could bide her time.

After her morning ablutions and dressing in another simple daytime gown, she practically floated downstairs for a late breakfast. All was right in her world.

She was about to enter the dining room when her father called out to her. "Jo, please join me in my study."

Her stomach dropped at his request. As a rule, the only discussions which occurred in his domain were those of significant import. That, of course, meant this would likely not be a pleasant discussion.

Jo took a deep, steadying breath and straightened her bodice. "Of course, Father."

She stepped into his overtly masculine room, with its dark wood and dark fabrics. Despite the sun streaming through the window, it was all very heavy and gloomy. She hated this room. This was where her father had informed her of her first marriage, and it was impossible to miss the fact her mother sat silently on the sofa near her father's desk. This could not be good.

"Jo, please sit down. Your mother and I would like to speak to you about a particular matter." Her father looked very puffed up this morning, as though he had news of great import to discuss.

She repressed the urge to sigh. "Very well, Father. What did you wish to speak to me about?"

"I have received and accepted an offer for your hand in marriage from the Marquess of Whitestone."

Silence fell like a deafening clap.

For a moment, the air was sucked from the room, from her very lungs.

She was an independent woman. A widow! He didn't have the right to accept a marriage proposal on her behalf. "I'm afraid you will have to rescind your acceptance. I am uninterested in his offer of marriage."

"The devil I shall!" Her father's voice boomed through the small space, utterly filling it. "You will marry the Marquess and help your sister make an advantageous match, or I shall force her to marry the old codger."

Jo gasped. "But Father, she is just about to make her come out. You cannot force her to marry some old man for...for...for what? It cannot be his fortune, I have heard no such—."

Her father laughed. "Egads! No. The man's coffers echo when he dares to open them. No, we are the fortune he needs. He has the respectability of a title that will lift this family out of obscurity. We shall no longer be new money, but will ascend to the rank we deserve. To the heights of nobility."

Jo felt the blood drain from her face. This was something her father had always spoken of: this bettering of the family. Her marriage to her now deceased husband was his first attempt at just that. It seemed his second attempt would bear far greater fruit. "And I suppose my inheritance from my first husband will be included as my dowry for this farce of a marriage?"

"Why shouldn't it? You're no longer my dependent. I'll not foot the bill of yet another dowry. Perhaps you can try to keep this husband alive for more than a few years. I'm not sure I'd be able to convince a third man to marry you if a second dies under your unsatisfactory care."

She looked to her mother, desperate for support, but her father cut her off before she could speak. "You'll find no support there. Your mother knows better than to question my decisions."

Jo had never heard her mother openly question her father, but she'd also never seen her mother so cowed as she saw now. It stole her breath to realize her mother might be as unhappy as she herself had been in her first marriage. But she had been married to her father for five and twenty years!

"You are a despicable bastard." Jo glared at him and rose. "I'll never forgive you for this." With that, she stormed from the room.

Appetite gone, she grabbed her coat and flew from the house out into the morning cold. Her chores be damned! Tears coursed down her cheeks as she ran toward her place of refuge—the gamekeeper's hut.

Jo burst into the space only to find it cold and empty. Dismayed at first, she realized she'd left home much earlier than planned. Linc and Arthur wouldn't be there for a while yet. Unwilling to sit in the cold, she gathered some chopped wood from outside and carried it to the fireplace. She fumbled with the kindling more times than she could count, but she eventually got a fire going and had the place warming up. With that done, she sat down on the bed and allowed herself to cry.

She should have expected her happiness to be short-lived.

Sometime later, she awoke to gentle hands stroking over her back as a warm baritone called her name.

"Jo. Wake up, Jo." Arthur hovered over her.

Jo sat up, took one look at his handsome face, and burst into tears once more.

Arthur gathered her into his arms and sat down with her in his lap. "Tell me what's wrong, Wood Sprite." He stroked her back and held her close.

Linc sat down next to them. "What is it, Jo? What has you so upset?"

Tamping down her tears, she tried to dry her face and pull her thoughts together. "My—my father has promised my hand in marriage to some lord."

Linc and Arthur stiffened. "He cannot do that. You are a widow, he is not your legal guardian."

She sighed. "True. But he knows I shall not leave my sister Rebecca—Becca—to marry this man instead of myself. He will force her if I refuse."

The men cursed softly. Then Arthur spoke. "What if you had another offer?"

She tipped her head to the side and contemplated him. What would her father do if another man with a title made an offer? One who didn't require her fortune. Would he be greedy enough to switch horses mid-race? "I am not certain.

My head says he sees himself as a principled man and is unlikely to be tempted. My heart hopes he might be lured by a good connection that doesn't require my fortune." She hesitated. "And there is my sister to consider. He has threatened to give her in my place." She sighed, defeated. Her father had boxed her in quite nicely.

Was she cursed in marriage? Would she never be allowed to marry for love?

Arthur cleared his throat. "I'm not wealthy. I'm rebuilding my fortunes. But I am capable of taking care of a wife. And Linc—"

"No. No, I couldn't do that to Becca." Jo's heart swelled with emotion even as she shook her head. She dared not name it—it was far too early and pointless besides. But that these men might attempt to come to her aid and offer to marry her was overwhelming. She reached up to cup Arthur's cheek in her hand. "You." She did the same to Linc's with her other hand. "And you, you are both amazing. How could I be so fortunate as to stumble upon such wonderful men, and in the woods, no less?"

Linc grinned and winked at her, dark blue eyes sparkling. "Fortune has always favored me."

Arthur chuckled. "I was just lucky enough to be standing next to him."

Jo laughed softly. "Thank you both for your wonderfully gallant offer. But no, I cannot marry you." Then she reached up and kissed Arthur, letting her tongue tangle with his.

As their kiss deepened, Linc pulled her hand from his face and pressed in behind her. The three of them got lost in their burgeoning new feelings and the bittersweet moment.

Chapter Eight

A rthur was nervous. In fact, he thought he might cast up his accounts at any moment. After all, it wasn't every day that a man called on the father of the woman whose hand he intended to ask for. Especially one who had—strictly speaking—rejected his offer.

But he couldn't sit by and do nothing. What if they lost Jo forever?

He looked over at the man with whom he had shared the beautiful woman—thank God he had him by his side. If they did indeed lose their Wood Sprite, he wasn't sure where that would leave him and Linc. At least as friends, if nothing else, though he fervently hoped for more.

Hand shaking, Arthur reached up and knocked. The sound of the knocker rang out loud and true. Perhaps there was a bit more echo than there should be? He chuckled at his own flight of fancy as they waited for someone to answer their call.

Eventually the door opened, revealing an older woman who was tidy in appearance, despite her harried expression. "What can I do for you, gentlemen?"

"Please tell Mr. Marshall that the Earl of Dunmere and Baron Lincolnshire wish to call upon him." Arthur waited a moment. Then a few more. But the woman hadn't departed to search out her employer to alert him to his guests. "Is there a problem?"

"Mr. Marshall expressly stated he would not be receiving visitors today. Besides which, it's far earlier than his normal receiving hours."

"Well, I must insist you go find him. This is a matter of the utmost importance." Arthur stared at the woman, who simply stared back at him. The insolence!

"I'm afraid I cannot do that, my lord. The family is very busy this morning and are not to be interrupted." She seemed dead-set against delivering his message.

Linc stepped forward. "Good morning, my lady. Do be a dear and tell us where Mr. Marshall might be found just now." He unleashed a dazzling smile on the poor woman.

Arthur had to fight back a snicker at how quickly she was bamboozled by Linc's smile and good looks. Women always seemed entranced by him, he thought as he shot his gaze heavenward in exasperation. All the same, he was not un-willing to take advantage of the man's ability to charm the ladies.

"Oh well, I'd dare say he's in his study, my lord." She smiled at him for a moment, but then quickly snapped back to herself. "But you still can't go in there, my lords."

Linc dialed up the blinding smile. "Surely you cannot mean to keep us from our very important business?"

"I—I'm sorry, my lords. But I'm afraid I must." Her voice rose in pitch and she started wringing her hands.

Linc moved closer to her, closer still. "I'm certain he would wish to hear what my friend Lord Dunmere has to say." Suddenly he was easing her away from the door as they moved into the house. "In fact, I'm positive he would wish to speak to us." By that point, they were in the hall and Arthur was able to brush past the maid-cum-butler in search of the study. "You've been a gem. Now run along, so you don't get into any trouble."

With that, Linc fell into step just behind Arthur as they wandered down the hallway. After knocking on and opening a couple of doors only to find empty rooms, they knocked on one and gained a response.

"I said I was not to be disturbed," a gruff voice barked at the closed door.

Arthur utilized Linc's more brazen approach, opened the door, and stuck his head inside. "There you are. Right where one would expect you to be."

A startled man looked up. "Eh? Who the devil are you?"

Arthur stepped inside and allowed Linc to join him. "The Earl of Dunmere, at your service." He swept a bow, straightened up, and waved a hand toward Linc. "And this fine gentleman is the Baron Lincolnshire." Linc bowed as well and then rose. "I've come to speak to you about your daughter."

A speculative gleam came into the man's eye. "Have you now? I imagine you spotted my lovely Rebecca in the village and have come to inquire about her availability?"

"Actually, I am here about Mrs. Josephine Fulton. I should like to ask for her hand in marriage." Arthur decided to get to the point, since the man was both mistaken about which daughter and had yet to offer them a seat.

All the little things Jo had mentioned were suddenly adding up. The chores she had to do, her father's unwillingness to hire staff, the housekeeper answering the door in lieu of a butler, his forcing Jo to marry against her will: the man really was new money, though Arthur would wager they were just on the cusp and living above their means.

It was sad that the man chose to put money and status above the welfare of his flesh and blood. How had Jo turned out so innocent and kind?

The man's eyes dulled to a flat green shade that held no interest or care. "I'm afraid that one is spoken for. In fact, as a result of that, I am about to be on my way to London. The women already traveled ahead earlier this morning."

Arthur glanced at the clock on the mantle, aghast. Earlier that morning! It was only half-past eight, a ridiculously early hour for calls but a monstrous time to make ladies travel. He must have pushed the women out the door at first light. No wonder that poor maid looked so harried. "Mr. Marshall, I'm an earl. I can give your daughter—no, both your daughters—access to my noble friends, and all that comes with it. I can even say I have a modest income that will allow me to support my future wife in comfort."

"You're too late. A deal's a deal. She belongs to Whitestone now, or she will before the sun sets." The man stacked a few papers on his desk, not even deigning to look up.

"But you must procure a license," Arthur pressed, his chest tightening with panic.

"It was procured weeks ago. The wedding is today. Speaking of which, I need to leave." The man stood, revealing his bulging middle and less than impressive height. "Unless you'd consider Rebecca? I'm yet to receive a satisfactory offer for that chit."

"I told you, I'm only interested in Josephine," Arthur growled at the repulsive man.

"Suit yourself. Since you two managed to show yourselves into my home, I assume you can show yourselves out as well?" He turned his back on them and gathered some documents from his credenza.

Furious, but with little recourse, Arthur and Linc strode from the room and the house. Outside, they mounted their horses and rode for Arthur's home in silence. The only question was, how quickly could they pack and get back to London? How would they even find her? And could they do it all in time to stop a wedding?

It was midafternoon by the time they reached town. Before leaving they had sent a telegram to their friend, Stonemere, before they caught the train and by the time they'd arrived in London, he had a footman waiting to meet them at the station with the address they required.

Determined to save their Jo, Arthur and Linc rode straight to the crumbling townhouse that belonged to the Marquess of Whitestone. Tossing their reins to a groom who happened to be out front, they raced to the front door and knocked soundly until the portal opened.

A butler appeared in worn, but immaculate livery. The uniform was likely of the finest quality twenty years ago, not unlike the man wearing it. "Sirs, how may I help you?"

"We are looking for Mrs. Fulton, we were told she could be found here." Arthur resisted the urge to plow through the flimsy obstruction of a butler and search the house from attic to cellar for their Jo.

"I'm afraid Lord and Lady Whitestone are not home. They've left on their honeymoon." The devastating news was delivered in the blandest of tones.

Arthur reeled back. Only the steadying hand of Linc on his shoulder kept him upright.

"Do you wish to leave a calling card?"

Arthur felt his mouth open and close a few times, but no sound would come out.

Linc grabbed him by the shoulders. "No, thank you."

They retrieved their horses and Arthur found himself heading somewhere. Where precisely, he did not know; Arthur merely followed Linc's lead.

Gone. She was married off. Their Jo, the woman he loved. She now belonged to another man. There was an ache in his chest where his heart should be.

As they arrived at his townhouse in the city, Arthur looked over to see Linc was just as upset. "What do we do now?"

Chapter Nine

L inc wanted to lift his head up and howl his anguish to the sky—or at least to Arthur's roof. There was a gaping hole in his chest where his heart should be. Certainly, it still beat. His blood pumped through his body. He breathed, but it all seemed rather overrated in his estimation, perhaps even unnecessary at the moment.

Jo was married.

"What do we do now?"

Arthur's question still rang in his ears as Linc turned his attention to the devastated man. *Bloody hell.* There was no time to wallow in his own mire of self-pity. Arthur was in much more agony over this. The man had puffed himself up to marry the woman, only to be burst like an over-inflated balloon.

Letting out a sigh, Linc slapped his friend on the shoulder and nudged him down the corridor toward the man's study. "We drink, Arthur. That is what we shall do now."

Determined to numb the pain of loss, Linc splashed two healthy portions of whisky into the cut crystal tumblers that matched the decanter sitting on the sideboard. He handed one to Arthur and took one for himself. They each stood there a moment, awkwardly staring at each other, clearly at a loss for any kind of toast or, more aptly, any words of wisdom.

"Fuck it," Linc murmured and then tossed back the contents of the glass.

Arthur followed suit and grabbed the decanter to refill their drinks. They quickly took refuge on the sofa in front of the roaring fire and proceeded to get soused.

It was sometime later—precisely how long he was not sure, for Linc had lost track of time. They sat there working their way through another bottle of whisky after having finished off the partially filled decanter earlier. He looked over at Arthur and couldn't help but smile. The man was far too handsome for his own good. Dark to Linc's own light, they were a study in contrasts. Whereas he was known for laughs and fun, Arthur was more serious. Whereas he went his own way and did as he pleased, Arthur tended to get along with everyone, ever the charming companion.

And despite all that, Linc found the man deeply attractive. He'd have never acted on it were it not for their interludes with Jo, but now he couldn't but help but need Arthur. Need his touch. His cock stirred with interest.

Arthur sat low on the couch, sprawled in a slightly depressed but despotic pose that nonetheless held an air of command. As though he were a powerful man who had been thwarted. It was a rather enticing display, if Linc were honest with himself.

Suddenly, his companion lurched to his feet with a roar and smashed his glass into the fire. They had long ago shed the civility of their coats and waistcoats, sitting in their rolled-up shirtsleeves.

The man's corded forearms pressed against the mantle as he rested his forehead on them. "We were too fucking slow! Too sure of ourselves and the outcome."

Linc shrugged. "How were we to know her father was bastard enough to sell her out from under us?"

Arthur snorted. "Because she told us, you fool. She told us he'd threatened to use her younger sister in her place if she didn't cooperate." He cursed and spun around. "But instead of running for Gretna or riding directly to his house and demanding her hand in marriage, we made love to her together, we waited until the next morning to attempt to secure her hand."

Linc unfolded from the couch. "I dare say we calmed down the distraught woman we care deeply for, and went to call on her father in a civilized manner. We played by the rules Society has. In this case, it was to our detriment." He set his whisky on the mantle and laid a comforting hand on Arthur's shoulder, trying to ignore the feel of the muscles playing under his fingers, the way they bunched and loosened as the clock ticked relentlessly in the background.

A hard glint came into Arthur's glassy gaze. He swayed for a moment, not quite steady on his feet. "I'm done living by Society's strictures. All it has ever brought me is heartache."

Before Linc could say a word Arthur had reached for him, hauled him into his arms as their lips crashed together.

It was a heady kiss. A heady, drunken kiss—but for a few moments, Linc could say his heart ached a little less. Arthur seemed to feel the same way as he pressed the kiss deeper, his tongue exploring Linc's mouth with a rapacious persistence that had his cock standing up and taking notice.

Linc moved his hands from Arthur's waist to the front of his shirt, opening the buttons one at a time, very slowly. Once he finally had skin exposed, he reached inside to run his hands over the man's chest. Linc enjoyed the softness of a woman's body, but the feel of all Arthur's muscles enticed in a very different way. Watching him chop wood had only highlighted how much he appreciated the differences.

Pulling his shirt off over his head, they barely stopped kissing. Linc took care of his own shirt as Arthur seemed too focused on exploring his mouth to manage any clothing.

Skin to skin, Linc pressed closer to him, letting their hard cocks—and they were both hard as steel—grind together. The friction was a delicious torment he could stand for only so long before he needed more.

Breaking their kiss, he dropped to his knees in front of Arthur and opened the man's trousers. Reaching inside, he pulled out the man's weighty cock and stroked it with one hand as he rubbed his own through the fabric of his pants. Arthur stood there with his head tipped back and eyes closed, clearly lost in the sensations.

"Arthur, look at me," Linc gave the explicit command. He needed the other man to be with him in the moment. He refused to let him pretend this was someone else sucking his cock.

Arthur looked down and offered a small smile. The first he'd seen from him in hours.

Then Linc swallowed the head of Arthur's cock into his mouth, taking the salty, sweet tang of the dripping pre-cum with it. He was greedy for more, never wanting this moment to end. Taking him deep into his mouth then his throat, he reveled in the masculine groan he ripped from Arthur's chest.

"Oh, God Linc." Arthur's hand sunk into his hair as he palmed his head.

Satisfaction that his man understood who was loving him settled in Linc's chest as he continued to work the baron's length. Soon the man's hips were thrusting into his face, matching the rhythm he'd set. Pushing Arthur's undergarments down further, he exposed his balls and gently cupped them as he continued to suck his cock.

Then Linc pulled away, suddenly unwilling to end things so soon. He wanted more from him: wanted to feel him wrapped around his cock as he sank deep into his tight arse.

Rising to his feet, he grabbed Arthur's neck and hauled him in for a kiss. Their tongues twined as they dueled for control. It was a battle of wills that he wouldn't lose, not this time.

When Linc had wrestled him into submission, he finally broke off the kiss. Drawing his lips along Arthur's stubbled jaw, he murmured, "I want to fuck you."

Arthur's breath hitched, but he didn't respond.

For a moment, Linc wondered if he might be pushing the man too hard, that he didn't feel what he did.

But then Arthur hissed his response, "Yes."

Linc's gut tightened in excitement. He'd thought about taking Arthur's arse so many times as they'd all cavorted at The Market. Now he would have the opportunity to sink into him. "Here or your bedchamber?"

Arthur cast his gaze around the room for a moment before refocusing on him. "My bedchamber. I don't think I have the needed supplies here."

Linc nodded. "Lead the way."

Arthur bent down and drew up his trousers before closing them enough that they could walk through the house without utterly shocking any of the staff, should they run in to anyone. Quietly, they made their way through the town-house and up the stairs, Linc's heart hammering. Within moments he would be sunk so deep into this gorgeous man that—

They had just stepped inside Arthur's bedchamber when his valet appeared. "Can I assist you with your—" The words ceased as he took in their shirtless states.

"No, thank you, Travers. We came up here in search of a..." Arthur seemed to draw a blank on why on earth the two men were approaching the master's bedchamber.

"You're sauced! We came to taste the particular bottle of whisky you keep in your room, remember?" Linc stepped around Arthur and chuckled a little.

"Yes." Arthur recovered with a shy grin. "It's a particularly good bottle. Travers, you may find your own bed when you are ready. I shall be fine on my own tonight."

Travers looked slightly aggrieved at his dismissal. If he was anything like Linc's valet, he was very particular about what happened to his master's clothing when he removed them. Clearly knowing Arthur was likely to leave what few items he still wore strewn about at best, crumpled on the floor at worst, had the valet in an unhappy state.

Alone again, with the door of Arthur's bedchamber firmly shut, Linc wasted no time in re-engaging where they'd left off. Lips and tongues tangled once more, he worked Arthur's trousers back open and then down his thighs. Next went his underwear, which wholly impeded his progress in almost as annoying a fashion as a lady's corset.

With Arthur stripped, Linc broke the kiss. "Grab the salve and climb on the bed."

"Not yet." Arthur reached for the front of Linc's trousers and opened the first button.

Linc pushed his hands away. "If you touch my cock right now, I'll not make it inside your tight arse and I really, really want to be inside you. So grab the bloody salve and get on the bed and do what you're told."

With a soft grunt of annoyance, Arthur went to his bedside table and pulled out a jar before being obedient and clambering onto the bed.

Satisfied his direction was being followed, Linc turned his focus to his own clothes and quickly shed them. He stood at the foot of the bed and looked at Arthur's well molded physique. The man was no athlete, but he was put together quite well, and his newly formed muscles were taking shape in a way that had been garnering Linc's notice for the last couple of months. "On your hands and knees, please."

The man rolled over and lifted into position, causing his muscles to flex and bunch.

Linc bit back a groan of delight.

"Please, fuck me, Linc. I need to feel something other than this misery." Arthur's voice had just enough of a pleading tone to push Linc's desires harder.

Linc crawled on the bed behind him and took the globe of each cheek in his hands. "Do you know how long I've admired your arse? Wanted to sink into it?" He leaned over and bit one, causing Arthur to jerk at the unexpected nip.

"No, and I don't bloody care at the moment. I need you. Now." Arthur pushed back into Linc's hands as though trying to urge him to get on with it.

"Arthur, slow down. This is your first time, isn't it?" Linc needed to be sure. He suspected, but he needed to confirm. He had to make this good for Arthur.

"Y-Yes, but it doesn't matter. I need you inside me," Arthur urged, his voice rough with desire.

But Linc refused to rush. He planned to enjoy this moment, to linger in the connection; not just because it dulled the pain of their loss, but because he wanted Arthur in his own right. Even without Jo in their life, he still wanted the other man.

Slowly, he opened the jar and scooped some of the salve out. Taking the dollop, he dropped it between Arthur's cheeks and then rubbed over the crinkled hole before he sank a finger inside. As the heat and tightness engulfed his digit, he doubted if he'd survive breaching Arthur's arse without spilling early.

"Oh shit, Linc." Arthur moaned.

"That's just one finger, Arthur. There is so much more to come, so much more. Are you ready?"

Chapter Ten

Arthur's mind stuttered and stopped. *A single finger?* He felt so full.

"Arthur? Are you still with me?" Linc's voice seemed to come from a long way away.

"Yes, God yes. I just—" Before he could form the next words, Linc pulled his finger out and sank what felt like four back in. "Bloody hell!"

Linc chuckled. "Breathe through it, my man. That's only two fingers."

Arthur took a deep breath and blew it out. *Fuck.* He had wanted Linc to fuck him. Got hard at the idea of it. But, holy hell, he had not been prepared for what it would feel like to take something—anything—up his arse.

Linc started gently working his fingers in and out and the discomfort morphed into a pleasurable fullness. Then he pulled out, but he must have opened his fingers, because the stretching and burning was back.

His companion continued to impale him with his fingers and, after a few more minutes, added a third. Arthur knew this because Linc had made a point to inform him, not that he was counting. By that point, his hips were bucking to meet each stroke as though seeking more. As his body adjusted, Arthur wanted that sense of stretched fullness back—wanted to feel possessed by Linc. In this moment, he appreciated whatever comfort he could find.

"I think you're as ready as I can make you." Linc's voice was thick and a little rough, as though he had some gravel caught in his throat. He sounded as turned on as Arthur felt, which was only amplifying the experience.

"Yes, please. Fuck me." Arthur didn't care that he was begging. He knew there was something lacking about just having Linc's thick fingers buried inside him. He wanted more. No, he needed more.

After a bit of shifting on the bed, he felt something prod against his hole.

"When I push in, you push out. It will help you take me," Linc said gruffly, before he was doing as he'd promised.

Arthur's body tensed as Linc pressed inside of him. It fucking hurt. God, it burned.

"Push out," Linc said again in a low murmur.

Focusing on the timbre of his voice, Arthur managed to relax his body as he tried to push against the intrusion—and suddenly Linc was inside him. His sphincter felt stretched to the limit, and he thought for a moment he wouldn't be able to actually do it, but Linc was in.

"Now I'm going to push deeper. Work—work my way in." Linc's voice sounded strained, as though he was struggling for control.

"Deeper?" Arthur was having a hard time following. Wasn't he already in?

"Just the head of my cock is in you. I need to slide deeper," Linc growled. "Want to feel you wrapped around my massive cock."

As he spoke those dirty words, Arthur's body screamed, *yes*! even as his head shouted, *no more*! With the two parts of him at odds, he barely noticed as Linc started pushing deeper.

It wasn't until his body took over that he realized the man was half buried inside of him. "Oh shit, Linc."

"Fuck yes, you feel so good. I knew you would." Linc's voice sounded stiff now. Was he as close to the edge as Arthur was? "Just—just a bit more."

Arthur could feel him deep inside, could feel every inch of Linc's cock as it filled him up in a way he'd wanted for so long. Suddenly he could feel Linc's hips pressed to his arse, their flesh meshed together.

He was full of Linc.

"I'll hold still a minute so you can adjust. Tell me when I can move." His lover sounded like he spoke through gritted teeth.

Arthur's head spun, but he knew he wanted to feel Linc move now, not later, as he leaned on his elbows and tried not to blow. "I'm ready. Fuck me."

Linc sighed gustily, as though relieved Arthur demanded he move. He took hold of Arthur's hips and pulled back. The slide out was strange, like they'd lost some connection but before long Linc was sliding back in.

Arthur moaned as the first tingle of pleasure rippled through him. *Fuck yes*. He wanted more of that. "More, Linc."

Linc maintained his steady pace. "I don't want to hurt you."

Arthur groaned and sucked in a breath as he pushed back into the next slow, steady thrust. "Please! I need more."

Linc picked up the pace, sliding in and out of his body, his balls slapping against his man with a constant rhythm that had Arthur pushing back into each thrust. His cock seemed to sink deeper each time and just as he bottomed out, Arthur felt him stroke over a spot inside him that grew from a tingle to a steady thrum of pleasure.

Soon they were fucking hard and a little wild as they got lost in the moment. Linc reached down and stroked Arthur's cock, causing the sparks shooting through his body to multiply.

"Fuck, Linc. I'm—I'm going to come."

"Do it. Come for me, Arthur." Link continued to stroke him as he shuttled in and out of his arse, still hitting that spot deep inside.

"Fuck!" Arthur cried out as pleasure unlike anything he'd ever experienced cascaded through his body, causing his limbs to shake and his toes to curl. His cum shot out on the bedclothes and all over Linc's hand as he continued to work his now softening cock.

And yet still Linc resumed sliding in and out of his arse as he let go of Arthur's softening cock. Looking back over his shoulder, wanting to watch him come, Arthur gasped as he watched Linc lick his load off his fingers and hand.

Not missing a beat, his lover continued to pump into his arse for one, two more strokes. "Bloody hell! Yes!"

Arthur felt his cock stir as he ran the image of Linc licking his cum off his hand before coming inside him through his mind. He'd have that image to pleasure himself to for years to come.

Then Linc collapsed on his back and pulled him down onto the bed with him, remaining buried inside him for the moment.

"Thank you for that," Linc murmured.

As they lay there together, Arthur's thoughts drifted toward what came next. He hesitated as he considered what this meant for him and Linc. Were they...together now? Was he ready for that?

But he had no answers. Not yet.

Arthur was grateful to wake up alone when Travers came bustling in as he normally did. He hadn't considered just how awkward it would have been for the valet to walk in and find him and Linc in bed together. Between the whisky and the grief, he just hadn't been thinking clearly.

Fortunately, Linc had been, because at some point he slipped out of Arthur's room and into his own, leaving Arthur to be dressed by his valet and step downstairs alone.

"Good morning." Linc looked up from the newspaper as Arthur walked into the breakfast room.

"Good morning," Arthur replied, more out of habit than any real sense of goodness about the day. He reached for the pot of coffee, a preference they'd both gained from their friend Lord Stonemere.

"Do you have any plans for today?" Linc asked as he nudged his empty cup toward Arthur.

Arthur stared at the man, dumbfounded. *He couldn't be serious, could he?* "Well, there was the small matter of rescuing Jo from her bondage. But otherwise, I might go for a ride through Hyde Park later."

Linc's head snapped up at the sarcasm Arthur couldn't contain. "Jo? Arthur, I'm not sure you understand. There isn't anything for us to do. She has married someone else to protect her sister. We have no ability to interfere, especially if that interference is not wanted. Dare I say, it is not. If it had been, she would have come to us yesterday morning."

Arthur growled at his friend and lover. "Unless she had been unable to come to us. What if her bastard of a father had locked her away?"

Linc looked stricken for a moment, but his face quickly settled back into its normal arrangement. "Arthur, surely you can see that as resourceful as she is, she is not one to be locked away unless it was by her own choosing. No door or lock would have kept Jo from us if that is what she had chosen." Linc looked down at his hands, now clenched in his lap. "She simply didn't choose us."

Arthur's gut twisted. Was this about physical barriers or emotional? "I'm not ready to accept that. You may come with me or you may remain here, but I am returning to Whitestone's townhouse today to find her. We know her father had threatened her sister. Our Wood Sprite would never sacrifice her so she could be free. The question remains, is there anything we can do to save her now?"

Chapter Eleven

February 1862

J o, now the Marchioness of Whitestone, sat in the rundown drawing room of her new husband's townhome. They'd just returned from their honeymoon, spent mostly at his country estate.

Fortunately, she both enjoyed the country and winter. Less fortunate was the company that she was forced to endure. Whitestone was tolerable, though far too advanced in years for her taste, but his sister and her son had passed by uncivil and careened straight into rudeness almost upon meeting her.

Fortuitously, her new relatives had remained at Whitestone Manor when her husband had been called back to the House of Lords for an important vote. The Marquess had waved farewell that morning after bidding her to get to work on refurbishing the house to her liking. *Now his coffers have been replenished,* she thought sourly. *With my money.*

Jo sat alone, staring at the drawing room without the faintest clue where to begin. Had the man bid her to reorganize his library, she would have rolled up her sleeves and gotten to work straight away. But decorate? A house? Perhaps she should have paid greater attention to those lessons her mother had tried so desperately to impart on her. Her last husband had had a staff which ran like a well-oiled machine. They had required nothing of her beyond the occasional approval of a menu—and even that normally had gone to her husband. Perhaps she should have looked at a few magazines now and again, instead of assuming she'd be free to go her own way after her first husband's death. Clearly, she had miscalculated.

A knock preceded the opening of the drawing room door. "Excuse me, my lady. Lords Dunmere and Lincolnshire are here to see you." The butler—what was his name again? Bell! Mr. Bell stood there looking very aggrieved that she had two male visitors.

"They are?" Jo's stomach gave a little flip. What on earth were they doing calling on her? How did they find her? Well, there was only one way to find out. "Please show them in."

A few moments later, the very two men who she'd thought she might never see again were standing in her shabby little drawing room.

Once Mr. Bell exited the room, Jo rose to her feet and ran over to the men. "Arthur, Linc!" She hugged each man she had once thought to spend the rest of her life with, though no more, considering her newly married state. "It is so good to see you both."

The men hugged her back, Linc rather stiffly, and Arthur with a bit more warmth. "Jo, it is good to see you looking well." Arthur smiled at her.

"Marriage seems to agree with you." Linc's words came out stilted and stiff as though he was holding himself back.

Her joy at seeing them withered a little. She'd known they'd be hurt once they found out, but truly, she hadn't been allowed a chance to tell them. If they'd listened to her, they'd have realized she had no choice. "Well, I wouldn't go that far,

Linc. But it is certainly better for me to be here than my baby sister." She let one brow lift as she eyed him.

Darting a look at the closed door, she wondered just how private they truly were. It mattered naught, really. Nothing inappropriate would transpire between them now. She may not love her husband, but she respected the vows she took.

"I'm sorry if my disappearance and marriage hurt you both. When I returned home that afternoon, my father leveled an ultimatum. I marry Lord Whitestone, or Rebecca would. She has just turned twenty, still a young woman who dreams of falling in love." Jo took Arthur's hand and squeezed it until he looked at her. "I couldn't steal that from her in pursuit of my own happiness. I secured a promise from my father that he would allow her to marry where she chose, and in return I would marry Whitestone. In the end, I would have been miserable knowing she'd been married off to Whitestone—or someone like him. I had to protect her."

Arthur reached out and touched her shoulder. "Of course you did. But will your father hold to his end of the deal?"

Jo nodded. "Strangely, he prides himself on keeping to his agreements. It is the one thing I cannot fault him for. So yes, I expect he will allow Becca to marry where she wishes. I just hope she is smart enough to marry well."

"Jo," Linc said before hesitating. "Is...your husband awful?"

Jo smiled a little. "No, he's not awful. He's just old and set in his ways. I don't love him, not like I..." She let the words hang there unspoken. It would do none of them a spot of good to finish her thought aloud.

The moment grew thick with tension as the three of them stood there, touching, but not really touching. Not as they all would have preferred. They were connected one last time.

"We could take you and run away. To America." Arthur offered, almost in a whisper, as though too afraid to fully voice the suggestion.

"No," Jo replied, as a tear welled up and slipped down her cheek. *This man.* He broke her heart. "That's not the woman I am. Not the kind of woman I hope you would want in your life. I took a vow, and I shall uphold it until the end." She released Arthur's hand and turned away from Linc's touch. "Perhaps this would be easier if we did not see each other again." She walked to the front window that overlooked the street. "I fear I find this far too painful to endure."

There was a choking noise behind her as she watched the hustle and bustle of people going by on the street. A pained moan came low and mournful. Then finally, movement.

"Goodbye, Jo. If you ever have need of us, we shall be there for you. No matter what. No matter when." Linc's solemn words felt like the final blow to her heart, but there was nothing else she could do.

She was married now.

Linc led Arthur from the townhouse and out onto the street. After weeks of stopping by daily to see if she was at home, they had finally found her in. Hope had sprung eternal, only to be squashed by painful reality.

But he had little time to wallow, he had Arthur to consider. "White's?"

"No. I think someplace more private is definitely in order." Arthur looked fragile, as though he might shatter.

Or was Linc projecting his own state of mind on his friend? "Yes, probably best."

A short while later, they were once again ensconced in Arthur's study with multiple bottles of whisky, a roaring fire, and their mutual sorrow. For a long while they sat there drinking, neither saying a word.

Finally, Arthur broke the silence. "We knew her for such a short time, yet I feel as though a limb is missing."

"It is an oddly physical ache for what is largely an emotional loss. Though she had spent so little time between us, perhaps it was more than a physical bonding than we realized?"

"So it would seem." Arthur's words slurred a bit.

Long after the sun sank and the whisky ceased to flow, Linc helped Arthur up to his bed. There they both stripped and lay together, holding each other as they tried to forget the woman they loved. The woman they'd lost.

The next morning, just as the sun had enough nerve to peek through the heavy curtains guarding the window, a knock sounded at the bedroom door.

Linc moaned and rolled over, reaching for Arthur. "Thank God I locked the bloody door last night."

Arthur shoved Linc's arm away and shot out of the bed while making an urgent shushing sound.

Confused, Linc sat up, suddenly more awake. "What's the matter?"

"They might hear you!" Arthur whispered, panic making his eyes open wide as his gaze darted around the room as though looking for a suitable hiding spot.

"Who might hear me? Your servants?" Linc was still feeling a bit confused, between the too early hour and the aftereffects of last night's over imbibing. In fact, there was a distinct headache forming right between his brows.

"Yes!" Arthur all but hissed the words. "I cannot be found with a man in my bed!"

Linc wanted to curse, having assumed they were past these types of pretenses—at least in Arthur's own home. "My apologies." He stood from the bed stiffly and began pulling on his clothing. "I had no idea we would continue to sneak around, even within these walls."

"Hush!" Arthur snapped.

"My lord? The door appears to be locked." Travers announced the obvious to all and sundry as he knocked at the door.

"Yes," Arthur replied as he pulled his sleep shirt on over his head. "I didn't wish to be disturbed last night."

Linc finished gathering his things and moved to the door that joined the master's chambers. It would have been the future countess' rooms, but under the circumstances, it seemed a perfect place to hide until the servants departed.

"Linc—" Arthur's voice called out in hushed tones.

"Don't." Linc cut off his excuses and slipped away quietly. He didn't need more disappointment piled on top of yesterday's heartache.

Chapter Twelve

March 1862

Avoiding Linc was proving bloody difficult for Arthur. It didn't help that none of their circle was aware of their estrangement. The Lustful Lords were marching right along, pairing off and falling in love, with no notion of what had occurred between him and Linc. And they certainly had no idea about...*her*.

Arthur's gut clenched. He couldn't even conjure her name, let alone speak it.

He was at yet another ball and there was Linc, smiling and beguiling the ladies with his charm. *The bloody*—

Arthur sighed. He wanted to hate Linc, but sadly, he knew it was his own fault they were apart. His own fears and insecurities held him back. It had been one thing when—he nearly choked on her name—when Jo had been there as a buffer. But there had been no denying that the night he'd let Linc take him, there had been something between them, even without her there.

Now the man was parading around London's ballrooms as though he didn't have a care in the world. And damn him to hell, Arthur couldn't look away. Couldn't stop watching. The way Linc's dark blue eyes sparkled with mischief. His sly, puckish smile as he said something undoubtedly outrageous to the young miss he was dancing with.

Something primal and needy inside of Arthur demanded that he make Linc bow to him. Make him kneel before him and take whatever he chose to give him. The notion was so strange and foreign he nearly recoiled physically as he stood next to his friend Lord Stonemere and his brother-in-law, Lord Brougham.

"Are you well, Dunmere?" Cooper, Lord Brougham, stared at him.

"I think I shall take some fresh air on the balcony. It's a bit stuffy in here." Arthur made to leave the group he stood with.

"Arthur, do be sure to dance with a few of the eligible ladies." His sister, Emily, Lady Brougham, gave him an arch look. "You did promise to make an *effort*."

Refusing to say anything—after all, he had promised to make an effort to find a match, but that had been before Jo and Linc—he chose to nod in acknowledgement. What could he say to his sister?

Soon he found himself in the frosty night air on the balcony where only those seeking escape from the evening's entertainments or some form of privacy would venture. He moved to the far end of the space and melted into the shadows, happy for the reprieve.

"There you are, Dunmere." An all too familiar voice followed him into the shadows.

The two men stood in silence as Arthur's body warred with his upbringing and societal expectations.

"You know, you can't avoid me forever." Linc's voice held a note of sardonic humor.

Needled by his mocking tone and cool sense of confidence, Arthur looked at where the moonlight shone down on Linc.

"You're the one who walked away. What makes you think I've been avoiding you?"

"I've seen you at the last three balls I've attended, yet each time I visit with our friends, I find you conspicuously absent." Linc let one silvery brow lift in question. "And I left because you hurt me. Staying would only have led to more hurt, on both our parts."

"A coincidence. As good etiquette dictates, I ensure I do my duty and dance with a few of the ladies. It just so happens to have aligned with the times you chose to greet everyone." Arthur tried to sound as nonchalant as he wanted Linc to think he felt about it. Not that he had carefully timed each absence from the group to avoid any awkward meetings, which, of course, he had. His cock twitched, highlighting why that strategy had been so very necessary. "And I suppose you are right. I—" Arthur swallowed, guilt swamping him. "I did not handle that moment well. I'm sorry if I hurt you. You're my friend first and foremost and I would never wish to do that again."

But he would one day, won't he? Because he'll have to marry. Eventually.

Linc edged closer to him, crowding him in the darkened corner and drawing him from his thoughts. "Good. I should hate to think that you were dodging me. Evading this thing between us."

Arthur growled, his earlier instinct rising to the fore in a most unexpected surge. He snaked out a hand and fisted it in Linc's hair as he drew the man closer. "I thought you were past sneaking about."

"I was caught off guard and rather hungover. It wasn't the moment to discuss your obvious concerns. But when I looked for you later in the day at a reasonable hour, you had hied off to your country house." Linc sounded hurt, perhaps even a tad resentful.

"I-" Arthur hesitated, trying to remember what he'd thought that morning. "I was still so fuzzy from the night before and the way you left, I assumed you were done with me."

Linc lifted a hand to his face. "Wary perhaps, but not done. You returned to London but did not seek me out. I thought to give you the space you seemed to desire." He appeared to swallow, his throat bobbing with the motion. "You...you are all I have left. I didn't want to overstep more than I had. I thought—hoped—you would come to me when you were ready. But you haven't."

It was too much to bear, too much to hear without acting. Arthur took Linc's mouth with his own and the kiss was one of possession. Ownership. Their tongues tangled and twined but Linc sank into it, melted in to him: submitted to him.

Arthur turned him and pinned him against the stone railing. Their cocks had both grown hard. His own pulsed and throbbed with need as they rubbed against each other. A low groan escaped one of them, Arthur wasn't sure who, as the kiss lingered and slowly ended when the need to breathe took over.

He rested his forehead against Linc's. "We need to talk about how this might work, but I've been miserable without you this past month. It's bad enough being without Jo. I don't want to lose you as well."

Linc inhaled sharply. "We should talk. I know discretion is important to you, but I refuse to be relegated to shadowed corners and back alleys." He huffed a laugh. "Well, any more than is necessary." Linc tucked his nose into the crook of Arthur's neck and inhaled deeply, as though he needed his scent to sustain him. "Take a few days to think about it. Let me know when you are ready to discuss the possibilities." Then the handsome man slipped away as quietly as he'd appeared.

Arthur stood there in the dark, reeling. The taste of Linc lingered on his lips as he tried to imagine how he might configure his life in such a way to fit a man such as Linc. He would have to marry eventually to carry on the title, but suddenly the thought didn't seem so bleak. After all, they had found Jo, who had loved them both. Was it possible they could find another woman who could feel the same?

Chapter Thirteen

A Few Days Later

Linc strode into The Market and looked around the main salons. Arthur was nowhere to be found, but that didn't exactly surprise him. They had agreed to meet at midnight and it was only a few minutes past eleven. Linc had been restless sitting in his rooms, watching the clock. He thought at least here he could find some distraction, either in the form of socializing with the ladies or in a card game. He had no particular preference for which, just that the time pass less slowly.

Before he allowed himself to be diverted, he sought out Madame du Pompadour's right-hand man. "Good evening, Phillippe."

"Good evening, my lord." Phillippe bowed. "How may I be of service?"

"Can you arrange the Blue Room for Dunmere and I? We may send down for a few of the girls as well once we're settled." Linc staunchly tried to ignore the fluttering in his stomach. *He would not be nervous about this meeting.* It's not as if Arthur had told him to be on his way. He would've carried on with a stiff upper lip like the good Englishman he was.

But that hadn't been the case. At least not yet. Arthur had agreed to meet here. That had to mean he intended to carry on. *Good God, he hoped so!*

"Very good, my lord." Phillippe bowed again and hustled off to see to the requested arrangements.

Nearly an hour later, as Linc folded on yet another losing hand—he was far too distracted to be playing cards—the very person who was drawing his focus waltzed into the card room. Arthur was looking very dapper in his black evening suit with a swallow-tail coat, black waistcoat, white shirt, and white tie. Never mind the fact that every other man in the room, including himself, wore the exact same evening dress.

"If you will excuse me, gentlemen." Linc stood as the other men at the card table nodded and bid him good evening. He crossed to the bar where Arthur was ordering a drink. "Excellent timing. I required a reason to step away from that table and cease my losses."

"Happy to be of service." Arthur picked up the glass the bartender had placed before him and saluted Linc. "Other than a few losses, how has the rest of your night been?"

"Interminable." Linc opted for honesty.

Arthur chuckled. "I felt every tick of the clock like a physical touch. Tap. Tap. Tap. Midnight could not come soon enough. Why did we think this was a good time to meet?"

Linc laughed. "I was a bloody fool. I have no idea what I was thinking. Shall we head upstairs to talk? I reserved the Blue Room when I arrived earlier."

They chatted about the latest gossip as they climbed the stairs, keeping the conversation light. When they were finally alone, Linc poured himself a drink, repressing the urge to immediately taste Arthur once again. Drinks in hand, they finally sat down in the two wing chairs by the fire.

"I suppose we should come to terms about this arrangement between us."

"Agreed." Arthur took a deep breath. "You need to understand right from the start, at some point, I shall have to marry. I have a title to pass on."

"Understood. Not everyone is in the position I am. I'm perfectly happy passing my title on to my cousin or his heirs, eventually." Linc took a sip of his drink.

Arthur nodded. "For now, it may be easiest if we meet here. I...I don't wish to put either of our staffs in a difficult position."

Linc considered the suggestion for a moment. "That makes sense. Eventually we may find it more convenient to meet at one of our homes, but for now I see the sense in your suggestion. I'd also like to suggest we leave the door open to sharing a woman as we did with Jo. If we meet someone we both care for, we might find the arrangement works for us."

"I'm afraid I am not prepared to open up to a woman like that again. At least for now, I'd rather the two of us find our footing first. Then we could consider bringing in someone if we found her to be as perfect for both of us as Jo seemed. As I said, I will need to marry." Arthur shrugged and took a long drink from his glass. "I know there is this attraction between us. There is no denying it. But I feel I should warn you off of any emotional entanglements. I simply must marry, my bloodline demands it. Once I do, I fully intend to commit to the marriage."

Linc stuffed down the disappointment rearing up inside. Arthur was right; it made little sense to allow emotional entanglements. They could enjoy each other. They were friends. But that was all it could ever be, nothing beyond the physical. "Understood and agreed."

Arthur grunted his response and drained his glass. Then he stood up and stretched before he removed his coat. "Can I get you a refill?"

Linc looked at his still half-full tumbler. "I'm good, I thank you. I want a clear head for what comes next."

"Agreed." Arthur pulled a cigar out of his pocket and held it out toward Linc. "A smoke then?"

Linc shook his head. "No, thank you." His father had enjoyed cigars, and he still liked the pungent aroma, but it was not a habit he had ever indulged. He supposed it was better than Arthur having another drink. The man seemed to be indulging more lately, between the loss of Jo and the strain between them. Hopefully that would change soon.

He sensed a certain tension building in the room now they were agreed on terms. Sitting and watching Arthur, Linc's arms and legs vibrated with a restlessness he could only attribute to desire. Perhaps also a bit of nervousness. Arthur had an air of confidence Linc had noticed more and more in the rest of his life. Now it seemed to be spilling over into Arthur's intimate moments, and Linc found it damned attractive. A commanding presence that seemed to draw him in and hold him captive.

He would never have described himself as the submissive type. He'd been a lord for far too long, and though he was not perhaps as dominant as Stone, he certainly was one to state his needs and expectations without hesitation. This feeling of wanting to serve Arthur, at least in a sexual capacity, felt strange. Strange, but not unwelcome.

Arthur moved to lean against the chair with his cigar still unlit in his hand. "Strip for me, Linc."

The vibration in Linc's limbs became a full-on quiver as he stood up, excitement thrumming through him. He commenced removing his clothing, letting Arthur watch.

His lover spoke. "I watched you from across various ballrooms for weeks, all the while wishing your clothing to perdition."

"It was too bad you kept your distance for so long." Linc let one brow lift, punctuating his rebuke. "But I suppose this more imposing version of you may be my recompense for all that silent suffering."

Arthur barked out a laugh. "When have you ever been silent about a bloody thing?"

Linc flashed a smile, the devil inside him rearing its head. "I bit my tongue bloody every time I stood there watching you sweep some chit around the ballroom while I wished— we could be alone again." He removed his shirt and tossed it over the chair. He cursed himself mentally for the near emotional slip. Arthur was right, he needed to hold himself back or he would be hurt. "I most certainly kept my lascivious thoughts to myself as I remembered how it felt to fall to my knees and suck your cock. I most definitely did not share with anyone how I wished it was your hand wrapped around me when I lay in bed alone stroking my cock."

Arthur cursed as he set his unlit cigar down and closed the distance between them just as Linc dropped his last bit of clothing to the floor. Their mouths fused as their tongues met and tangled. A low moan escaped from him as Arthur gripped his cock and stroked, though he managed to maintain enough focus to work the buttons on Arthur's waistcoat. Once he had that open Linc pushed it off his shoulders, momentarily disrupting the maddening stroke of the hand on his cock. Then he unfastened his lover's trousers and pushed them past his hips. With Arthur's cock freed, Linc dropped to his knees and took him hungrily in his mouth.

He relished the way Arthur filled his mouth, pushing into his throat; the way Arthur thrust in and out, taking him as his hand sank into his hair. It was highly erotic and made him want to take more.

But then Arthur withdrew. "I have plans that do not include my coming down your throat—not tonight."

Linc smiled. He sincerely hoped Arthur's plan aligned with his own needs, but he supposed he'd live if they didn't.

"On the bed, on your elbows and knees." Arthur's directions were crisp, but held a hint of the strain it was causing him to shift their positions.

Linc complied, lowering his head and elbows to the mattress as he waited for Arthur to join him.

He didn't wait for long before he felt the heat of Arthur closing in behind him. His balls drew up in anticipation as he waited for a touch. Any touch.

Then he felt it. The soft caress of a fingertip as it traced between his arse cheeks. He took a shallow breath and savored the gentle touch, the way his entrance clenched in need.

The finger returned, this time cool with salve as his lover pushed past the tight ring of his muscle. Linc quivered with pleasure as Arthur's digit slowly sank inside him. It was wonderful, wonderful and not nearly enough.

But patience would serve his ends far better than trying to hurry the man.

"I love the way your heat engulfs my finger. It makes me crave that same sensation around my cock." Arthur's voice was raspy, as if he hadn't spoken in months.

"Yes," Linc hissed in response. *God, he wanted that, too.*

Arthur chuckled and withdrew his finger before pushing back inside Linc with what felt like a second finger. Once deep inside him, Arthur spread his two fingers, causing the ring of muscle to stretch, pulling out, stretching him wider and wider. The burn was delicious and had Linc whimpering in pleasure. When he pushed back in, it was with yet another finger. He moaned as he took them and still craved more.

"That's it. Open for me," Arthur murmured as he worked them in and out.

"Please," Linc groaned. "I need you inside me. Need to feel you—you filling me up. Stretching me."

"Fuck," Arthur cursed as he pulled his fingers free of Linc's body. "I wanted to take my time with you, but now all I can think about is being inside of you."

Linc felt the pressure of Arthur's cock as he pressed against his rear entrance. His body stretched, the burning sensation melding into the pleasure as the darkly handsome man slid inside him. Did precisely as he'd asked. "God yes!"

Arthur thrust his hips, thrusting in and out of Linc and causing the most delicious friction. Then he pushed deep on random strokes, hitting that spot deep inside him that caused fireworks to spark.

That deep penetration, combined with the feel of Arthur's big hands gripping his hips as he plunged inside him, had Linc fighting for control. He didn't want this to be over too soon. He wanted to revel in the sensations this man stirred deep within him. He wanted to feel this forever.

"So tight, Linc." Arthur growled. "So. Hot. Around. My. Cock." Each word was punctuated by a deep sudden advance.

"I haven't"—Linc gasped, knowing the words could change everything—"been fucked since you."

Arthur groaned behind him and thrust harder—and on a powerful stroke, Linc exploded. He came hard and long as Arthur reached around to stroke his cock for him. With the last of his pleasure being wrung from him, he fought to stay up on his knees.

Only then did Arthur set up a fast pace, pounding into him until his own orgasm came in a shout of pleasure. Finally, they collapsed onto the bed in a heap of limbs.

"My god I missed you—this, I mean," Arthur murmured as he remained buried in Linc's arse.

"Missed you too," Linc muttered and then held his breath for a moment before slowly releasing it.

It seemed this not being emotionally invested business was going to be much harder for both of them than they realized.

Chapter Fourteen

April 1862

Jo sat in the coach with her husband, George Downs, Marquess of Whitestone. They were finally back from their surprise second honeymoon, on the Continent. She'd thought their sojourn in the country to be their honeymoon, but then Whitestone had announced a surprise tour of Europe and in truth, it had been a restful trip without Whitestone's family in tow.

Butterflies danced in her belly as the vehicle rocked side to side. She'd been feeling poorly all day, but had pulled herself together so she could attend their first ball as a married couple.

"Josephine, if you are feeling poorly, you do not need to attend the ball tonight. I can send you home and have the coach come back for me." Her husband reached over and tipped her face up toward his with a finger under her chin.

She let her lashes drift down to hide the turmoil that burbled beneath her placid surface. In the last three months, she had come to like him very much. He was proving to be a kind and attentive husband, if not a man she was in love with. She tried to remind herself that she was very lucky. Her father could have chosen any number of horrible men to sell her off to. It just so happened that this man was gentle. "Thank you, my lord. I am feeling much recovered and would very much like to attend this evening."

He grunted. "Very well then. Should you find yourself taking a turn, do let me know."

"Of course." Jo doubted she'd say a word, not until she'd had time to search the guests for two in particular. She was hopeful she might see Linc and Arthur at the ball, even if only from a distance.

Half an hour later, she found herself moving through the receiving line to greet their hosts. Once in the ballroom, her husband directed her over to his brother's wife, who stood with her daughter-in-law.

"Lady Agnes Downs, Mrs. Beatrice Downs, you remember my wife, the Marchioness of Whitestone." Whitestone gave her hand a squeeze as the two women curtsied to her.

"Lady Downs, Mrs. Downs. I am pleased to see you all again." Jo darted a worried look at her husband. She had not mentioned to him the less than warm welcome she'd received from the women at their wedding reception, nor his sister and her nephew's treatment at his country house. It seemed no one in the family would welcome her.

She supposed she couldn't blame them; besides being new money, she also represented the likelihood that her husband's brother, Lord Downs, would not inherit the title of Marquess. That is, if she was capable of bearing him a child.

Her gut churned at the thought. Whitestone was kind enough, but his family were a pit of vipers. The thought of raising a child in the midst of such people worried her. She sighed. Of course there was little to worry about at the moment. Possibly never. After all, she'd never fallen pregnant with her first husband, and the man had tried. Repeatedly.

Unaware of her distress, her husband continued, "If you don't mind, I shall leave my wife in your capable hands.

Agnes, I would appreciate you guiding her through the festivities, as she is still learning who is who and how to navigate these waters."

"Of course, my lord. We'd be happy to guide your new bride." Agnes curtsied to her brother-in-law and attempted to smile at Jo as Whitestone made to depart their little group.

"Excellent!" Whitestone turned and bowed to Jo. "I shall collect you for the first waltz later."

"Thank you, my lord." Jo curtsied to her husband and watched his retreating back as her heart sank.

It was hard to ignore his family's blatantly ingratiating behavior—particularly when it changed in a trice once he was gone.

The coldness of Agnes' brown, glittering eyes sent a shiver of alarm down Jo's spine as she faced the women. She had suspected when they'd met during her reception, but now she could say with certainty she did not like the woman. Not one bit.

Agnes cast a critical eye up and down her form. Jo had liked her deep blue gown when she'd dressed that evening. It paired beautifully with the sapphires that her husband had given her while they were on their honeymoon. It would seem Agnes did not share her appreciation for her gown.

"I can see I need to take you in hand, my dear." Agnes waved her fan in front of her face even as she added insult to injury by not addressing Jo properly.

"I'm sure you must have a great deal of advice to offer." Jo offered a slash of a smile.

"Indeed, I do." Agnes puffed up, oblivious to the sarcasm lacing Jo's comment, and leaned over to speak far too loudly with her daughter-in-law. "I see that American girl who caused such a scene at the Lytton ball has arrived." She snapped her fan closed. "The gall of that girl to show her face."

The pair huddled together to gossip about the poor woman, which allowed Jo to slip away. She sidled to the outer edge of the ballroom and sought a vantage point that would allow her to spot her quarry, but circling the space, she found no perfect spot to hide. Instead, she came across the two men she had hoped to see. Spotting a potted fern, she slipped behind its fronds and attempted to blend into the wallpaper as she watched them from behind.

The pair stood together, one dark head leaning against the blond. Jo wished she could hear what they spoke about, but instead settled for appreciating them in profile. Staying tucked behind the plant allowed her to watch as their hands brushed in an ever-so-subtle gesture that spoke volumes to her. Then one of their friends joined them, saying something that caused them all to laugh. Her heart squeezed, momentarily stealing her breath.

Realizing she had been gone quite a while, Jo eased back around the ballroom to where she had left her husband's relations. There she found the snobbish women still gossiping about the other attendees of the ball. She slid back into place beside them. Pulling her fan out, she gently stirred the warm air of the ballroom.

"Where on earth have you been?" Agnes leaned around her daughter-in-law to address Jo. "I was just about to send for Whitestone."

"I slipped off to the retiring room for a few moments." Jo was surprised the woman had even noticed she had disappeared.

"It's not safe for you to wander about on your own." Agnes looked pointedly at her. "There are rakes and rogues a plenty at these events. Why, I even saw some of those Lustful Lords traipsing about."

"I'm sorry, those who?" Jo wasn't sure what the woman was prattling about.

"Precisely my point. How can you know who to avoid and who to speak to at these events? You require my guidance." She tipped her head ever so slightly toward a group of men and women who seemed to be enjoying themselves. "You'd do well to steer clear of *that* group of hedonists. The Lustful Lords are trouble, not the type of people the Marchioness of Whitestone should associate with." She sniffed delicately as if to punctuate her point.

Jo stared at the group Agnes had indicated, shocked to see Linc and Arthur among them. Nonplussed, she replied honestly. "I was not speaking to them."

"And well you shouldn't," Agnes stated flatly. Her daughter-in-law, Mrs. Downs, nodded in agreement.

Deciding that silence would hold her in greater stead, Jo bit her tongue as the ladies continued on with their gossiping. Ignoring their pointless conversation, she angled herself slightly behind Mrs. Downs so she could watch the group Agnes had indicated.

The group seemed...friendly. The women were all dressed in the first stare of fashion and the men impeccably turned out. Handsome to a man, she wondered why they were called the Lustful Lords. Agnes suggested they were rakes and rogues, but that was not how she thought of Linc and Arthur. They had been her protectors, her lovers—they had never taken advantage of her. In fact, she'd been shocked when they had appeared on her doorstep in London, trying to save her from her fate.

When a countess greeted their group and drew Agnes into a conversation, Jo seized the opportunity, daring to ask, "Excuse me, Mrs. Downs?"

The woman was the nicest of the family, so it was no surprise when the pretty brunette turned and offered her a small smile. "Yes, my lady?"

"Why do they call them the Lustful Lords?" Jo asked. Curiosity now mixed with her earlier upset stomach to churn in a nauseating ball. Did she truly wish to know the answer to her question? What would it change?

Mrs. Downs giggled. "Because they were all confirmed bachelors and rogues—at least, until the last two years. They've suddenly all fallen in love and married."

Jo felt all the blood leach from her face as her stomach twisted. *Had they been married men?* "All of them?"

"Well, all but three. I'm not sure which three are still unwed." Mrs. Downs glanced over at the group.

With the blood rushing back to Jo's face, relief flooded her body. *So not married.* Well, she had to assume they were two of the unmarried three. Didn't she?

What little she knew of the men did not support the idea of either of them being married while they had engaged in such vigorous erotic activities with her—though that obviously no longer mattered, now she was a married woman.

Waving her fan once more, Jo smiled back at the woman. "They must have married extraordinary women."

"Oh yes! The ladies are nearly as notorious as their husbands are now. I've heard they are friends with a woman who once ran a brothel."

Jo gasped. "Oh my!"

"It's amazing, really. Despite all the rumors about them, no hostess would dare leave them off her guest list."

Agnes said something that pulled Mrs. Downs back into their conversation, leaving Jo to consider what she had learned. They knew a former brothel owner? How fascinating! More than ever, Jo wished events had unfolded differently.

As she stood there alone with her thoughts, her earlier wave of nausea returned. Working her fan faster, she leaned toward Agnes. "I'm afraid I am not feeling well. I believe I shall go find Whitestone."

"He'll likely be in the card room. One of the footmen can fetch him for you." Agnes said as she turned to greet some of her friends who had just arrived.

Grateful for the escape, Jo turned and went in search of her husband. It would seem she needed the carriage.

The next morning Jo laid in bed, her stomach not feeling well once again. She finally conceded, after much nagging from her maid, that it was probably best to call for the doctor. In her gut, she suspected what was wrong but voicing it—saying it aloud—would be bittersweet.

The doctor finished his exam and closed his bag. "My lady, I am pleased to inform you, that you are with child."

Jo mustered up a small smile for the doctor. "I was fairly certain that was the case. Thank you for confirming."

He patted her hand. "I know you don't feel well just now, but that should pass before long. Try eating some dry toast or crackers in the morning to help settle your stomach."

"Thank you, doctor." She let her eyes slip closed as he turned to leave.

Despite the nausea churning with the dollop of sadness inside her, Jo pushed the errant feeling aside and hauled herself out of the bed to ring for her maid. She needed to dress and find her husband with their news. He would certainly be pleased to hear that she now carried his child.

The question was, would she bear him the coveted heir...or a girl?

Chapter Fifteen

June 1862

Arthur leaned over Linc's shoulder, peeking into the hallway of The Market as they watched Matthew Derby, the Marquess of Flintshire, speaking to Mrs. Rosalind Smith in the hallway. They were speaking rather low and urgently when he waved at her. "We're down here."

Mrs. Smith was the widowed sister of Lady Julia Wolfington who had married their friend and fellow Lustful Lord, Grayson Powel, Viscount Wolfington. She looked past Flint's shoulder and blinked. It appeared that she'd somehow missed the fact they were looking on. She grabbed Flint's hand and marched him down the hall into the room they were leaning out of.

She quickly scanned the space before she dragged Flint over to a chair at the table and pointed. "Sit."

Then she turned to Linc. "I need fresh water, bandages, and if they have some salve, it would not come amiss."

Jokester that he could be, Linc saluted her smartly and marched out of the room.

Arthur stood there, watching everything unfold until she turned to him. "Pour me two fingers of brandy or whisky in a glass."

He moved across the room immediately. As he was busy selecting a glass and pouring the requested drink, he could hear the murmur of low voices. It appeared Flint had been in pain since he'd arrived at The Market, fresh from another dockside bareknuckle fight. He carried the glass of whisky over and set it down on the table.

Flint reached for it, but Mrs. Smith swiped the glass filled with amber liquid before he could wrap his hand around it. "That's mine."

She tossed the contents down her throat and, handing the glass back to him, said, "A refill, if you please."

"Mrs. Sm—"

She waved a hand at Arthur. "The next one is for medicinal purposes." She turned her focus back on her patient. "And I do not mean for you to imbibe. I'm sure you've had quite enough to numb the pain already."

Arthur returned to the sideboard to pour a second glass when the door of the room opened again and Linc appeared, followed by a small troop of servants who deposited their offerings on the table. He joined them, delivering the whisky as well.

"My lords, thank you for your kind assistance. Perhaps you could give us some privacy while I see to his injuries?" She looked first at Linc, then Arthur, and finally, she dragged her gaze to the door of the room in a clear request.

With a smirk and a nod, Linc nudged Arthur as he stood there in surprise. In short order, they hustled out the door.

In the hall, he stopped and looked at Linc. "Did she just toss us from our room?"

Linc laughed as he closed the door. "Indeed she did. But no matter—we have more important business to attend to. I saw a fine specimen downstairs. I think we should grow better acquainted with her, if you're game to try again? Something light and fun, as we discussed."

Arthur swallowed and nodded. It hadn't taken either of them long to grow comfortable with each other. Perhaps too comfortable. And as much as he enjoyed being with Linc, he was curious if adding a woman to the mix ever again would be possible. He couldn't help but wonder if what they found with Jo was an anomaly.

But then, this would be something light. Fun. Not an actual candidate for their third.

In the main salon, Linc led him over to an attractive blonde sitting amidst a bevy of admirers. "Miss Samantha, may I introduce my good friend, Arthur?"

He took her hand and bent to kiss it. "A pleasure to meet you."

"Oh my, I believe the pleasure is all mine." She spoke with a soft American accent that held a drawl he knew came from the southern part of the country. It was enchanting.

"Might we invite you for a drink with us, in a more private setting?" Linc suggested, to the dismay of more than one man who had been paying court to her.

"As long as Madame has approved that, I'd be happy to join you." She simpered from behind her fan.

"Give me a moment to secure a room for us." Linc nodded and moved away. As he passed Arthur, he murmured, "See if you can help her extricate herself."

"Of course." He nodded and looked back to Samantha. "Miss, may I help you stand?" He leaned over and offered her his hand.

"Thank you, my lord." She smiled and rose. "Gentlemen, it has been very diverting to sit with y'all. I do hope y'all will come back to see me real soon."

The men stood as well and bowed slightly. Once Arthur had her free of the group, he could see she was a petite woman, though not as much as their Wood Sprite had been.

Pushing the wayward thought away, he focused on the lovely woman at his side. "Have you been in London long? I don't recall seeing you here before."

"I'm new to The Market, though I came to your lovely city a few months ago." She smiled, but there were shadows in her lovely blue eyes.

Linc strolled up. "I've secured the Red Room for us." He turned his focus on Samantha. "With Madame du Pompadour's blessing."

"How perfectly lovely." Her smile brightened and turned sultry. "I feel certain you gentlemen will be more than capable of showing a lady such as myself a pleasurable evening."

In their room, Linc and Arthur worked together to strip Samantha's copious outer garments. Down to her virtually sheer chemise, it was clear she did not need her corset to create her curves. Her breasts were just a bit more than a handful, topped with nipples that looked like ripe berries. Her waist nipped in before rounding out to generous hips. Arthur's cock rose to attention as he and Linc shed their own garments. Once Arthur dropped his trousers and underclothes, Samantha dropped to her knees and took his cock in her mouth. It had been months since anyone other than Linc had wrapped their lips around his length, so the soft lusciousness of her lips surrounding his cock was a little shocking and very pleasurable.

Linc was at his side, turning his face toward him for a long, deep kiss. Their tongues tangled, intensifying the sucking sensation on his cock.

When she released him, she seemed to notice their kiss. "Oh my I do declare, I believe this is going to be a highly diverting evening."

Linc broke their kiss and smirked. "It can be as diverting as you wish."

Arthur reached over, wrapped Linc's cock in his hand, and stroked it as he said, "If you might be interested in managing both of us at the same time. If not, we're happy to mix things up."

She fanned herself with her hand. "I believe that may be the most inflammatory offer I've ever received. I don't know why people say you lords are a bunch of prigs."

"Can't imagine, love." He stroked Linc's cock once more. "Now show him how magical that mouth of yours is."

She did as he bade and sucked Linc's length into her mouth as Arthur watched. Linc moaned while he hung on to Arthur as though his knees might give out. After a few minutes, she pulled off Linc's cock and stood up. Standing before them, she pushed the straps of her chemise off her shoulders and let it slide to the floor.

Arthur was ready, past ready to be inside her. "Arse or cunny, Linc?"

"Arse. I want to feel that bulbous round backside pressing against me as I fuck her." Linc grinned.

Arthur groaned as he imagined feeling Linc slide against him as they both filled Samantha. "Not a problem for me."

"Sounds delightful," Samantha purred as she climbed onto the bed.

Bloody right, it sounded delightful. Arthur followed her on to the bed. He moved up to the headboard and positioned himself so he lay in a partially reclined position. Then he donned a French Letter before he helped her straddle his cock. As she slid down, memories of doing this with Jo intruded, nearly spoiling the moment. Arthur pushed the impossible desire away and focused on the woman at hand. As Samantha slid down onto his cock, she sighed softly.

Then Linc pressed in behind her. Arthur could feel him preparing her to take him, his long fingers sliding in and out of her arse as he faintly brushed against Arthur's cock. she lifted, moaned, and leaned forward as Linc pushed inside her, stretched her. Arthur knew how delicious that felt, the fullness of having Linc inside him. For a brief moment, he wished the woman wasn't here, that it was just the two of them.

Once Linc was in, they moved. With Samantha up on her knees, Arthur was able to push up into her with short strokes as Linc pulled out. Their cocks rubbed over each other inside of her, adding heat and friction to the experience. Though they both wore French Letters, it was all intensely pleasurable. Never one to leave a woman—even a professional—unfulfilled, Arthur leaned forward to lick and suck at one of her nipples. Leaning on one hand to hold herself up against the headboard, Samantha used the other to lift her breast to his mouth.

Linc pumped inside her, shoving in and pulling out. "I-I can't hold on."

Arthur was close as well, but he refused to permit himself climax. "Not until Samantha comes."

She moaned.

"Come for us," Arthur demanded, sucking hard on her nipple as he pushed up inside her.

"Yes," she cried out as her body spasmed around his cock. "Yes, I'm coming!"

With that, Arthur pumped once, twice more, and then his balls tightened up and he came with a shout of pleasure.

Linc was a hair behind him, his yell of release melding with his own. As they all caught their breath, his gaze met Linc's, and he saw the same pang of sorrow he felt in his own chest.

They loved sharing a woman, but it was quickly becoming clear that just any woman wouldn't do. How would they ever find a woman to replace Jo?

Chapter Sixteen

July 1863

Arthur sat in his study, looking through his correspondence. He was to meet Linc at their club later and then they would likely retire to Arthur's home, since he had taken steps to ensure his staff's discretion. They'd given up meeting at The Market not long after their last encounter with a woman between them. While he cared deeply about Linc, there was only one woman he wanted between them.

And she was no longer theirs.

Pushing aside the painful memories, he tried to focus on the letters his secretary had left on his desk for his attention. But there was a knock at his door.

"Enter."

"Your sister the Countess of Brougham is here to see you, my lord, " Harris, his butler, announced.

He repressed the sigh that wanted to escape. If Emily was there, it couldn't mean anything good. She normally only came to see him when she wished to harass him—in that loving way only a sister could—about one thing or another. Usually about his marriage prospects. "Please show her in."

"Very good, my lord." Harris bowed and swept out of the room.

A few minutes later, his sister swept in, looking elegant in her apple green walking gown. "Good, you're home, Arthur."

"Indeed I am, Em. What can I do for you on this fine summer day?" He settled back into his chair, resigned to enduring whatever she was here for. As if he did not know.

She settled into a chair across from him, her skirts swishing with an authority he couldn't remember her having before she'd become a countess. "Arthur, I'm here about your promise to me. The one you have not been holding up your end of the deal on."

Arthur groaned. Out loud. He should never have made her that promise to find a wife—but he'd needed her to marry the Earl of Brougham, for her own reputation.

Her gaze narrowed. "Do not do that. You promised me you'd look for a wife and I have left you alone for a good while. No match making. No hints. No nudges."

He closed his eyes. How could he tell her? How could he explain it wasn't his fault? He raised his hands to his head. "Em, I know. And I have tried. I swear it."

"How Arthur? How have you tried?" Her hazel eyes glinted green as her gaze drilled into him.

"I've danced with ladies." Arthur resisted the urge to cross his arms and pout like a petulant child.

"You have, but that is all you have done. One dance each, with a few eligible ladies. Nothing more. Not one of them warranted a second dance?"

"No." He met her stare. "Not one."

"How is that possible? What are you looking for in a wife?"

He sighed. "It's not as simple as you think."

Arthur's gut churned. Should he tell her? Should he reveal his deepest secret? A truth he hadn't even shared with the person it most concerned?

"Then help me understand. What are you looking for? Perhaps I can help you find it?" His sister looked earnest, not angry.

Silence stretched between them. Long and thick with tension.

He cursed and jumped from his chair to pace. "Em, I need to tell you something. I don't know how you will feel about this. And I need to ask you to keep what I tell you private."

He continued to walk back and forth in front of the enormous fireplace. He could feel her gaze on him, nearly a physical touch.

"Whatever it is, Arthur, you can trust me."

"I know, I do. But it's still new to me. Something I am wrestling with in some ways."

Emily rose and came to him, cupped his cheek in her hand. "I love you, Arthur. You could never tell me anything that would change that."

He laughed worriedly. "Be careful. You never know how much I may test such a vow."

"It can't be worse than you discovering I was a jewel thief." Emily dropped her hands and clutched them in front of her as she stepped back. "Tell me."

"I met someone. Two someones, to be honest." He offered her a wry smile.

"And you can't decide?"

"I had no need to choose. I love them both and I believe they love me. Well, at least one of them I'm fairly certain does. The other is unavailable."

"I don't understand." She stood staring at him, confusion and distress playing out across her face.

"I'm in love with another man—"

Emily gasped in shock.

"—and a woman." Arthur wanted to groan out loud as he voiced his truth. He'd denied it for so long because he knew the challenges loving a man created. He had a title to pass on. He needed to marry, sire heirs, yet he loved Linc.

He had yet to tell the man, but deep inside, he knew the truth.

"Oh, dear." Emily stepped back and flailed for the nearest chair.

Seeing her need to sit, Arthur grabbed her arm and helped her find her seat. She'd gone most pale.

He knelt at her side. "Em, are you well?" Blast, he shouldn't have told her.

"I'm fine. I've been a bit under the weather lately. Nothing serious." She tried to put him off.

"Lady Emmaline Brougham, you will not sit here, demand my secrets, and expect me to accept such a vague response." Still kneeling, he looked up into her face. "Tell me what is wrong."

She smiled sweetly. "Nothing is wrong, it is just...I am with child."

Arthur grinned. "A baby?"

"Yes." She smiled back. "A baby. We think he or she will arrive just in time for Christmas."

"Congratulations!" He hugged her close. "What wonderful news!"

His sister's joy beamed from her face. "It is, but we haven't told anyone. You're the first." Her face grew stern. "And you are sworn to secrecy until we formally announce the news."

"My lips are sealed. But I am truly happy for you."

"Thank you. Now tell me about this man—and woman you are in love with." His little sister was already acting more like a mother, focusing on the important things. Her child would be well cared for, and most importantly, loved.

Arthur sighed and stood up. "I'm in love with Linc."

"Oh, that's wonderful!" His sister sounded genuinely happy for him.

"It's taken me a long time to come to terms with how I feel. It's not how we were raised. It's not even legal." He let those words hang in the air for a moment. "But I can't deny how I feel, though I haven't told him yet."

"Do you think he suspects?" she asked gently.

"I've just come to a place where I can admit the truth. It's been difficult for me and I didn't want to say something I didn't truly mean or that I felt I might wish to take back later."

"You have become a very thoughtful person. I am sure he will be glad to know you waited until you were certain." Emily was not at all appalled, it seemed. "Now, who is this woman?"

Arthur fell into his seat. "We met her last January and the three of us fell in love. She was a widow, with her own fortune, but her father forced her to marry a peer for his title. I tried to offer for her, but I was too late."

"Oh, no!" His sister empathized with him in a way that soothed his still ragged soul.

"She is married now, with a child. There is no hope we might all be together, so Linc and I are trying to find what happiness we can together." Arthur shrugged. "So I dance with ladies at balls, and truthfully, we have looked for someone who might stir those feelings in us again. But as of yet, we have not found anyone."

"Oh Arthur." His sister stood and went to him. Pulling him up and out of his chair as she wrapped her arms around him. "I am both happy and sad for you. I am thrilled you have found someone to love, but sad you lost the woman you both embraced."

"Thank you. As you can imagine, it is imperative that you keep this to yourself. I'm trying to find the right time to tell Linc how I feel, and well, with her, there is no hope." His heart pounded in his chest as though he'd been galloping across the countryside.

"Of course. Your secret is safe with me. After everything we've been through? I should think I've proven I'm quite capable of keeping secrets." His sister gave him a pointed look.

"Indeed you have, my little jewel thief." A sigh of relief escaped him. Now he just had to figure out how and when to tell Linc.

A few days later, Arthur and Linc went for a midday ride through Hyde Park to break in Linc's new mount. It was not the fashionable hour, but it did allow for them to gallop, and with fewer people, the less likely the colt would be to become skittish.

Well, that had been the hope. Linc had pulled a little ahead of him when they heard a woman cry out.

The next thing Arthur knew Linc had yanked back on the reins of his horse, causing the colt to rear up. A scream sounded from the woman—and he saw it. A white fluff of fur was bolting into the field, having crossed the path. Linc had fallen off his horse and landed flat on his back but the dog was still hot-footing it into the field and toward the tree line on the other side.

With a curse, Arthur looked over at Linc who waved him on. He swerved his stallion to the left and took off after the dog, quickly passing the animal and leaping from his horse to snatch the panicking snowball. The dog squirmed in his arms then began licking his face as he grabbed the reins of his horse and walked back to where the woman knelt over Linc.

She stood as he approached and reached for her dog, freeing Arthur to check on Linc.

Kneeling at his side, he bent over his lover—no, the man he loved. "Linc!"

Linc lay there with his eyes closed, unresponsive. Arthur patted his cheek, trying to bring him around, but had no luck.

Turning to the woman who hovered nearby, Arthur asked, "Do you have any smelling salts?"

"Oh! I do. My Aunt Ida frequently faints so I keep some in my reticule." She pulled out the little tube and passed it to him. After breaking it beneath Linc's nose, the man's eyes fluttered as he moaned.

"Bloody hell! Get that stench away from me." Linc pushed Arthur's hand away.

The woman gasped. "Such language!"

Arthur grinned at Linc before turning to look up at the woman. "Madam, please excuse my companion. He is not quite himself after such a fall."

"Very well." Her tone was begrudging and her face pinched, but she said no more.

Returning his focus to Linc, Arthur pressed him to the ground when he tried to sit up. "Stay put a moment more. You took a nasty spill."

"I'm fine, let me up." Linc frowned and attempted to sit up again.

"Is he feeling better now?" The woman still hovered nearby. "I'm terribly sorry. Fluffy surprised me and escaped, I nearly fainted when she bolted under your hooves."

"I'm fine. Just glad I didn't trample the poor little creature." Linc rubbed his forehead.

Arthur helped him up slowly. Once he'd gained his feet, he handed the injured man his hat after he dusted himself off.

Linc nodded and plopped it on his head before he turned to the woman. "I do hope Fluffy will recover from her ordeal."

The woman smiled a bit. "Thank you. You've been very understanding." She turned and left the pair of them, crooning to her dog as she went.

"Shall we make our way to your house, Arthur? I believe you live closest to the park, and I'm not sure I'm up for more galloping today." Linc took hold of his horse's reins, which had been dangling to the ground.

"I should think so," Arthur agreed before they ambled carefully toward his home.

All the way back to his house, he fretted over Linc, who continued to assure him he was hale. By the time they arrived in Arthur's study, he was frazzled by having imagined Linc's neck had been snapped in the accident. He closed and locked the door before pushing Linc against it. "You scared me to death today."

Linc grinned. "Worried about who could stand to pal around with you if I was gone?"

"You bloody fool! You could have snapped your neck! I love you, I would have been devastated to lose you!" Arthur crushed his lips against Linc's.

Their tongues twined around each other as his surge of emotions overflowed. Taking Linc's face in his hands, slid his tongue deeper to explore. To taste. Soon Linc went soft against him, giving in to the sensuous kiss that had gone from claiming and needy to soft and languorous.

As their lips parted so they could breathe, Linc smiled. "I love you too."

Arthur's heart skipped a beat or three as they stared at each other. However this had happened, he would not deny how he felt. He wanted to embrace the happiness and this man was the center of it all.

Linc looked at him with uncertainty and then took a breath. "What now?"

Chapter Seventeen

August 1863

Linc was...happy. He was in love with a man who returned his feelings and they were going to tell their friends. It was a big step.

Straightening his cravat, he then smoothed down the lapels of his coat before knocking on the door of Arthur's home.

His butler opened the door. "Good afternoon, Lord Lincolnshire."

"Good afternoon, Harris." Linc walked in. "I assume he's in his study?"

"Yes, my lord." Harris bowed and closed the door.

"Excellent. I know the way." Linc nodded and wandered off to find Arthur. He was a bit early, but they had wanted a few minutes to review how they would tell everyone. He walked into the study and found Arthur standing, staring out a window. The sun streamed in, lining his tall, lean body. Linc knew well how much strength was contained in that whipcord body. It was something he relished about the other man. "Hello, Arthur."

He turned to face him. "Oh good, you're earlier than expected." He crossed the room to greet Linc, placing his hand on the back of his neck and pulling him in for a kiss.

After a few moments, Linc pressed his hands to his chest and pushed back from the drugging kiss. "Cease, or I shall have to greet our friends with a raging cock stand."

Arthur laughed. "Very well. I'm glad you came early. I have just found out my neighbor is selling his townhouse."

"And this is important because...?" His gut told him this was important to Arthur, but he wasn't sure why.

"We've barely been together officially for two months and you are ignoring me." Arthur shook his head. "I may have to punish you for such carelessness."

Linc laughed. "You wouldn't punish me."

A hungry gleam appeared in Arthur's brown eyes. "Oh, but I think I might. I've been having delicious fantasies of reddening your arse before I fuck you."

Linc's breath hitched in his chest. He was no true masochist like Flint, but he enjoyed a good spanking now and then. That Arthur was expressing an interest in such a thing was inspiring news. He loved it when the man became dominating and growly. He reached down and adjusted his hardening cock. "Not helping, Arthur."

His lover smiled at Linc, an almost feral grin. "Not helping who? I'm feeling quite good about this little chat. Though I do digress." He took a breath and a step back.

Linc drew in more air and tried to focus on willing his cock to go down.

"Lord Warrington lives next door, and he is putting the place up for sale. That means you could buy the house and we could create a door between the two homes so we can pass through undetected."

Linc looked up at Arthur in surprise. "How devious of you. That is good news!"

"Indeed, it is. I'll send a note over immediately to set up a meeting." Arthur strode over to his desk and pulled out a sheet of paper. He quickly scrawled a note, sanded it, and sealed it. Then he tugged the bellpull.

While he was writing the note, Linc poured them each a glass of whisky. He assumed Arthur felt much the same, but he really needed something to help settle his nerves. Arthur took his glass and sipped. "Thank you. About our guests—"

A knock at the door sounded and Harris appeared. "Yes, my lord?"

Arthur handed him the sealed note. "Please have a boy run this next door to Warrington."

Harris took the note and bowed. "Very good, my lord."

A short while later, Arthur and Linc stood in his front salon, surrounded by all the Lustful Lords and their wives. Stone, Cooper, Wolf, Flint, and Lucifer all stood together chatting. The ladies were broken up into two clusters. Theodora, or Theo to her friends in this room, and Emily were colluding in the corner because, where Theo was concerned, there was always a plot. The other group comprised Julia, Ros, and Amelia.

Refreshments were wheeled in on two carts and then his staff retreated.

"Emily, would you mind doing the honors?" Arthur motioned to the two carts.

She smiled at her brother. "Of course. Theo, if you'll pass out sandwiches and cakes, I shall pour."

With the ladies busily passing out refreshments, Arthur herded the men back to where the women were sitting. A few minutes later, with everyone settled again, Arthur looked at Linc and nodded.

Linc cleared his throat and brushed invisible crumbs from his coat as he stood up. "Arthur and I would like to share some news with you all."

Everyone looked up expectantly.

Arthur stood up and took Linc's hand in his. "We've fallen in love."

The ladies all grinned as the men looked to Emily, perhaps to gauge her reaction first. Once they saw her grin, they all stepped forward to congratulate them. There were hugs and backslaps all around.

Once everyone settled back down and returned to their tea, Emily spoke up. "So, please tell us all the details."

Linc deferred to Arthur on this, since it was his sister.

"When we took off to my hunting lodge last year, Linc and I became close. It was an unusual series of events, but we ended up having feelings for each other."

"Last year!" Theo set her tea down with a clatter. "How are we just hearing about this?"

Arthur turned a bit red. "I was—"

Linc reached over and squeezed his hand in support.

"I was having a difficult time coming to terms with how I felt. Our relationship is not the norm, and it took me some time to accept how I felt. I'm very lucky that Linc was so patient with me."

"Well, as patient as one can be with an unmovable obstacle," Linc laughed.

"Yes, it was a trifle difficult for that period where we were not speaking. Frankly, we are both surprised the lot of you missed that rift. But then I suppose you all were so busy falling in love yourselves." Arthur waved a hand toward the group.

Ros grinned. "Do share these unusual events. I smell a story."

Linc nodded, resigned to share the more painful part of their story. "Arthur and I...we met a woman. She is an amazing, vivacious spirit who completely bowled us both over. In the course of sharing her, we found ourselves falling in love with both her and each other."

"But where is she? Did something go wrong?" Julia asked, looking around the room.

Linc cleared his throat. "Unfortunately, her father forced her to marry a lord for his title. We tried to rescue her, but her father moved too quickly. In the end, we lost her."

Arthur leaned against him for a moment. The pang of Jo's loss still reverberated through his very soul—through both of them.

"Oh no! That's awful," Julia crooned as she popped up and stepped forward to hug the pair of them.

Once she stepped back, Linc nodded and tried to swallow the lump in his throat. "We are doing our best to find happiness together. Telling you all is a big part of that."

"I just found out today that the townhouse next door is coming up for sale. I plan to buy it so we can be closer to each other. Under the circumstances, it's the best we can do." Linc couldn't help but smile at Arthur. He relished the love and happiness he found there, despite their loss.

Arthur smiled back. "We should probably speak with our respective staffs, as discretion will be a critical attribute in anyone who works for us."

"An excellent point. But we digress." Linc looked pointedly at him.

"Indeed. All of this is to say, we'd like you all to come to dinner tomorrow night. A meal to celebrate our finding each other and the love that has blossomed between us." Arthur's grin was huge.

Everyone agreed without hesitation, and it felt good to know their friends would support them. Now they had the rest of their lives to enjoy together.

What could possibly go wrong?

Chapter Eighteen

May 1867

Jo's heart was about to leap from her chest. Her palms were sweaty and her knees weak. *Perhaps this was a bad idea?*

It had been so long since she'd spoken to either of them. Occasionally she saw one or both from across a ballroom, but never had she dared to speak to them. She feared her husband would see the truth if she had and—though she had not loved him—she was loathe to hurt him in such a fashion.

But everything had changed.

Sucking in a breath of the cool spring air, Jo braced herself and knocked...and waited. It seemed to take forever for the butler to answer the door.

Finally, it swung open, revealing a middle-aged man wearing simple but elegant livery of black and white. "How may I be of service, my lady?"

She started at the honorific. "How do you know I am a lady?"

The man smiled serenely. "Your clothing betrays you, my lady."

Her brows drew together. "I could be some rich nabob without a title."

"You could, yet I would treat you with the same respect until you made yourself known to me." The man let one eyebrow lift in punctuation. Then he waited.

Jo smiled. "Fair enough. Please would you tell Lord Dunmere that Lady Whitestone is here to see him, Mr.—" She handed over her calling card, unsure what to call the man at the door.

The man took her card and inspected it. "Harris, my lady." Then he bowed before closing the door.

The next time the door opened, it was not Harris, but Linc. "Jo?"

She had been watching the people passing by on the street, so turned at his voice. "Hello, Linc." She smiled hopefully and waited to see what he would say.

Before he could spit out a response, Arthur was there, pushing Linc out of the doorway. "Jo?"

Again she smiled, still standing there on the front stoop. "It's me."

Before she knew what was happening, Arthur was grabbing her hand and dragging her in the house.

She supposed she shouldn't have been surprised to find the pair of them together. It seemed one was rarely found without the other, at least in her experience. Once the door was closed, she found herself being embraced then passed to the other man, over and over again.

Happiness fizzed inside her, bubbling up into a laugh Jo simply couldn't contain. It felt so good to be welcomed with such warmth and affection after so many years apart. So many years spent pretending the barbs and icy animosity of her husband's family didn't matter.

Finally, Arthur set her back from him and blocked Linc from grabbing her once more. "Enough, or the poor woman will think we've gone mad."

She laughed delightedly. "Never! You two were ever the most wonderful pair to spend time with. I couldn't possibly think you mad."

Linc grinned. "It is so wonderful to see you again." He turned to Arthur. "But we are being poor hosts, making the poor thing stand here in the hall." He turned back to her. "Please, take off your cloak and come sit with us." He helped her remove her cloak and handed it off to Harris. The butler took the coat and turned to disappear. "Harris, send in tea and cakes, please."

"Very good, my lord." Harris bowed and departed into the bowels of the house with her cloak.

Jo was ushered into a beautifully decorated salon done in shades of green with dark wood trim. It was both masculine yet welcoming to the fairer sex, an impressive balance to strike. They arranged themselves on the various couches and chairs available so they sat in a perfect triangle that allowed them to see and speak with each other.

Just like old times.

"How are you doing?" Arthur ventured once they'd settled.

"I am well. Perhaps better than well now." She offered a sunny smile that felt as though it would be perpetually plastered on her face when in the company of these two men.

Linc tried to look casual as he lounged in the chair across from her, but she could feel the tension emanating from him. "What brings you here after such a long absence from our lives?"

"Linc! That is no way to welcome our bosom friend back to us," Arthur chided from where he sat, his deeper tones rolling through her and causing sensations she had long forgotten were possible.

Just then a sharp knock sounded, interrupting whatever response Linc had been about to supply. The door of the salon swung open, and a maid wheeled in a cart laden with tea and cakes as requested.

Nervously, Jo smoothed the deep purple sarcenet skirt of her walking gown. *Would they wish to rekindle their understanding?* Even if their amorous feelings had long since faded, she had cherished their friendship. But so much had changed, for them and for her. She did not wish to intrude where she was no longer wanted. After five years of feeling like an intruder, she wanted to be wanted.

Finally the maid had poured and passed out tea to each of them, as well as a plate with an assortment of delicacies to taste. Once they were alone again, Jo cleared her throat. "I am just out of mourning from my husband's passing. And I wished to take the opportunity to renew a few friendships my marriage had not allowed me to maintain. If that is not a welcome turn of events, I completely understand." She fell silent, her hand trembling as she lifted her tea to her lips.

Arthur glanced at Linc, who nodded slightly, then he cleared his throat. "I believe I speak for both of us when I say we would be delighted to renew our acquaintance with you. This is a very welcome turn of events." Arthur smiled gently and took a sip of tea.

"I am thrilled to hear that. I was afraid that after so much time had passed, you two might have forgotten me. We knew each other for such a brief time." Jo hesitated, not sure if she should say her next thoughts, but she was tired of holding her thoughts in after five years of biting her tongue. "But...but remembering our time together sustained me through the dark days of my marriage."

"Was it all terrible?" Linc asked, pain seeping into his voice as though the thought of her misery hurt him physically.

Jo shook her head, trying to gather her thoughts. "No, not all of it. My marriage allowed my sister, Rebecca, to marry for love. She has been happily wrapped in marital bliss for the last four years."

"But what of you?" Arthur asked, concern causing his brow to furrow.

"Honestly, Whitestone was not a bad husband, he was just—" *not you two*, hung on her lips, but she didn't wish to push. "Well, he was just a typical English husband. He had a mistress and other than getting an heir on me, left me be. He was never intentionally cruel, and he was even kind at times." Her lips tipped up on one side in a wry twist. "His family, on the other hand, was awful to me. Are awful to me. If they weren't cutting down my decorating or fashion choices, they were ignoring me as though I didn't exist. When I became pregnant, they turned particularly nasty. But now I am a widow, I am no longer forced to tolerate them as often as when my husband was alive."

"Bloody hell," Arthur said as he set his tea down with a clatter. "Had we known..."

Jo smiled softly, the warmth of his concern wrapping around her chest. "Had you known, you could have done nothing to aid me that would not have made things worse." She took a bite of a cake and moaned at the delicious lemony flavor that burst over her tongue.

The men grew still as their gazes riveted to her. Jo opened her eyes and realized they were staring. Her cheeks grew warm. "My apologies. The cake is divine."

Arthur licked his lips, and all but growled, "Not a problem."

Linc almost choked, ending up in a coughing fit. Arthur rose and slapped him on the back.

Jo took another bite, suppressing the moan this time. The pair of them were still devastatingly handsome and had her senses reeling. She had merely come to see them to renew their friendship but as she sat there, watching them interact, the memories came flooding back. How it felt to be pressed between them. To have them filling her, pleasuring her together.

Heat infused her face, spreading down Jo's neck as the memories continued to come unbidden. She had to set her plate down before she dropped it and tried to calm herself.

A chuckle from the direction of the pair drew her attention.

"Arthur, I do believe our Wood Sprite has begun having wayward thoughts again." Linc's sparkling eyes belied the desire she could sense rolling off him.

"My apologies. I was just remembering old times. I would not presume to expect things to be as they once were." Jo fanned her face, wishing the floor would open and swallow her whole.

"Why not?" Arthur asked, his low voice more gravelly than she remembered.

"I have no idea if either or both of you might be engaged elsewhere, though I shall admit to watching for banns or marriage announcements." She looked at her fingers, knotted in her lap.

"Jo, look at me," Arthur demanded, drawing her gaze from her lap. The power of his voice rolled through her, shaking her to her core. "Neither of us is spoken for. In fact, we are, but perhaps not in the way you would expect. We are committed to each other, despite the limitations of society."

A small gasp escaped her. "You are together? And people know this?"

"Our closest friends do, but we are not trying to flaunt our unusual relationship before the Ton. I can't imagine the shock if Arthur swept me into a waltz in the middle of Almack's." Linc laughed heartily.

She joined him in the laughter, imagining the whole scene. "Yes, that would be a sensational bit of gossip. I suspect it would travel the Ton in record time."

"Yes, and to the magistrates as well, I would imagine," Arthur said. "But more importantly, what were you imagining just now, Jo?"

Could she tell them? Could she not? "I- I was remembering how it felt to be pressed between you both." The words escaped her in a near whisper.

"Where has our bold little Wood Sprite gone?" Linc asked as he rose from his chair. "I remember the woman who read naughty books and demanded what she wanted from us."

Jo's gaze tracked him as he prowled over to where she sat. With Linc as a distraction, she hadn't noticed that Arthur had done the same on her other side. Suddenly she found herself hauled up off the settee and into Arthur's arms.

"If you do not want this Jo—do not want *us*—speak up. Because we never forgot about you, and I am tired of pretending my cock hasn't been hard and throbbing with desire for you since you walked through the door."

"Yes," she said on an exhale of breath. "Oh, kiss me, Arthur."

"Linc, lock the door." Arthur demanded before his lips crashed down on hers.

His tongue swept in and explored her mouth as his hands roamed over her back and down to her bottom. Behind her, she felt the heat of Linc pressing against her as Arthur moaned into her mouth. *This was what she remembered.* Being surrounded by masculine heat and firm bodies made her feel protected. It was wonderful.

Arthur broke their kiss and turned her to face Linc, who captured her mouth. He pushed past her lips and allowed his tongue to explore.

Kissing him was different from kissing Arthur. His exploration was gentler, more searching and less a storming of her defenses. Jo enjoyed both. Letting his care and concern sweep through her as their tongues dueled, she melted into Linc. Then she felt fingers on her buttons, unfastening the smart jacket of her walking gown. Once it had been peeled off they started on her blouse and skirt, each of them taking one of the garments.

It was amazing how quickly a woman could get undressed when two determined men were at hand.

Corset tossed by the wayside, Linc tugged her chemise down and sucked one nipple into his mouth. She arched and moaned as sensation blitzed her body. Arthur pressed behind her, the bare skin of his chest pressing to her back. She sank her fingers into Linc's golden hair as he moved from one breast to the other, licking and sucking.

As pleasure bombarded her, Jo wondered how she'd survived without this, without them for five years?

Chapter Nineteen

Arthur tugged her pantalettes down Jo's legs and groaned. Her body had changed with childbirth, her arse growing rounder, softer, more inviting. He grabbed two handfuls and squeezed, enjoying the new fullness. Then he reached around and pulled Linc's mouth off her breast. "Don't be greedy, Linc."

Linc flashed him a sheepish grin.

As Arthur turned her into his arms, he looked at Linc, desire whipping up from smoldering embers to a full flame. "Strip." Then he focused on pushing Jo's chemise down over her hips to puddle on the floor. "Kneel facing the back of the couch."

The need to demand more burned deep inside him. He wanted to do everything. To touch her everywhere. To bring to life his every fantasy—his every dream. He stripped the remainder of his own clothes and knelt behind her. Taking a cheek in each hand, Arthur opened her to him, exposing her glistening pussy. She was already wet and ready for them.

Leaning forward, he dragged his tongue from her clit up over her opening to push inside. Jo's sweetness burst on his tongue, sending him reeling. He had decided his memory had embellished how good she had tasted, but with confirmation on his tongue, it was hard to deny the accuracy.

"Suck my cock," Linc rumbled somewhere above him. A jostle of movement. "Fuck yes."

Arthur continued feasting on her, swiping his tongue over her clit again and again before sliding his tongue inside her core. Seeing her lips wrapped around Linc's cock as she caused the blissful look on his lover's face only heightened Arthur's arousal. Add that to her moans and groans, and his cock was at full staff as he worked her over.

Then she let out a long, low moan and shook. She released Linc, moaning, "Yes! Yes I'm coming!"

Arthur redoubled his efforts, forcing as much pleasure through her as he could as she rode his tongue. He lapped her juices, relishing the sweetness as she came.

While the shudders of her orgasm subsided, Arthur stood up and plunged deep into her pussy in a single stroke. She cried out at his intrusion, causing him to stop.

"Bloody hell! Did I hurt you?" Panic dripped from his tones.

Jo held Linc's cock in her hand as she caught her breath. "No, it's just been a few years since I've been with a man. Once I had my son, my husband left me alone. Before then, sex was purely for getting an heir on me."

Arthur grunted and tried to ignore the deep satisfaction that she hadn't been with anyone since she fell pregnant. Many Ton wives sought lovers once an heir was provided. That she hadn't? That stirred the dark caveman part of him he tried to suppress. Then he drew back and pushed inside of her once more, Jo's moans heightening his senses as he filled her. "That's it. Take my cock while you suck Linc's."

Licking her gently swollen lips at his command, Jo returned eagerly to Linc's length. This time he sank a fist into her hair, mussing the pins which had remained despite his earlier attention, and slid his cock in and out of her mouth. He matched Arthur's rhythm, the pair of them stroking in and out at the same time.

Together they fucked her, working her over to all their mutual delight. As Arthur sank into her over and over, he spread her cheeks to see the tight sphincter of her anus, imagining how tight she'd feel when he fucked her there.

Realizing he was too close, Arthur released one arse cheek and reached down to find her clit. "Come for us, Jo. Come on my cock while you swallow Linc's cum," he crooned to her as he neared his own release.

"Fuck!" Linc cried and shoved deep in her mouth as he pumped his hips.

Jo swallowed his load greedily until her second orgasm ripped through her, forcing him to finish on her tits as she reared up. Arthur continued pumping into her, but held her by her shoulders, bearing her to Linc as he finished. Then his own orgasm surged as his balls tightened up and the tingling at his spine shot out through his limbs.

He pulled her to him and twisted so he sank on the settee with Jo still in his lap as Linc came around and plopped down next to them. Together they sat, stroking her and recovering.

Linc's world had been turned upside down by the sudden return of Jo. Sitting naked in his front salon with her soft skin under his fingertips was a dream come true. A very dirty, very satisfying dream.

As they sat there, he couldn't help but imagine them spending more time like this in the future. His heart lurched in his chest. *He would do anything to make that idea a reality.*

Jo licked her lips. "I believe I mentioned I have a son."

"I vaguely recall you stating that at some point." Linc smiled lecherously at her causing her to blush prettily.

"Behave, Linc." Arthur chided in a deep, sonorous tone. "Yes, Wood Sprite, you did mention that."

"He's the most wonderful of boys and I would very much like to introduce you both to him. He needs good male role models in his life. The men in my husband's family are not what I would call good men, they are greedy and pompous arseholes. I do not want my son to turn out like that."

"We would love to meet him." Linc sat up. "He is important to you, so he is important to us. Not to mention I'm always on the lookout for a new pal."

Arthur rolled his eyes at his silliness.

Jo laughed. "Of course you are, Linc. Perhaps we could meet in the park soon?"

"That can be arranged," Arthur said. "You tell us when and where, and we shall be there."

"Excellent!" Jo looked more than pleased. Then she glanced at the clock on the mantle. "Damnit, it's getting late. I had best dress and get home. Matthew shall be up from his nap soon, if he isn't already." She stood and began sifting through the clothing piled on the floor.

Linc rose and pulled on his trousers, then turned to her. "I make an excellent ladies' maid."

"If I recall correctly, you most certainly do." Jo turned her back to him with her corset pressed to her middle. He deftly laced her up then helped her with the remainder of her clothing.

Arthur had dressed himself and laid Linc's clothes on the settee so he could quickly don the rest while Jo repaired her hair as best she could.

"I'll ring for Harris to bring her cloak." Arthur said.

"Thank you. I'll dash up to my bedchamber when I return home to make sure I am fully presentable." Jo worried her lip.

"I'll have my butler bring the carriage around so she needn't walk," Arthur said as the pair worked on setting themselves to rights.

A short while later, Jo stood in the foyer once again and they were politely bidding her farewell. Once she was bundled into the carriage, Linc turned to Arthur. "This really happened? It wasn't another drink driven dream?"

Arthur smiled. "It happened. I don't know where this goes, but she appears to be back in our lives. I hope for good?"

Chapter Twenty

J o sat in her nursery playing with Matthew, the young Marquess of Whitestone. Though he was all of four years old, her son was extremely smart. More endearing than that, he looked remarkably like his mother. The only feature her son had taken from his father was his Romanesque nose.

He was busy stacking blocks and gleefully knocking them down when a knock on the door sounded.

Bell entered and executed a perfunctory bow. "Lords Dunmere and Lincolnshire are here to see you, my lady."

"Thank you, Bell. Please see them into the salon and I shall be right down." She dismissed the butler as she stood. "Abigail, I believe it is time for his mid-morning nap."

"Very good, my lady." The young woman curtsied before kneeling down on the floor to help Matthew put his toys away.

Jo stepped into the hall and found a looking glass where she peeked at her reflection to ensure her coiffure was in good repair. With that, she quickly made her way downstairs to greet her guests. As she all but ran into the salon, stopping so swiftly that her skirts swished about her ankles, she couldn't help but grin at the two men she saw.

Of course, she knew it was them, but her joy at seeing them once more was difficult to contain. "Linc, Arthur, don't you two look wonderful today?"

Linc grinned at her. "We do look rather smart today, don't we?" He smoothed down his blue silk waistcoat as though very pleased with himself.

"You really are too much, Linc," Jo laughed, and shook her head as she made her way to the bellpull.

"Ignore him. He's feeling very pleased with himself." Arthur grinned. "You, on the other hand, look lovely."

Heat swept into her cheeks as she absorbed the compliment. She very much wished to throw herself into his arms and demand a kiss. Instead, she turned as a housemaid entered the room. "Harriet, please have Mrs. Bell prepare tea."

"Of course, my lady." The maid curtsied then scurried away, closing the door behind her.

Alone at last, Jo quickly moved to hug Arthur, who wrapped her in his arms and kissed her warmly in greeting. Not to be outdone, Linc was there to collect her with a similar greeting.

"Please sit down, won't you?" She waved them toward the settees and chairs grouped in the center of the room.

"How are you feeling?" Arthur asked. The way he narrowed his gaze suggested he was concerned about her answer.

Jo dipped her head with a small smile playing across her lips. "I am well, if a bit sore."

Link darted a worried gaze toward the door. "Were we too rough with you?"

She couldn't help but laugh. "Of course not, silly. It has simply been many years since I've been with a man. I was bound to be a little sore today, and the cost was well worth the price of admission."

Both men seemed content with her response, though Linc grinned mischievously. "Well, Arthur, I suppose we should make a better effort next time."

Before Arthur could respond a knock on the door sounded, and Harriet returned with their tea. Jo dismissed her and handled the pouring duties herself.

Arthur sipped his tea. "I hope we didn't interrupt anything important with our unexpected visit."

"Not at all. I was just in the nursery with Matthew, but Miss Stevens, his nurse, just put him down for his morning nap." She took a sip of her own tea and then picked up a small sandwich.

"We would still love to meet your son. I'm sorry we missed him today." Linc's eyes glowed with a warmth and sincerity that eased her previous worries about intruding into their lives.

"Of course. We shall be in Hyde Park tomorrow afternoon around two o'clock near the Round Pond. Matthew adores feeding the ducks."

"We shall be happy to join you." Arthur spoke with an easy confidence she couldn't remember him having when they'd first met years ago. Nonetheless, it was a development she appreciated very much.

Then there was a ruckus at the door of the salon. She'd set her tea down, standing to see what was going on, when the door swung open and Bernard, her brother-in-law, strode into the room—much to the dismay of Bell.

"What the bloody hell is going on in here?" Bernard demanded to know.

Shocked to her core, Jo stood there, her mouth agape as the man halted in the middle of the room.

"Who the bloody hell is this?" he roared.

Finally regaining her composure, she stepped around the settee to face her brother-in-law as Linc and Arthur both rose. "Bernard. I'm afraid I wasn't expecting you today." She waved her arm toward Arthur and Linc. "I'm entertaining guests."

The man was puffed up like a peacock as he once more made blustering demands. "I can see that you are entertaining gentlemen. I'd like to know who the bloody hell they are?"

Jo clenched her teeth. "This is the Earl of Dunmere, and Baron Lincolnshire. My lords, may I present Lord Bernard Downs, my brother-in-law. Now if you don't mind, Bernard, we were having tea. Perhaps you could come back at a later time."

Bernard sneered at the two men behind her. "The bloody hell I shall—I can see the vultures circling already. You two need to leave immediately."

Jo gasped in utter shock at such rudeness. "Bernard, I absolutely demand you cease this at once. This is my home. These are my guests. You are the one intruding."

Bernard took a step toward her, his face a mask of fury. "Listen here, Lady Whitestone. This is my family home—my brother's home—and as the patriarch of the family, it is my duty to see that all is well and as it should be. A lady entertaining gentlemen callers alone is absolutely unacceptable. Should this get out, it would be a stain on my family's reputation and name."

Arthur cleared his throat and stepped up behind her. "Now see here, Lord Downs. I don't particularly care for the way you're speaking to Lady Whitestone. She has done nothing wrong. We are simply old friends who have come for a visit."

The man sneered, "It is unseemly."

Jo huffed, then turned to Arthur and Linc. "My lords, perhaps we could reconvene this visit on another day? I apologize for cutting our tea short." She tried to offer them both a reassuring smile.

She assumed she'd failed, since neither man moved.

Arthur looked at her worriedly, clearly hesitant to leave her alone with her overbearingly pompous brother-in-law, but she knew there was no way she could resolve the situation with both of them still there.

"It would seem there is some family issue that needs to be addressed. Again, my apologies for this untimely interruption."

Arthur nodded and stepped forward, taking her hand and bending over it to kiss her knuckles. "My lady. If you're sure you will be well?" he hesitated.

She smiled and nodded. "All will be well. I shall speak to you both soon."

Linc followed suit, holding her gaze for a moment before he bent and kissed her hand. Then the two made their way to the door of the salon as they glared at Bernard.

Once they were gone, Jo whirled on the man, resisting the urge to slap him across the face for his disrespectful and rude remarks, but she knew that would lead to no good. "Now, Bernard, if you would like to discuss the issue you seem to have, calmly, I shall of course oblige you out of respect for my departed husband."

Bernard curled his upper lip with disdain. "You were nothing but a broodmare for my brother, and I refuse to allow you to bring dishonor to our family name and reputation. I insist you cease entertaining gentlemen callers in my brother's home unchaperoned."

She huffed a laugh. "Unchaperoned? I'm no green girl. I've buried two husbands and borne a child. I shall not be dictated to like I am some young chit out of the schoolroom."

"I'm afraid you are mistaken about the circumstances, *Lady* Whitestone."

She was coming to detest the way he said her title, with far too much emphasis on the lady. As though she were not worthy of the moniker.

But Bernard wasn't finished. "As I am the one who holds the financial purse strings of this house and this family, you will, in fact, do as I say—if you care to continue to eat, have a roof over your head, and clothes on yours and your brat's back."

Jo blanched, her face draining of all warmth as confusion colored her every thought. She struggled to understand what he was suggesting. As far as she knew, her finances were in her hands. She had been present at the reading of her husband's last will and testament, after all. "This is an outrage. I shall speak to my husband's man of affairs at once and sort this out. My inheritance from your brother is mine—outright. What is not mine belongs to my son, the Marquess of Whitestone. Since I am his mother and legal guardian, you have control neither over my finances nor his."

Bernard laughed, low and sinister. "Since *my nephew* is not yet of age and my brother's man of affairs won't do business with a woman, it will be up to me to manage your finances. So whether or not you like it, I quite literally have all the control I require over your finances."

Jo's stomach turned as she imagined what the next few years might be like under his thumb.

"Now, if you'll do as I say, I suggest you go have a lie down. You seem a bit overwrought, my lady."

Furious, she stormed out of the salon and upstairs to her bedchamber. This simply would not stand. Perhaps she could enlist Arthur and Linc's assistance to deal with her former husband's man of affairs, if the man wouldn't do business with a woman.

Regardless, this was certainly not going to be the end of things, not by a longshot. She'd had enough of overbearing men and their poor decisions where she was concerned. The question was, what could she do, short of marrying another man? Her gut twisted. Even the thought of marrying Arthur—not that he had asked formally, mind you—made her nervous. They'd only just reconnected. Could she trust him with her future—and what of her heart?

Chapter Twenty-One

The Next Day

Jo arrived on Arthur's doorstep much earlier than she'd intended, but Bernard had appeared in her dining room along with breakfast. Unable to stomach a meal while pretending to be civil to the man, she had finished her cup of tea and announced she had somewhere to be. She stood and hurried upstairs to change her morning gown for a walking one before she gathered Matthew.

With her son in tow, she had walked toward Hyde Park before she hailed a hansom cab and directed the driver to Arthur's home. Once there, her nerves expanded in her stomach as she considered that neither man might wish to entangle themselves in her mess.

Unable to stand on the front stoop all morning, Jo finally knocked.

The door opened, and a butler appeared. "Good morning. How may I be of service, my lady?"

Her tongue felt thick in her mouth as she struggled for words. Any words. "Good morning, Harris. Lady Whitestone, to see Lord Dunmere."

The man opened the door wide and stepped back. "Please come in and I shall let Lord Dunmere know you are here."

Surprised by the alacrity with which he admitted her, she walked through the door, tugging Matthew behind her. "How is your family, Harris?"

Her question must have caught him off guard because his smooth, elegant step stuttered. "They are well, my lady. My father is just recovering from a cold. Thank you for asking."

"I'm glad to hear he is doing better. Family is very important." *Well, as long as one can stand to be around them.*

She kept that last part to herself. Not everyone married into an insufferable family, nor were they born with parents such as hers. At least she had Becca.

He led her toward an open door off the foyer. "Please take a seat in the salon. Would you like tea or perhaps something to nibble on?"

Jo's stomach rumbled loudly, causing Matthew to gasp. "Mummy!"

Cheeks heating, she looked at the placid man and offered a slight smile. "Tea and sandwiches would be lovely, thank you. We were a tad rushed at breakfast."

"Very good, my lady." Harris bowed and left her and Matthew in the sun-drenched room.

A few moments later she heard heavy footsteps. The door burst open, admitting Arthur and Linc. She had obviously disturbed them at breakfast, or some other morning ritual because both men were in their shirtsleeves, no waistcoats or coats to be seen. And Linc was here? In Arthur's home? Were they living together so openly?

"Jo! How delightful to see you," Arthur greeted her warmly as he crossed to where she'd risen. "I see you've brought your son with you." He pulled her into a hug before she could say or do anything. He then spoke low and urgent in her ear. "Are you well? We were terribly worried when we left you yesterday."

Joy and a sense of warmth seeped through her at his concern. "I am well, but couldn't abide the company I would have had to keep at breakfast this morning." She whispered her response, hoping to protect her son from her adult concerns.

As soon as Arthur stepped back, Linc swept in for a hug. "You look lovely this morning."

"Thank you." Her hands fluttered up to her cheeks to try to cool the twin flames that heated them. "I apologize for dropping in unexpectedly."

"Nonsense!" Linc smiled warmly at her. "I don't think we've formally met your companion."

"This is my son, the Marquess of Whitestone." She gently took her son by his shoulders and nudged him forward. "Matthew, this is the Earl of Dunmere and Baron Lincolnshire."

"Hello." Her son greeted them shyly.

"It's very nice to meet you, Lord Whitestone," Arthur said formally and bowed to the boy before ruining the whole display with a wink.

Matthew giggled and tucked his face into her skirts.

"Well, I certainly hope you two plan to spend the day with us. If not, Linc and I shall be forced to do some very dreary grown up things instead."

Jo hesitated, hating to intrude on their entire day. "I don't know." She bit her lip.

"We were promised an outing to the park, if I remember correctly. And I believe there is a circus that has taken up residence in Hyde Park. They have a large tent with lions, and tigers, and bears!"

Arthur's excitement was contagious and spilled over to her son. "Mummy, may we please go?"

"Yes mummy, may we?" Linc looked down at her, his eyes sparkling with mischief.

She laughed. "Well, we wouldn't want to force these two into dull activities they'd rather avoid. So, yes. We shall go to Hyde Park and see the circus!"

Linc carried Matthew in his arms ignoring the small pang of memories long past. The sweetness of the boy asleep reminded him of his late sister—a memory he resolutely pushed aside—as they returned to Arthur's townhouse. They'd spent a delightful afternoon at the circus watching the little boy grin and laugh at each new animal or act that appeared in the center ring. Jo had smiled the entire time as well, which made his heart squeeze. She was still a beautiful woman, maybe more so now. Motherhood agreed with her, not to mention the changes it had wrought on her body. Her breasts were fuller now, her hips more rounded, and her arse had filled out. He had fallen for the Wood Sprite, but found himself just as enchanted by the lush woman they were rediscovering.

Inside the house, Jo reached for her son. "I should get him home."

Arthur took one of her hands and turned it palm up as he planted a kiss in the center. "Stay?"

It was both a demand and a question, one that resonated with Linc as well.

"I can have Nancy sit with him as he naps in the nursery." His dark gaze bore into her, revealing the need and desire he felt. Linc knew because an identical flame lived within him.

"You have a nursery?" Surprise colored her question.

Arthur smiled, a sultry grin which made Linc's cock take notice. He recognized the look as one redolent with erotic promise.

"I do. Between my sister's child and the other of our group's children, it seemed reasonable to have a place for them to sleep when we all gather here. Will you stay?" Arthur pressed another kiss to her palm.

Jo sighed softly as she watched his lips on her skin. "Yes," she whispered on a gentle exhale.

"I'll take him upstairs if you'll send Nancy to me?" Linc started up the stairs.

"She'll be right up. Then you can find us in our room." Arthur's voice rumbled with desire.

Linc carried the boy into the nursery and had just tucked him in one of the small beds when their housemaid cum nursemaid, Nancy, appeared. "I've got him, my lord."

"Very good, Nancy. Please let us know when he wakes up." Linc nodded and left her to her watch.

He slipped into their bedchamber—he and Arthur slept there most nights—hiding in the shadows as he quietly closed the door. There he found Arthur and Jo in a passionate kiss, and hesitated. Were the dynamics shifting? Was he becoming extraneous?

Arthur looked up, breaking their kiss. "Don't lurk there in the shadows, Linc. We need you."

Warmth filled his chest as Linc strode forward, and Jo turned into Arthur's arms as though she'd been waiting for him to come. They both had.

With her body pressed to his, Linc sought out her mouth. Tentatively, Jo slid her tongue along the seam of his lips, seeking entrance. With a groan, Linc let her in and tangled his tongue with hers. She whimpered and melted into his body as Arthur worked on unhooking her bodice. As it loosened and gaped, Linc drew it down her arms, momentarily breaking their kiss.

Arthur unfastened her skirt and untied her petticoats, letting them puddle around her ankles. Linc unfastened her corset cover and peeled it off her arms as Arthur spun her around and took her mouth in another searing kiss, Linc continuing to work her laces loose on her corset. Finally peeling the restrictive layer free, they had her down to her pantalettes and chemise. Linc untied and let her drawers drop with the rest of the fabric puddled at her ankles.

Finally Arthur broke their kiss, grabbed her under her arms, and lifted her free as he spun her toward the bed. Linc began working free of his own clothes while Arthur peeled Jo's chemise over her head and tossed it to the side. "On the bed, love."

Jo crawled up and reached to remove one of her garters.

"Leave them." Arthur's voice sounded almost rusty. He must have been as turned on as Linc was.

Gratefully naked, Linc joined her on the bed as they watched Arthur finish stripping. Linc had appreciated the changes in Arthur's physique himself, but turned his gaze to Jo to enjoy her reaction. Her green eyes glowed with appreciation. Previously they had been so swept up in their reunion; he doubted she'd had a chance to truly appreciate the sight of Arthur's form. There was no doubt she was taking the time now.

"He's changed a lot since we were together all those years ago," Linc murmured softly, for her ears alone.

"Oh, he has. How did I miss that fact the last time we were together?" she asked. The husky timber of Jo's voice sent shivers down Linc's spine.

"I'd say it was the fact that neither of us was willing to let go of you for longer than, say two seconds, once we got you naked." Linc grinned cheekily at her, then flicked one of her distended nipples.

Unwilling to wait longer, he leaned over and sucked the rosy tip into his mouth as she watched Arthur finish undressing. Jo's soft moan of encouragement had his cock jerking in response as Arthur crawled on the bed. He quickly joined in, sucking her other nipple into his mouth. They continued licking and sucking at her breasts until a hand fisted Linc's hair and pulled him off. Then Arthur swooped in and kissed him, their tongues dueling for control almost from the start. He loved the rough way Arthur handled him and how it contrasted to Jo's gentle touch.

When Arthur broke their kiss, Linc looked at Jo to find her eyes glassy and her breathing choppy.

"My God, that is unbearably sexy." Her words came out in a breathy exhale.

"Linc is an excellent kisser, isn't he?" Arthur grinned at her.

"He is, but watching you two devastates a woman's senses."

"Well, we can't have you completely devastated, not just yet, anyway." Linc winked at her.

Desire flickered over Arthur's face. "Recline against the headboard."

Linc happily went, loving nothing more than when Arthur exerted his authority in bed. He leaned back against the padded headboard and stroked his cock.

Arthur helped Jo up to her knees. "Now sweetheart, I want you to straddle his hips and sink down on his cock, but facing away from him."

Jo cocked her head curiously, but followed Arthur's directions. Being an arse-man, this was a favorite position of Linc's. Jo's derrière wasn't overly large, but it was most certainly round and soft. He grabbed a cheek in each hand and watched as his cock slid into her tight little cunny from behind. He couldn't resist stroking a fingertip over the tight pucker of her rear entrance to stimulate the nerves found there, causing Jo to groan loudly.

"Mmm. Very nice." Arthur was down between their spread legs, watching him slide inside of her. Then a jar of salve landed on the bed next to Linc. "Feel free to play back there while I have a little fun here. Jo, your job is to ride his cock, no matter what either of us does to you."

Jo's head tipped downward to where Arthur was. "Yes, sir." Then she rose slowly on Linc's cock.

"Fuck!" Linc cursed as her heat sank back down on him. She lifted again, but this time her movement was jerky.

"Oh, Arthur!"

Jo's exclamation was the only indicator Linc had of what was happening, since he couldn't see anything. But then, when just his tip was inside her entrance, he felt Arthur's tongue lick up the length of his cock which was exposed.

"Good God, man!" he groaned.

"Don't you two stop," Arthur growled.

"Y-Yes, sir," Jo replied as she sank back down onto Linc's cock.

Arthur continued licking at her pussy and Linc's quivering cock as she slid up and down his shaft. The sensations were incredible as his balls tightened. As a result, it was minutes later that he spotted the salve he'd been given, though it was difficult to focus on that and not the pleasure Arthur was delivering with his tongue as they fucked.

Grabbing a dollop of the viscous lubricant, Linc pressed a warm digit against her sphincter again, this time sliding his finger inside her. As the heat of her backside engulfed his finger while her pussy surrounded his cock, Linc thought he might explode.

"Do not come, Linc." Arthur's terse order had him pulling back on the orgasm he could feel rising up. Linc silently added a second finger to her backside, continuing to open her up, as Arthur continued, "I plan to be inside her arse when we all come. But Jo, you may come if you need to."

She moaned in response—or perhaps it was because Arthur was back to using his tongue on them again. "Oh God, Arthur—Linc—it's too much."

Arthur seemed to redouble his efforts, Linc gritting his jaw at the blissful sensations. *He wasn't allowed to come.*

"That's it, Jo. Come for us. Come on my cock and Arthur's tongue." Linc encouraged her, even as his own orgasm was growing harder to hold back. Then he added a third finger to her arse.

"Yes! Don't stop," she cried out and began furiously pumping her hips on his shaft.

Arthur groaned and Linc could feel his tongue lapping at his cock and then his balls as her juices dribbled down. "Fuck Arthur, if you don't stop, I'm going to come."

"She tastes so good on you. Do. Not. Come. Or there will be consequences," Arthur commanded.

But the bloody man continued lapping at Linc's sack and Jo's pussy, based on her continuous moans and the twitches of her channel wrapped around Linc's cock. "Fuck, I can't hold it!"

Linc grabbed Jo's hips and lifted her up just enough so he could slam into her from below. He pumped once, then again, and on the third time he came, pumping his seed up into her tight cunny.

To both their delighted surprise, Arthur kept licking at them as his load dribbled down his cock to join her juices, refusing to stop sucking and licking until Jo came once more, her body contracting around Linc's cock. Finally, she came down from her second high and Arthur let her climb off of Linc's lap.

Jo lay in a heap next to Linc, whose heart was still racing from the intense orgasm.

Arthur looked at him and shook his head. "You disobeyed an order, Linc." Suspecting what was to come, Linc couldn't muster up any regret—and he had guessed right. "On all fours. Now."

Linc obediently rolled over and pushed up to his hands and knees.

"Now, move between Jo's legs. If she wishes it, you may lick her cunny while I spank you. You've earned yourself 10 strokes."

Linc couldn't help but grin up at her as he got into position, but Jo shook her head.

"I'm much too sensitive right now," she murmured.

"Very well then, Linc. Sounds like a spanking and no pussy for you." Arthur tried to sound stern, but Linc could hear the grin in his voice. "Count until she lets you between her thighs."

Arthur rubbed his hand over Linc's arse, warming up the skin before the punishment. Linc's softened cock stirred at the touch.

Then the first spank landed and heat spread out over his left cheek.

"One." The next one landed on his right side. "Two."

The next came in quick succession and caused heat, quickly followed by pleasure, to radiate through Linc's body.

"Three. Four."

Linc looked up to find Jo biting her lip as she watched the two of them. Desire shone in her green gaze and a quick glance down showed him she was turned on by the spanking.

"Five."

Clearly unable to resist any longer, Jo grabbed Linc by his hair and tugged him down toward her wet pussy. Linc happily lapped up the length of her wet slit as the sixth and seventh spanks landed, sparking fire through him. He could taste himself mingled with her sweet-tart taste, and it only made his half-hard cock grow stiffer. Between the pleasurable spanking from Arthur and Jo's wet pussy, he was going to be ready to sink inside her again—or him—in no time.

The rightness of the moment, being caught between the two people he loved most in the world, hit him hard. Harder than the eighth spank that landed across both his cheeks.

"Mmmm, Linc, that feels so good." Jo tightened her grip on his hair as her breathing grew choppy.

The final two swats on his arse landed, bringing Linc's cock to full staff.

Arthur reached down and stroked his dripping, aching shaft. "Not sure that was much of a punishment, but I am pleased with the results." He shifted around the bed and started kissing Jo as Linc continued licking her cunny.

Linc loved this, and as he imagined doing this with Arthur's cock embedded in her pussy, his orgasm surged to the fore. He immediately pulled off her clit, causing Jo to break her kiss with Arthur to complain.

"But I was close, Linc. Don't stop, damn you!"

"Oh no, I want to feel you wrapped around my cock when you come the last time," Arthur growled.

Jo nodded enthusiastically at that notion. "Oh yes, please."

"Linc, lay down and let her straddle you. I want to be inside that hot, tight arse of hers."

Linc did as he was told, laying on his back as Jo straddled him and once again sank down on his cock. She felt so good wrapped around him. This time she leaned forward over him, allowing him to lick and suck on her delicious nipples as Arthur got into position behind her.

"Her hole is already open a little from your fingers, Linc. Very nicely done." Arthur's approval was a buzz in the back of his head as Jo moaned. "God, she's so tight. I've got the tip inside her." Their lover continued to report his progress to them both.

Jo ground down on Linc's cock.

"Hurry, I'm close already," he groaned.

"Hold on, almost there," Arthur gritted the words out as he pushed deeper into their woman's tight rear entrance.

Linc could feel Arthur's cock sliding inside of her, inch by inch, through the membrane that separated them. It felt amazing to feel him inside of her at the same time.

Meanwhile, Jo panted through Arthur's intrusion. "Oh God! I'm so full of you two."

"Ah!" Arthur exclaimed in triumph as he was fully seated inside of her. "Your arse is like a bloody oven, but it's snug around my cock, Jo. More so with Linc's cock stuffed inside your sweet cunny." She moaned at his dirty words. "Now we're going to fuck you and fill you with cum," Arthur growled out and drew back, sliding out of her arse until just his tip was inside.

Linc waited, enjoying the feel of Arthur's cock sliding over his. Then, as Arthur pushed back inside her, he pulled out of her pussy.

Jo cried out. "Bloody hell!"

Arthur smiled at Linc as they continued to time their thrusts. Soon Jo was being stuffed full of cock in an alternating rhythm that ensured each of them enjoyed their shared connection. With every slide in or out of her cunny, he could feel Arthur sliding inside her arse. Their thick cocks rubbed over each other, again and again, their pace picking up.

Before long Jo moaned, "I'm coming!"

Her body clamped down on both their cocks, squeezing and letting go with each powerful pulse of her orgasm. Linc gritted his teeth and held on through the delicious spasms. Then, with a nod from Arthur, they proceeded to pound into her body, every thrust timed to drag over Arthur's cock until they both panted.

Finally Linc cried out, "Fuck! Yes!"

His orgasm slammed into him, ripping up his spine from his balls to burst through his chest as he pulsed his load deep in her pussy. Arthur thrusted twice more then groaned as he too finished buried deep inside of their Jo.

They had certainly shared a woman since Jo, but none ever felt as right between them as she did.

Linc lay there with the pair of them draped over him and relished just how good it felt to be loved by these two people.

Chapter Twenty-Two

Later That Day

J o sat in Arthur's carriage with Matthew at her side, thinking back on her unexpectedly pleasurable afternoon. Still
sleepy from his nap, her son sat snuggled into her side. The
carriage pulled to a stop, and the footman opened the door
and helped her down. With Matthew's hand in her own, she
entered the townhouse to find a strange man in the foyer.

"Welcome home, my lady."

"Who are you and where is Bell?" Jo stopped and stared at
the man.

Where the bloody hell was her staff? Why was this strange
man answering her door? Determined to find out what was
going on, she turned on her heel and walked past the un-
known man.

The stranger trailed behind her. "My understanding is that
Mr. Bell is no longer employed here. I am Mr. Jasper, my
lady."

Jo burst into the kitchen and spotted the cook bent over
the fireplace. "Mrs. Adams, what is going on around here?"

A woman stood up and spun around to face her but she
was not, in fact, Mrs. Adams.

"Who the bloody hell are you?" Jo winced as she glanced
down at Matthew, but pressed on. Her concern for what
had happened to the staff she and her late husband had put

in place far outpaced her concern for her son hearing the profanity.

"I-I...I'm Mrs. Paulson, my lady." She curtsied and looked past her to the man from the foyer—Jasper, was it?

Fury rising inside her as suspicion bloomed, Jo turned around to face Jasper. "Who precisely hired you?"

The man cleared his throat as color rose in his cheeks. "I believe Lord Downs oversaw the changeover of staff."

Jo choked, "The *changeover* of staff?"

"Yes, my lady." Jasper had the good grace to look uncomfortable as he affirmed the information.

"Where is Lord Downs at the moment?" Jo asked, anger making her voice shake.

"I believe he is in the study, my lady."

With a growl of fury, Jo stormed out of the kitchen and up the back stairs to the nursery. There she found yet another servant she did not recognize.

"Matthew, I want you to stay here with this," she looked up at the unsmiling woman, "this nice lady. I'll be back shortly to check on you." Jo motioned for the other woman to follow her into the hallway. After shutting the door to the nursery, she looked at the woman. "I do not know who you are, but I am leaving my son here for now. I expect you to ensure he stays safe until I return."

"Yes, my lady." The woman nodded somberly.

As assured as she could be that her son was safe, Jo went in search of her brother-in-law finding him, as promised, in the study.

She stormed in without knocking, letting the door bang loudly against the wall. "Where the bloody hell are my servants?"

Lord Downs looked up with derision on his face. "I told you, Lady Whitestone, I control the finances now. I have replaced your overpaid staff with individuals who come at more reasonable rates and who understand who is in charge around here."

She blanched. She had thought his blustering was just that: blustering. That he would have the audacity to dismiss her staff and replace them with his own hires was outrageous. "Bernard, do not think for one moment that this is the end of this matter. This will not stand."

"The decision has been made." Lord Downs stared back at her, an impassive expression on his face.

"We shall see," Jo seethed and spun around to leave.

Determined to take immediate action, she stalked into the dining room and into the butler's pantry. "Mr. Jasper, I am afraid your services are no longer required. Please see Lord Downs, he will provide you with a reference and three months' wages."

"I see, my lady." The man looked mildly concerned but resolute. He nodded and went in search of Bernard.

Feeling at least a little better, Jo headed upstairs. It was growing late, and she needed to check on Matthew. After seeing that he was tucked in bed, she went to her own bedchamber and met the new woman who had been hired to be her lady's maid. She seemed nice enough, but Jo remained skeptical of all the servants hired by Bernard, and the unpleasant man himself.

The next morning Jo made her way down to breakfast and found two unwanted individuals. Bernard sat at her table drinking tea as Jasper filled a plate for him from the sideboard.

Gritting her teeth, Jo took a seat. "Coffee, please."

Jasper cleared his throat as he set a plate in front of Bernard.

"We are no longer stocking coffee. It is a vulgar drink and inordinately expensive." Bernard sniffed then slurped tea from his cup.

Grinding her teeth now, Jo bit her tongue. "Tea then, Jasper."

"Very good, my lady." He bowed and poured her a cup of tea and set it before her. "Breakfast, my lady?"

"I find I'm a bit off this morning. I shall skip the morning meal." Her stomach roiled as she sipped the tea and nearly spat it out. "I'm sorry, what in the world is this? I've never tasted such vile stuff."

Bernard peered at her. "We are cutting costs around here. The tea you prefer is far too costly. I've ensured we are stocking a more cost effective blend. That will be all, Jasper."

Jasper nodded and retreated from the room. Jo sat there, stunned at how quickly and easily Bernard had taken over her household. The embers of fury sparked to life deep within her breast, but her morning's fight was not over.

"Josephine, I would appreciate it if you ceased attempting to fire my employees." Bernard said as he set his knife down and looked at her.

"And I would appreciate it if you vacated my home with said employees," she smiled delicately.

"This is a family home. It does not belong to you. It belongs to my family. The one you married into, as a convenience to my brother."

"Regardless, my son is the one who bears the title now. It is our home." Jo pushed her tea aside. "I believe I shall check on my son, the actual head of this family. Don't hesitate to see yourself out."

She left the breakfast room and went to find her son before her temper got away from her. He was playing quietly by himself overseen by Miss Kelley, the new nursemaid, keeping an eye on him as she straightened up his drawers.

Content that he was well and had breakfast, she headed out. Jo needed to replace a few of the linens she and Mrs. Adams had identified as too worn recently. She had also been intending to select a couple of new gowns, now she was out of mourning.

Jo entered into the linen shop and had selected the new tablecloths and napkins when the clerk leaned toward her and said in a low voice, "I'm afraid your line of credit is late on payment, Lady Whitestone."

Shocked and terribly embarrassed, Jo's cheeks turned pink. "I'm sure there is some mistake. I'll send word around to my man of affairs to ensure you are paid."

"Of course, my lady," The man agreed and smiled before he packaged up her purchase.

Next she went to the modiste's. Jo walked in, ready to forget her worries and do a little shopping. She was busy looking at dress designs in a private sitting room when the owner of the shop stepped inside. "It's lovely to see you again, Mrs. Atwell."

"And you as well, Lady Whitestone. My condolences again on the loss of your husband," she murmured in concern.

"Thank you. I was looking to arrange for a few new gowns, now I am out of full mourning." Jo smiled softly.

"I am excited about the opportunity to dress you again. When do you need the dresses by?" Mrs. Atwell asked, a smile gracing her hawkish features.

"I'd like to have them in two weeks."

"Excellent. Now, let's see which designs have caught your eye."

By the time Jo was done with her errands, all was feeling back to normal in her world. Now she needed to hope that Bernard had vacated her home as requested.

Chapter Twenty-Three

A Week Later

Linc and Arthur stood in the front salon of Jo's town-home waiting for her to appear. She walked carefully into the room and smiled warmly at them before closing the door behind her.

Concern reared up in Linc as she flew across the room and into their arms. Smothering her face in Arthur's chest, Linc pressed against her side and wrapped a comforting arm around her. She wept silently for what felt like an eternity.

Linc swallowed, a little overwhelmed by her seeming grief. "What is wrong, Wood Sprite?"

She lifted her tear-streaked face and offered a tremulous smile. "I'm worried, and was feeling very alone until you two arrived."

"What has you so concerned?" Arthur asked as he stroked a hand down her spine.

She drew in a deep breath and made to step back from their embrace. They both released her, though Linc took her trembling hands in his and sat with her on the settee. Arthur crowded in on her other side, the three of them buried by her skirts as they crammed on the small piece of furniture that was built for two.

"Take a deep breath and tell us what is going on," Arthur encouraged again.

Linc darted him a warning look to be less pushy, but he understood the deep-seated desire to fix whatever had upset Jo.

She cast a wary glance toward the door. "It's...it's Bernard. My brother-in-law. He has replaced all of my staff with his own hires—I attempted to release the new butler, but was thwarted by the odious man. He suggested the other day that I was not in control of my household any more now than I was when George was alive. I assumed he was being a bully, not that he could actually do anything to control my household."

"The bloody bastard!" Arthur swore as he rose.

Jo jumped to her feet as well and placed a hand on Arthur's arm. "Please! You mustn't be so loud. Someone might very well be listening at the door." She cast another nervous glance in that direction.

Linc reached out and took her hand, coaxing her back down beside him. "We'll keep our voices down, Wood Sprite. We should move you and Matthew to Arthur's townhome immediately."

"Absolutely!" Arthur agreed.

But Jo shook her head. "No, I shall not give up my son's birthright. He is the new Lord Whitestone, whether my brother-in-law likes it or not. To move out of this house would be akin to forfeiting everything. Bernard and his loathsome brood would simply move in—he certainly cannot afford to maintain two households. I'm not even sure how he is doing so now. George always grumbled about how his brother was always asking for more allowance."

Arthur looked over at him. "I wonder where the income for the staff he has hired here has come from?"

"You can't possibly be suggesting that—" Linc was shocked at what he suspected Arthur was alluding to, but a sharp knock sounded and the salon door opened.

"My lady, there has been an accident in the nursery," the butler that Linc did not recognize announced solemnly.

"What? Oh, my God—Matthew!" Jo jumped to her feet and rushed out of the salon, leaving Linc and Arthur to follow in her wake.

They all rushed up the stairs and followed her flight up to the third floor and into the nursery. As they crammed through the doorway, they found Jo sitting on the edge of her son's bed, occupied by a crying boy. A nurse hovered nearby, looking less concerned than Linc thought was proper, under the circumstances. After all, the boy had clearly been injured while under her care.

Jasper the new butler walked in a few moments after them at a much more sedate pace.

Linc looked back over his shoulder at the man. "Has a physician been sent for?"

Jasper nodded. "Yes, my lord."

"Very good." Linc was glad to hear that even if Jo's staff were spying on her for Lord Downs, they were at least properly trained.

He nudged Arthur, and together they moved closer to Jo and Matthew.

The boy looked pale and scared as he cradled his arm. "I was heading downstairs when—" He cast a nervous glance up at his nurse. Linc couldn't see her face, but the boy went a shade paler. "When I suppose I tripped a-and fell down the steps."

"Oh, how scary!" Jo whispered as she kissed her son's tear-stained face. "Does your arm hurt terribly?"

He cradled it against his chest protectively and cast a glance about the room at all the adults. Then he thrust out his little chin, full of bravado. "Only when I move it."

Linc sighed internally and repressed an inappropriate grin. Poor stupid boy; lying about the pain wouldn't make it any better, and it likely would only make his softhearted mother more apt to coddle him. Not that she could blame him.

Arthur coughed and then stepped closer to Jo. "Perhaps you should send the staff on about their duties. I'm sure the doctor will be here soon."

Jo looked up in surprise, clearly not having registered all the other people in the room. As they had been listening to Matthew tell what happened, a few maids had filtered into the room, and it was starting to feel a little crowded. "Yes, please, all of you should go back to your duties. Thank you for your concern but everything is fine here. Jasper, bring the doctor up as soon as he arrives."

"Very good, my lady." The stiff man nodded and ushered the gawkers from the room.

As he tried to shoo the nurse out, Miss Kelley huffed. "My duties are in this room."

Linc shot her a considering look. She didn't seem at all distraught about what had happened.

"I'll look after my son for the moment. Your services are not needed here," Jo said, with an air of authority that had Linc's cock standing up and taking notice.

Ignoring his lecherous thoughts, he stepped aside as the nurse left the room, clearly put out that she had been dismissed.

Curious, Linc eased around to the other side of the bed and looked at Jo. "May I?"

"Of course," she agreed, though she looked confused.

"Matthew, think back to before. When you explained what happened, you seemed to hesitate. Was there something you wanted to tell your mother that you felt you couldn't?" Linc asked gently.

"Well," the boy hesitated, glancing at the door where everyone had departed.

Arthur walked over and closed it with a thud. "There now. It's just the three of us."

Matthew nodded. "I...I felt someone push me. I didn't trip at all," he said firmly as his mother gasped. Then confusion appeared to cloud his resolve. "But I don't know who it might have been. Nurse was in here putting my things away. I had slipped quietly out the door because I had heard Uncle Linc and Uncle Arthur were here. A maid came up here to tell my nurse."

Jo reached out and stroked his face. "Well, don't you worry about it. Mother will figure out what happened. For now, you need to hold still until the doctor arrives, then I think you shall have whatever you like for dinner."

A knock on the door sounded and Jasper entered. "The doctor, my lady."

Linc and Arthur retreated downstairs as the doctor tended to Matthew's arm. The doctor had determined in short order that it was likely broken and so sent for his casting materials.

Arthur paced his agitation, making the movement jerky. "I should marry her." He raked a hand through his hair.

"I quite agree you should, but I don't think she or the boy are ready for that change." Linc held up his hands in a universal sign of helplessness. "She's barely out of mourning, and it wouldn't look good to the gossips in the Ton."

Arthur sighed, his frustration clear. "You may be right, but I hate doing nothing to help her."

Linc stood and walked over to Arthur. Laying a hand on his cheek, he murmured, "Look at me. We aren't doing 'nothing', we are here supporting her the best way we can in the moment."

By the time Jo had tucked her son in after his dinner several hours had passed, but they had resolved to stay until they were certain that Jo was well. She had just walked into the salon to let them know Matthew was well when her brother-in-law walked in.

"What the bloody hell is going on here?" Bernard demanded, all puffed up in apparent outrage.

Furious, Jo turned on the man before either Linc or Arthur could say a word. "What is going on here? I'll tell you what is going on here. That incompetent nurse you hired to replace Mrs. Stevens let my son fall and break his arm. I want her dismissed this very minute, as I do not seem to have the authority to do such a thing in my own home."

Bernard stared. "I am certain Miss Kelley is quite competent, and that unruly child you've raised is the one at fault."

"Someone pushed him," Jo ground out, her voice nearly a growl.

Bernard snorted in disbelief. "What makes you say such a thing?"

"Matthew told me." She crossed her arms under her breasts and held her back rigid. She was quite clearly spoiling for a fight.

To Linc's irritation, Bernard outright laughed. "Did the child hit his head? I certainly can't imagine why Miss Kelley would do such a thing? That's outrageous."

"Nevertheless, I want her replaced at once. I do not trust her with my son," Jo insisted.

"I hardly think this is an appropriate conversation to be held in front of your," her brother-in-law glanced over and sneered, "*guests.*"

"They were just leaving. They were kind enough to stay with me throughout the ordeal this afternoon," Jo rebuked him subtly.

"Well, I think it is time for them to go." Bernard swept an arm toward the door of the salon.

Linc hated leaving her alone with this man once more, but he feared insisting on staying would only aggravate the situation. "If you are well, Lady Whitestone."

"I am. Thank you both for staying with me through this." Jo smiled warmly, but politely, as she took each of their hands and gave them a squeeze.

Linc had a pit in his stomach as they walked out of the house. He turned to Arthur. "Something is very wrong in there. I do not feel good about leaving her alone to deal with him."

"Agreed, but she is stubborn and has made her position clear. For now, we must bide our time and help her, however she will allow us." Arthur sighed as they stepped up into his carriage.

The question was, how long would she wait to allow them to offer help?

Chapter Twenty-Four
A Week Later

J o walked into the nursery and found her son Matthew playing with his truck while Miss Kelley sat nearby and darned some of his clothing. A week ago, in the wake of Matthew breaking his arm, Jo had tried to have the woman removed from her household. But Bernard had refused, citing the lack of actual evidence of the woman's involvement in Matthew's accident. Jo had pointed out that no one else was up there but her at the time and Matthew insisted he was pushed. Despite this, Bernard had flatly refused to believe her son.

As a result, Jo had remained at home with her son so she could monitor the situation. Nothing else untoward had occurred since then but regardless, she did not trust the woman—could barely stand to look at her. "Matthew, come here, please."

Her son rose, a little awkwardly as he managed the weight of the cast on his right arm. "Yes, Mother?"

"We must go out." She turned to look at Miss Kelley. "I shall need Lord Whitestone's coat."

"Oh course, my lady." The nurse eyed her almost suspiciously as she set aside her sewing and rose to find the requested garment.

"Where are we going, mother?" Matthew asked excitedly.

She felt a tad guilty about dragging him to run her errands, but she had put things off as long as she could manage. The gown she'd ordered from the modiste was ready, and she needed to go in for the last fitting—and the last thing she was going to do was leave her son here, at the mercy of Bernard's underlings. "We have errands to run and I have a gown fitting, but if you are a well-behaved boy, we shall stop for an ice from Gunter's Tea Shop."

"Very well." Matthew sighed as though he was very put upon by her request of him. "I suppose I shall come along."

Jo nearly snorted as she suppressed her laughter at her son's pained response, particularly because she knew how much he loved Gunter's ices.

A half hour later, she walked into Mrs. Atwell's dress shop with her son in tow. They were shown to a dressing room, where she sat down and waited for the girl to come in with her gown. After a few moments, Mrs. Atwell appeared.

"Lady Whitestone." There was a note of disdain in her tone, as though she was very cross about something.

"Good morning Mrs. Atwell. Is my gown ready?" Jo asked, after noting that the clothing in question was absent from the room.

"Well, it is, but there is an issue with finishing it." The woman sniffed.

"What issue might that be?" Jo was growing more concerned by the moment. Something was definitely wrong, but she wasn't sure what it was yet since the modiste was being a mite dramatic about everything.

"Your account and credit have been cancelled, my lady." The modiste stared down her nose at Jo as though she was incapable of paying her debts.

Jo's cheeks heated as she struggled to comprehend what the very annoyed woman was saying. "I...I don't understand. I have not cancelled my account with you."

"It seems your man of affairs has done so on your behalf. If you were not going to be able to pay for this gown, I don't understand why you ordered it. It is not as if I can afford to gift it to you. Now I must hope to find someone to buy a gown created for another woman," she huffed as she crossed her arms.

"I'll have you know I ordered that gown fully intending to pay for it. I have no idea what is going on, but I intend to get to the bottom of it. I shall be back for my gown in the next few days." Jo grabbed her son's hand as she stormed out of the dressing room and out of the shop. She found her carriage and ushered her son inside. There was little point in making her other planned stops. She felt certain she would find the same situation wherever she had accounts established. It was clear that Bernard was behind this, and that meant she had only one course of action available to her. "Take me to Lord Downs' home."

The man had not been at her home that morning, so he must actually be occupying his own. For a change.

She arrived at his unkempt Mayfair home. "Come along, Matthew. You'll wait in the hall while I speak to your Uncle Bernard."

"Yes, Mother. Then can we go to Gunter's?"

"Yes. We shall go for ices after I speak with Lord Downs." Jo smiled sadly down at her son and, not for the first time, wished he could be spared the odious family she'd married into. Or, more accurately, had been sold into. But it was his family by blood, if nothing else.

They entered the house and she deposited Matthew on a tufted velvet bench, then steamed right past the butler and into Bernard's study. To her horror, she walked in to find the man with one of the young housemaids on his lap and his hand down her bodice. The girl was fifteen if she was a day.

"Bernard!"

"Oh!" The poor girl turned a violent shade of red and escaped his clutches. "Excuse me, m'lady." She curtsied as she ran from the room, all while she kept her gaze fixed on the floor.

Jo wasn't certain how she managed to both curtsy and move so quickly, all without looking up to see where she was going.

Finally alone, she looked at her brother-in-law and found herself grateful that she had been sold to the elder brother, who either had the good sense not to prey on the help or the intelligence to keep his proclivities hidden from her. Bernard, however, looked utterly unperturbed that she had walked in on him in such a compromising position.

"To what do I owe the pleasure of you deigning to grace my home with your presence?" Her odious brother-in-law sat back in his chair and threaded his fingers together as he rested his elbows on the arms of his chair.

"I went to my modiste shop for a fitting today and was informed that my credit was cancelled. I assume the same is true with all the vendors where I had accounts."

"You would be correct. I did inform you that I would act as the head of your household until Matthew comes of age. As part of that, I am reining in your exorbitant spending."

Shock slammed into her. Of course, she shouldn't be; he had in fact told her he would take control. But this was too much. It was humiliating.

"You will need to provide a list of household needs each month and I shall review and approve any expenditures. As for your wardrobe, you will be allowed one new gown each Season, the same as my wife, Agnes. What is good enough for her is good enough for you."

Anger welled from deep within, spilling over like an erupting volcano. "Impossible. I am not extravagant in my purchases, nor do I pretend to be in the first stare of fashion. But one new gown at the start of the season is absurd for any passably fashionable woman, let alone a lady. Not to mention you haven't the first clue what it takes to run a household the size of my townhouse."

"I assure you, I am quite capable of properly managing a household's finances," Bernard sneered.

Jo's anger flared, white hot. *The man must take her for a fool!* "I think not. I can see that your own house is so poorly run that the rugs are threadbare in places, the windows require washing, and last time I dined here half the fine china was chipped. Outside of all of those issues, you are trying to take control of my finances and you have no authority to do so. I shall stop to speak with my husband's man of affairs. Clearly, I should have done so sooner so that there was no question as to who is in control."

He laughed darkly. "I take it you have not made the acquaintance of Mr. Whitaker. You will find that he does not do business with women."

Her gut clenched as fear set in for the first time. It was 1867, not 1767. How could the man, any man, be unwilling to do business with a lady?

"As you can imagine, he was quite pleased that I would manage my brother's accounts on your behalf." Bernard waved a hand toward the door of his study. "But by all means, please go visit the man and see for yourself." He stood up. "Do have a lovely day, Josephine."

Incensed he would be so familiar with her on top of trying to steal her money, she turned and stormed from his study, letting the door bang against the woodwork as she departed. In the hall she collected her son then departed the twice damned house.

There was only one place she could turn under the circumstances.

Jo knocked firmly on the door and waited. When Harris opened the door, she rushed inside. "Good day, Harris. I hope your father is getting on?"

The stoic man nodded. "Indeed he is, my lady."

"Excellent! I do wish to hear more about your family, but I need to find Arthur and Linc immediately."

"I believe they are in the study, my lady." Harris provided the information as he began walking in that direction. Jo followed closely on his heels, grateful for his prompt action. He knocked and opened the door. "Lady Whitestone, to see you both with some degree of urgen—"

She stepped into the room and turned to Harris. "Can you see Lord Whitestone to the nursery?"

"Of course, my lady." Harris nodded and took her son's hand in his as he led him from the room.

Arthur and Linc had both risen at her sudden appearance. "Jo, what's wrong?"

She flew to them, throwing herself into Linc's arms as he was the first one she reached. "It's—it's Bernard. That odious man has cancelled all of my credit with the merchants I frequent and has spoken with my late husband's solicitor, ensuring he has complete control over all of my finances. That is how he is paying for the staff he hired. He is using my money!"

"Sit down and tell us everything." Arthur urged after embracing her tightly. "I'm sure we can sort this matter out."

Half an hour later, after she had explained everything, Arthur sat next to her and growled, "Who is your late husband's solicitor?"

"Mr. Whitaker of Whitaker, Burrows, and Jones."

"I believe we owe the man a visit." Arthur rose with a tight jaw. "Jo, you should come with us. Matthew will be safe here with Harris and Nancy while we take care of business."

*

"Good afternoon Mr. Whitaker. I appreciate you seeing us without an appointment, but as you can imagine, this is a matter of some urgency." Arthur smiled smoothly as they sat down in the man's office.

"Of course, my lord." The obsequious little man bowed and took his own seat. "How may I be of service?"

"Baron Lincolnshire and I are concerned about Lady Whitestone's finances. She has come to us with some disturbing information." Arthur let one eyebrow drift up. "It seems her brother-in-law, Lord Downs, has established some sort of stewardship over her accounts."

The little man puffed up across the desk. "Well, Lord Downs indicated that with his brother's passing, he would oversee Lady Whitestone's accounts moving forward."

"I see." Arthur let the comment draw out, along with its subsequent silence. "Is there a particular reason Lady Downs is not being consulted over her own money?"

"Look, my lord," the man began, his tone somewhat patronizing. "I find in my experience that women tend to be overwhelmed by such financial dealings. It is better when they have a male relative manage such matters on their behalf. Her son is so young, she cannot possibly—"

"Is that so, Mr. Whitaker?" Jo shot him an arch look as she sat stiffly in her chair. "So it would be beyond my ability to manage any decisions related to my annual income, despite the fact that I manage the household budgets, maintain inventory, and handle all payments to household suppliers every month?"

"Surely you can understand, my lady..." The man looked abashed at being called out.

"Surely you can understand I do not appreciate having my finances usurped by an unwanted interloper who has replaced all of my loyal staff with underlings of his choosing? Or that I do not appreciate being cut out of decision making that is directly affecting my life."

The man of accounts cleared his throat in the awkward silence. "I assure you, Lord Downs only has your best interests at heart, my lady."

"You see Mr. Whitaker," Arthur cut in. "If you cannot see your way clear to assist Lady Whitestone as she should be, and without Lord Downs' interference, we shall have to aid her in moving her accounts to my own man of affairs, Mr. Dunraven. I am certain he will see his way clear to conduct business with Lady Whitestone while protecting her interests from grasping relatives who have no authority over her finances."

"Why...I...I... Yes, of course my lord." The man sighed and sat back in his chair in defeat.

"Now, I would like to begin this new arrangement by conducting a full audit of all decisions made by Lord Downs since my husband's death." Jo announced.

"Very good, my lady. We can schedule that for three—"

"I'm afraid you misunderstood me, Mr. Whitaker. We shall conduct that audit now." Jo gave him an imperious look.

"But my lady, I have other clients this morning," he objected, almost angrily.

"I shall not be deterred. I shall review my accounts immediately or I shall take Lord Dunmere's advice and move my accounts."

The man blanched. "Very well, my lady." He rang a bell which sat on his desk and a young, gangly man dressed in a clerk's sleeve protectors and apron stepped in. "Higgins, please send notes around to my morning appointments that I shall be unavailable today. Reschedule at their earliest convenience."

"Yes, Mr. Whitaker," Higgins replied and slipped back out quickly.

From there, they reviewed the ledgers pertaining to her accounts. By the time they left Mr. Whitaker's office, they had undone multiple decisions made by Bernard, including the firing of her previous staff.

Now she'd wrested control away from the grasping bastard, she needed to release his staff to clear the way for the return of her original people.

She just hoped this would be the *end* of the man's interference.

Chapter Twenty-Five

A rthur led Linc into the study while Jo went to check on Matthew. Pouring each of them a drink before he sat down with Linc on the couch by the fireplace, Arthur murmured, "I'm worried this won't be the end of things with Lord Downs. He was too sure of himself and far too bold for someone who would be the type to cower and run away at the first sign of opposition."

Linc nodded and sipped his drink. "I agree. He bears watching. Perhaps we should call in the Lustful Lords for assistance?"

Smiling softly, Arthur looked at the handsome blonde man he'd come to love over the last few years. "I was thinking along those same lines. The ladies would be an excellent support for Jo as well, and her son."

"Brilliant. I shall send a note around later asking them to meet with us here. I hope tomorrow isn't too soon for them." Linc's face pinched in concern.

"I'm sure everyone who is available will come. We can fill in anyone not able to make it." Arthur shrugged a shoulder. He then took another drink from his glass, letting the whisky burn as it slid down his throat. The warmth was welcome, even on a spring day.

"I must say, I found it rather stirring watching you deal with that bastard, Whitaker. Quite a masterful bit of maneuvering on your part." Linc set his glass down and moved in to seal his lips to his.

Arthur groaned as he tried to set his glass down and missed the table. As he grabbed the back of Linc's head to deepen the kiss, he heard the thud of the glass hitting the carpet. Hard chest to hard chest, their tongues tangled in an erotic kiss full of desire, need, and love.

Linc was trying to work his own coat off when a feminine gasp broke through their lusty kiss.

Arthur leaned around Linc and smiled at Jo. "Do come in."

"I didn't mean to interrupt." Her cheeks heated, but she stepped fully into the room and closed the door behind her. Pausing, she turned the key.

"Interrupt? We were merely getting warmed up while we waited for you." Arthur held out his hand to her. "I take it all is well with young Matthew?"

"Indeed. He's taking a nap."

She took his hand, and he drew her closer to them. "Wonderful. Now, turn around."

Jo did as he commanded, causing his blood to rush through his veins as it made its way further south. Her acquiescence was heady stuff, indeed. Almost as heady as when Linc did his bidding.

"Help me unfasten her clothing." Arthur glanced at Linc while he gave the directions and saw the light of desire flicker deep in his gaze as he nodded. They began loosening laces and unhooking things until they'd peeled Jo free of all but a thin chemise and her stockings. "Leave those. I like the look of her black stockings against her pearly thighs."

Linc grunted in agreement as he finished working his coat free of his arms while Arthur did the same.

Jo turned around, still standing in front of them, her chemise nearly turned sheer by the fireplace behind her. "I enjoy watching you two together."

Arthur stilled and glanced at Linc, whose eyes had darkened further at her words. "Would you...like to watch us do more than kiss?" Arthur asked cautiously.

They had generally focused on her since she'd come back into their lives, though they had not held back from kissing and touching each other. But did she wish to see something more? Perhaps one of them sucking the other off? Or would she like to see them fuck?

His cock throbbed at the idea of their Wood Sprite watching him take Linc's arse.

"Yes." Jo's raspy reply seemed to be wrested from her lips but then she kept speaking. "I want to see you two together in every way you have been since we were parted." She paused and Arthur swore her cheeks turned nearly magenta. "I often imagined you two together without me..." She hesitated. "I imagined you both when I was alone in my bed at night. When...when I gave myself pleasure."

Linc cursed softly and suddenly stripped himself as if his very life depended on it. Arthur had to admit that though they'd both halted when she'd spoken, he was now racing his partner to see who could get naked first. They shed their last items of clothing nearly at the same time.

Arthur looked up at her standing there, hovering over them. "Well, Jo...your wish is our command."

She moved toward the wing chair nearby, discarding her chemise as she went. Then she sprawled in the chair, her legs splayed wide, exposing her glistening cunny. "I enjoyed that kiss I interrupted when I walked in."

Arthur nodded and pulled Linc into his arms on the settee they still occupied. Their tongues twined around each other once more as Linc laid on top of him. Their cocks rubbed against each other as they ground their hips together in mimicry of their eager tongues.

"Yes." Jo's breathless whisper recalled their attention.

Then Arthur took over and pushed Linc back against the opposite arm of the settee they were on. He kissed his way down his chest, stopping to lick and suck on Linc's sensitive nipples.

"Harder," Linc demanded as he laced his fingers through Arthur's hair.

Refusing to take commands, Arthur instead blew cool air across one puckered nipple.

"You bloody bastard." Linc fisted his hand in his hair and pulled Arthur's head back. The pull of the strands and the man's strength made Arthur's cock throb. This was what he found so sexy about Linc. As good natured as he was, he allowed Arthur to have control. The truth was, it was his gift to him, and Arthur knew it. It was a gift he treasured.

"Let go or I won't suck your cock," Arthur demanded.

Jo whimpered, drawing their attention. She had one hand between her plump thighs, working her clit while her other hand plucked a hardened nipple. "Don't stop."

"Fuck," Linc groaned as he released Arthur's hair, his head flopping backward in submission.

Arthur chuckled, low and wicked. With Jo in his corner, Linc had no choice but to give in—even if he didn't want to in the moment. But he knew Arthur would make it worth it for him.

Sliding down Linc's legs, he let his knees hit the plush carpet as he grabbed the man's cock and wedged himself between the other man's thighs. Arthur stopped to watch Jo for a moment as she continued sliding her fingers deliciously in and out of her wet pussy. Then she pulled her fingers free and brought them to her lips.

"Holy fuck woman," Arthur growled as he watched her lick her juices from her fingers. He knew when Linc had seen what was happening from the way his cock pulsed in his fist and the low curse that crossed his lips.

"Suck him, Arthur. Suck his cock for me." Jo's command was all the nudge he needed to get back to what he'd been about to do.

Their woman wanted to watch him suck Linc's cock? He would deliver.

As Arthur swirled his tongue over the swollen tip, gathering the familiar salty, sweet taste of Linc, he moaned with unabated hunger. Then he opened his mouth and swallowed him in a sensual gulp. Arthur loved the feel of Linc pushing against his throat as he tried to take all of him. Linc slid his fingers back into Arthur's hair and flexed his hips to push deeper. He let him slide in until his throat stretched around him and he was rooted.

"Damn, that feels good. Take it. Take me," Linc growled as he thrust in and out of Arthur's mouth.

Arthur didn't consider his current position subservient since he was the one doling out the pleasure: he was responsible for making Linc feel good while Jo's fantasy was brought to life.

Linc continued working in and out of his mouth as Jo's groans grew louder next to them. The frenzy grew, as did

Arthur's cock. He wouldn't have thought it could get any harder, but his lovers were proving him wrong.

"Going to come." Linc gritted out as he continued working Arthur's mouth with his cock.

"Yes, come in his mouth." Jo's voice rang out as the first spurt of Linc's orgasm hit his tongue.

Arthur swallowed some of it as Linc continued to pulse in his mouth, his body shuddering with his orgasm. Then, with a mouthful of his cum, he pushed Linc's legs up toward his chest as Arthur stood. His cock ached with the need to come. It would not take him long once he got inside his lover. He let the cum drip from his lips to hit Linc's sphincter and the man shuddered beneath him, whether from exhausting pleasure or the anticipation of more, Arthur did not know.

Aligning his cock to Linc's rear entrance, Arthur pressed. The makeshift lube did its job as he eased inside Linc.

With the head of his cock past the tight ring of muscle, Arthur paused to look up at Jo who stared lustily, her eyes wide yet riveted to where he'd speared into the man he loved. Then Arthur thrust deep in a long steady stroke that made Linc and Jo both moan, her as she stroked her clit, Linc as he sank deep inside him.

Then Arthur lost what little control he'd kept. He plunged in and out of Linc with hard thrusts as he watched Jo pleasure herself.

"Yes! Yes! Yes!" Her fevered chant seemed to sync up with his thrusts.

Arthur knew he wouldn't last much longer—was amazed he'd lasted as long as he had, if he was honest.

Then Jo cried out one last time as her toes curled and he was lost.

Arthur thrust once more into Linc and exploded. His legs trembled while pleasure jetted up and down his spine. The room went a little fuzzy as he slumped over Linc's contorted body.

A few moments later, he became aware of the sound of panting in the room. The three of them were all trying to catch their breath. He pushed up a bit to ease his weight off of Linc who objected. "Don't go yet. I love having you inside me."

"I'm breaking you in half," Arthur chided good-naturedly.

As he collapsed back onto the rug in a sprawl, Jo sat forward in her chair. "That was incredible. Thank you for letting me watch."

"You are welcome. It was incredibly erotic." Arthur stared at her solemnly.

"Though your cheeks might be permanently pink after today," Linc chimed in as he sat up.

She laughed, but did not deny it. She glanced around at her discarded clothing. "I should probably get home. Matthew needs to eat dinner and get to bed soon." Jo slipped her wrinkled chemise over her head. "And I have a staff to dismiss."

Arthur got to his feet and helped her dress. "We should go with you."

"Bernard will not be there, and I need to do this part on my own. I need them to understand who is in control."

Together, he and Linc helped her dress until she was fussing with her hair while they donned their own clothes again. With everyone dressed once more, they sent her on her way, though not without some trepidation.

Linc looked at him, a crease between his brows. "You follow her home and be sure that bastard isn't there. I'll take care of sending word to everyone to meet here tomorrow."

"Excellent notion," Arthur nodded.

After all, Jo was quite mistaken if she thought they were leaving her to finish this fight alone.

Chapter Twenty-Six

The Next Morning

J o awoke to find her lady's maid had returned. Upon her arrival home the previous afternoon, she had informed Jasper that not only were his services no longer needed, but that those of the rest of the staff that came with him were also not required. She had then sent messages around to her old staff, asking that they return first thing in the morning if they were available.

And here was her familiar lady's maid, bustling about her room as though the last few days had not occurred. "Good morning, my lady. Shall I ring for your breakfast?"

"No, thank you, Olivia. I believe I shall take breakfast downstairs. Has everyone else returned as well?" Jo didn't bother to hide her happiness.

"Of course, my lady. We are all very pleased to be back in your service." Olivia smiled. "How about your spring green day gown?"

"That sounds lovely." Jo stretched and crawled out of bed. Half an hour later, she walked into the dining room and found the welcome sight of Bell awaiting her. "Good morning, Mr. Bell."

"Good morning, my lady. Lovely to see you today." The man actually flashed a small grin at her. "Mrs. Stevens is upstairs with the young Master, and Mrs. Adams is happily ensconced in the kitchen. As for the rest of the staff, a few had already found new placements, so we shall look to replace them as quickly as possible, but almost everyone was happy to return to their positions."

"Thank you, Bell. You are nothing if not efficient. I would be lost—I was lost—without you." Feeling all was right in her world, Jo settled into her breakfast.

By mid-morning, she had moved to her study to review the house accounts and sort out the rest of the mess Bernard had made of her home. She had just closed the ledger when the door to her study flew open.

"You meddling little bitch!" Bernard stormed into the room with Bell hot on his heels.

"My lady, I apologize. He stormed right past me—"

"It's fine, Bell. Perhaps ask Jeffrey and Richard to make themselves available to escort Lord Downs out once he's said his piece?"

"Very good, my lady." Bell shot a wary glance at the intruder, but obeyed and exited the room.

"Now, what can I do for you, Lord Downs?" Jo turned her attention to him, striving for a calm she did not feel.

"You and those rakes you acquaint yourself with went to Mr. Whitaker and undid all of my hard work!" Bernard was practically seething.

"Of course I did. It was not your work to do. In fact, it is not your money or your property to manage. My son is Lord Whitestone now, and as his only parent and legal guardian I am the one who's job it is to manage his holdings until such time as he comes of age. So, yes, I absolutely undid all the mess you made of things." Jo took a breath, pleased she'd managed to rein in her fury and keep her cool, though her hands trembled with the effort. "If that will be all, I shall see you once a quarter when we discuss your allowance. I would use the funds you currently have wisely as I shall deduct the money you diverted to your household out of the next quarter's allowance. I suspect that will not leave you a great deal to live on."

"Like hell you will! This is not over. Not by a longshot," Bernard fumed as a knock sounded on the door.

"Come in." The door opened, admitting the two rather large footmen she had requested. "Excellent. Jeffrey, Richard, I believe Lord Downs was finished. If you two will help him find his way to the front door?"

"Yes, my lady." They bowed and stepped forward to where Bernard stood, mutinous and angry.

When they laid hands on him and began backing out of the room, Bernard yelled, "You bloody bitch! I shall be back!"

Jo listened to him screaming all the way down the hall and out the front door. Satisfied that all was well, she dashed off a note to Arthur and Linc, letting them know the confrontation had occurred and that it had gone smoothly, then headed upstairs to check on her son.

That evening, Jo had Matthew brought downstairs to have an early dinner with her. They were sharing a lovely roast pheasant with potatoes, carrots, and asparagus, the last of which Matthew was refusing to eat. The boy was ever one to avoid his vegetables.

"Now Matthew, if you don't eat your asparagus you can't have any dessert," Jo urged him to eat.

"No. I don't like it." He pushed the unwanted vegetable away. Then a speculative look twinkled in his eye. "If I eat more carrots instead, can I have dessert then?"

She stopped to consider. It wasn't an unreasonable trade-off. "Fine—" A loud bang sounded in the entryway. She rose and went to the door of the dining room to see what was going on. There she found Bell and her two largest footmen scuffling with three men while a fourth stood by, watching.

Jo gasped, drawing the man's attention.

"My lady, I suggest you tell your servants to stand down before they are injured." The man had black hair so coated in pomade that it sat slicked to his head, paired with an ostentatious mustache which made him look rather villainous if he wasn't so physically attractive.

Before Jo could say a word one footman, Richard, was knocked on the head with a rather intimidating club. "Stop it! Bell, Jeffrey, stop fighting!"

The men continued to tussle a moment more, then everyone stopped. Bell straightened his livery, as did Jeffrey, but they ceased the scuffle.

"Now, what on earth is this all about?" Jo demanded as she straightened her spine and stared at the stranger.

That was when Bernard walked in. "Is everything sorted out, Richardson?"

"Not quite yet, my lord." The man looked at Bernard with a little distaste, then returned his focus to her. "My lady, I apologize for the disturbance, but Lord Downs has hired us to serve as guards for you and your son. Your servants did not give us an opportunity to explain. We have been hired due to an apparent threat to your safety."

Jo sniffed indignantly. "The only threat to my safety is the one posed by you and your men working on behalf of my odious brother-in-law. I am in no need of guards, you four may be on your way."

The man cleared his throat and looked from her to Bernard uncomfortably.

"I think not, Lady Whitestone," Bernard stepped in. "I received a report of a credible threat against the life of your son today. I have hired these men out of an abundance of caution. They will attend to you wherever you go."

"And as I told you this afternoon, Bernard, I am in control of my finances. You are not. I suggest you leave and take your lackeys with you." Jo pointed to the door, ensuring that her hand did not quaver.

Bernard closed the door behind him. "I'm afraid that is not how this shall play out, my dear. We are here to stay."

"Are you then? And what of Agnes? Won't your wife miss your overbearing hide?" Jo glared at him, furious, yet there was a large pit in her stomach as she watched her staff unable to protect her.

"Never you mind about my wife. Agnes has a choice, be pushed aside and replaced or get on board with my plan." Bernard glared at her.

"What do you mean pushed aside?" Fear skated down Jo's spine like icy fingers.

"I mean, she can be replaced by permanent means." Bernard paused for a moment as if just hearing himself. "Well well. Maybe that is the better solution? I get rid of my wife and marry you. Then you and the brat are under my control."

Jo gasped. Shock and horror tumbling through her. "You can't force me to marry you."

Bernard laughed. "My lady, of course I can. There are parsons who can be—shall we say—*persuaded* to marry a man and a woman without asking too many questions."

Fury and desperation clawed at her throat, nearly choking her. Then she drew in a dep breath and calmed herself. She had one last avenue to thwart this man. "Gentlemen, I hope Lord Downs has paid you in advance, as he is not solvent beyond the quarterly allowance which I provide him." She stared at the men pointedly.

The one called Richardson cleared his throat. "I'm afraid we insisted on payment up front, my lady."

"I could double his fee for you to leave," Jo tried again.

"I'm afraid the promise of the long-term work outweighs the short-term gain you offer, my lady. I'm a man of my word." Richardson tried to smile apologetically, then he shot a look of distaste at the man who had hired him. Regardless of his dislike of the man, he appeared prepared to follow through on his agreement with Bernard. What little physical appeal Richardson had was instantly lost.

Jo's heart pounded in her chest as she considered what she could do without risking anyone's life or safety. Her staff would be safe as long as she complied. She could figure out how to get away from these thugs later. She had to remain here to protect Matthew. "I see. Very well then. I am going to finish my dinner with my son."

With that, she turned and retreated for the moment. Finding Matthew hiding by the door of the dining room, she ushered him back to his seat and resumed their meal—and as they ate, she plotted their escape.

Chapter Twenty-Seven

Linc knocked on Arthur's study door. Opening a passage between their homes had proven a brilliant choice. He certainly enjoyed being able to move freely between the houses when he wanted to find Arthur, and he knew Arthur felt much the same way.

"Come in."

Linc walked in to Arthur's study and found the man in question sitting at his desk. "Hello."

"Well, hello there." Arthur smiled at him.

Linc cocked his head to the side. "Have you heard from Jo?"

Arthur shook his head. "I have not, but the confrontation only happened yesterday. I really had wanted to be present for that." He frowned.

"As did I, but she is rather headstrong." Linc's heart thudded in his chest as he thought of their Wood Sprite. He loved her rebellious ways. After all, that is what had brought her into their lives. "Needless to say, I'm worried we haven't heard from her since then. As we agreed before, I don't see that man letting this go. I know you watched from the street the first night for quite a while. It's too bad we waited to call in reinforcements."

"Yes, we should have called everyone when the bastard switched the staff on her. At least everyone will be here this afternoon so we can set up some kind of watch on her house. Let's pay her a visit. Just to make sure all is well." Arthur stood from his desk.

"That's what I was considering as well." Linc nodded.

A short while later, they were standing on Jo's front stoop. The door was opened by Bell, her original butler. The man looked at them but darted a glance back over his shoulder.

Linc's gut tightened.

"Good day, my lords."

"Good day, Bell. We are here to see Lady Whitestone," Arthur announced, almost as formally as Bell had greeted them.

Linc stepped to the right a tad and tried to lean against the portico wall. As he did so, he could see a man dressed in dark, rough clothing lurking behind Bell.

"I-I'm afraid Lady Whitestone is not at home to visitors at the moment."

Arthur squinted, as though confused. Which made sense. Jo was never not at home to them now they had returned to their understanding.

Linc was sure Arthur couldn't see the man lurking. "Yes, well, please let her know that we stopped by." He grabbed Arthur by the arm and dragged him away as he sputtered in confusion. Once in their carriage, he turned to him. "There was a man who did not belong skulking in the shadows behind Bell. Once again, something is very wrong in that house."

"Well, bloody hell! Why didn't we just storm in there then?" Arthur growled as he reached for the door of the carriage.

Linc pulled him back into the seat. "And if they are holding her at gunpoint? Her, and Matthew? Then what happens if we burst in there?"

Arthur sighed. "You're right. We need to understand what is going on and have a bloody plan."

"Exactly. At least everyone is coming by this afternoon. We can discuss our options then."

Jo sat in her bedchamber writing a note to send to Arthur and Linc. She needed their help now. This was, without a doubt, a situation she could not handle on her own. At the very least, she needed a place to hide.

She laid out all that had happened since dinner last night, down to Bernard's threat to kill his wife and marry her, though he had been quite clear that was a last resort, as he found her so distasteful. Jo shuddered. After all, the feeling was mutual.

She folded it up and pressed the note into Olivia's hands. "Now, you must be careful. I do not, under any circumstances, want you hurt for helping me."

"Those brutish bastards have taken over everywhere. We all want them gone and will help anyway we can." Her lady's maid cast a quick glance at the door then shoved the note down the front of her gown and into her corset.

"Thank you, Olivia." Jo embraced her but stepped back just as Bernard walked in.

"Get out," he snarled as he strode in. "Get out and close the damned door behind you."

Jo shrank back in genuine fear as Olivia scampered out of the room with a worried glance her way.

"Why do you insist on associating with such lowbrow trash as those Lustful Lords?" Bernard grated out. "I've told you, *Josephine*, keeping company with the likes of those reprobates looks bad on the whole family."

"I don't know who you mean." Jo straightened her spine, unwilling to cower before this man.

His arm raised up and then the sound of flesh meeting flesh cracked into the silence a moment before heat and pain bloomed on her left cheek.

"You bloody bastard!"

"That's the least of what I'll do to you and to that little bastard of yours. Is he even of my brother's loins?" Bernard had a fearsome snarl on his face as he took a step closer to her. Then he reached out and spun her around toward her little writing desk. "Those two bounders, Dunmere and Lincolnshire, have come to visit for the last time. I want you to write them a note explaining you have no desire to see them ever again. Cut ties with them, or you and your brat will regret it."

Face throbbing from where he had slapped her, Jo began drafting the required note. She wrote the words he dictated in the most awkward and formal manner she could manage.

They loved her. They would read it and understand. That, and her secret note would hopefully arrive not long after they received this one.

Arthur and Linc sat with Lords Stonemere, Brougham, Wolfington, Flintshire, and Portridge, although the latter still preferred to go by Lucifer.

"Gentlemen, thank you for coming on such short notice." Arthur looked at each of them in turn before continuing. "Linc and I cannot tell you how much your support means to us."

Stone nodded. "We've all been in your shoes at one time or another."

"Still, our situation is unique because we have so little information," Linc picked up the conversation. "Today, when we stopped by to check on Jo, we found a rather strange situation. Her butler wouldn't let us in, which is unusual. I noticed a suspicious sort lurked in the shadows behind him. I couldn't get a good look at the man, but he seemed to hover close to Bell as though to ensure he said nothing he shouldn't."

"You didn't see or hear anything else?" Wolf asked.

"That was it. As I said, we don't have a lot to go on." Linc shrugged one shoulder.

A knock sounded and Harris entered the front salon. "My lord, two letters have come for you from Lady Whitestone."

"Two?" Arthur was surprised, but waved Harris over. "Thank you."

He opened the first letter, breaking the Whitestone seal.

Dear Lords Dunmere and Lincolnshire,

I find myself rather unfortunately indisposed for the long term. It will be best for all parties involved if we remove ourselves from each other's orbits. I do hope you both will understand the need for this permanent parting of the ways.

With all sincerity,

Lady Josephine Marie Whitestone

Arthur snorted, finding the whole bit of correspondence contrived. He handed it to Linc. "Someone made her write this. I don't believe a word of what she says."

Linc took it from him and read. At the end, he snorted in turn. "Most definitely either forced to write it or someone has attempted to write it on her behalf. Though it appears to be her handwriting."

"Agreed. It is her penmanship. I wonder what the second note says?" Arthur opened the second piece of correspondence.

My dearest Arthur and Linc,

Last evening Bernard burst into my home with the assistance of four brutal men. They have been hired to "safeguard" me. They are of course, simply put, my jailers. Bernard has threatened—though I am still not convinced of his veracity—to dispose of his wife and marry me should I continue to prove difficult—though I believe that was merely a threat to gain my compliance.

I am confident I can escape out of my window with Matthew in tow, but once away from here, we shall need a place to hide. I trust one or both of you can assist me with this. I shall make my escape tonight while the household sleeps. I hope to see you soon.

All my love,

Jo

"Bloody hell!" Arthur passed the note to Linc. "There are four men working for Lord Downs and acting as guards, and so Jo has determined she will escape out her window tonight. We shall need to be there to help her slip away. The bastard has threatened to get rid of his wife and force Jo to marry him!"

Linc balled the letter up. "That bloody blighter needs to be dealt with."

"I could call on enough men to overpower her guards and rescue the both of them, if that is what you wish to do," Lucifer offered casually as he lounged in his chair. The man's calm coolness had a deadly air about it. "There is, of course, some risk of her or the boy being injured with that approach. But you would have the power to determine how you would like things to be resolved with the men in question."

"Do you believe she can effect an escape out her window as she suggests?" Wolf asked carefully.

"I have no doubt she will escape. The problem is, I do not know if she can make it happen on her own with Matthew's arm still in a cast. We need to be there to help her." Arthur sighed. "I suspect that if the men Lord Downs has hired are at all well trained, they will walk the grounds periodically. We should have someone watching to see if we can determine any schedule they may be keeping."

"I can take the first shift." Brougham rose to his feet. "I'll head over now, and you can send someone to relieve me in a few hours. By tonight, we should have a clear picture of their movements."

"Thank you, Cooper." Linc nodded as their friend departed. "I believe once we have Jo and Matthew ensconced here, we may need some additional support to protect her."

"I'll have my men cover that," Lucifer offered. "That will leave the rest of you free to move about as needed to handle Lord Downs."

"Excellent," Arthur nodded. "I think we have a plan."

It felt good to have his friends come to his and Linc's aid this way. He of course knew they would do so, but knowing a thing and seeing a thing is true is a very different experience. Particularly when it came to the unflinching loyalty of one's friends.

He'd been such a fool as a younger man, thinking the men he'd caroused with were his friends. *These men* here in this room were his genuine friends.

Now they just needed to rescue his and Linc's woman.

Chapter Twenty-Eight

Linc crouched in the bushes in Jo's garden and waited with Arthur. Together, they watched the back of the house for signs of movement inside. The lights were steadily doused throughout the first floor.

"She'll wait until everyone is asleep and then sneak out the back window, won't she?" Linc looked in Arthur's direction, peering into the shadows which surrounded them.

"I'm worried. If there are guards on all the doors, then she'll have to find another path of escape."

Just then, the dull thud of boots on the cobblestones sounded. They huddled deeper into the bushes and waited. The guard moved past them with no hesitation. They continued to crouch and watch as the lights on the second floor slowly went out, one by one.

About five minutes later, the same guard wandered through the backyard once more as expected, based on Cooper's report from earlier. He seemed to make a fairly regular circuit of the front and back gardens of the home.

The man came past them at least four more times as the house continued to settle into an eerie stillness. Fortunately it was a cloudy night, so there was little moonlight to potentially expose anyone making an escape.

Eventually, there was the creak of a window opening above them. Linc looked up and tapped Arthur on the shoulder to get his attention. He pointed up to where curtains now gently billowed out the window. A pit formed in his stomach as he imagined what Jo might be planning.

Linc cursed as he realized the guard would come by soon. "Arthur, the guard!"

"I'm on it. I'll ensure he can't raise the alarm." Arthur rose from the bushes and slipped out, keeping along the shadowed edges of the fence line. Then he waited in the deepest shadows.

Linc's gaze darted back and forth from where he thought Arthur was to the open window. Then he saw Jo and Matthew in the opening.

As they had feared, Jo's son was not nearly as intrepid as his mother. For long moments, the boy sat on the windowsill cradling his broken arm as his mother appeared to encourage him to slide over the sill. Twice the boy turned as though to climb back into the house and twice Jo soothed him and returned him into position.

Linc felt for the boy, but he was also quite confident that Jo wouldn't have chosen this avenue of escape if she'd had any other viable option.

Then suddenly a scuffle broke out where Arthur had been waiting—there were a few grunts of pain, and the muffled sound of a body hitting the ground. Linc held his breath as he waited for Arthur to appear.

Right about the time Jo finally eased Matthew over the edge and down a bit, Arthur strode toward where the boy was being lowered. Linc crept out of his hiding spot and joined him. Matthew spotted them and gave a soft squeal of excitement, as he often did, but Linc and Arthur both held their fingers to their lips and shushed him. He nodded and grinned as Jo continued to lower him to the ground with a sheet tied off around his waist.

Once the boy was in Linc's arms, Arthur quickly untied the knot and waved up at Jo to let her know it was safe to come down.

Linc passed the boy to Arthur. "Best get him to the carriage while I help Jo."

"Agreed." Arthur bundled the boy close to him and slipped out the back gate near the stable and into the mews where they'd entered.

Linc glanced back up to the window to find Jo dangling above him. The rope of bedsheets appeared to still be holding as she shimmied down the makeshift rope. Watching her make her way down the side of the house so easily suggested that her life in the country had her spending more time as a tomboy than one might have expected, based on their time with the woman.

A moment later, she was on the ground and in his arms. He resisted the urge to plunder her mouth right there and instead took her by the hand and led her the same way Arthur had gone.

Once they were by the stables, Jo tugged on his coat sleeve. "Where is Matthew?"

"Arthur has him safely in our carriage. Let's go." Linc urged her into the mews.

They carefully picked their way down the street, moving from shadowed doorway to shadowed doorway until they reached the carriage. Once there, he helped her up into the vehicle and joined her, stopping long enough to bark a short "drive" to the man wielding the reins.

"Oh, thank goodness you two came." Jo threw her arms around Linc's neck and hugged him fiercely before she moved to Arthur. Then she looked at her son. "And you, young man, you were so courageous!"

"It was a grand adventure, mother!" Matthew appeared thrilled now it was over.

"Indeed, it was." She smiled lovingly at her son as tears gathered in her eyes. Then she sniffed them back, glancing back and forth between them. "Are we headed to one of your London residences?"

Arthur cleared his throat. "No. Out of an abundance of caution and a strong sense of propriety, we've made other arrangements."

"What do you mean?" Jo seemed surprised and not a little concerned about this news.

Linc sighed. "Damn it Arthur, you should have just told her." He scowled at his lover then turned to Jo. "We've arranged for you to stay at Lord Brougham's house. With his wife and children in residence, we felt it was best for both of you, initially. Then we can sort out a better long-term solution."

"Oh." She sounded disappointed by that news. But it really was the best choice.

"We shall have some men helping with guard duty at the house. The others are our friends. Their women will spend time with you and help get you settled," Arthur explained.

A short while later, they were pulling up to the rear of the Brougham's house. Emily and Cooper were both there to greet them and usher them toward the back entrance.

"Good evening, Lady Whitestone. I hope you and Matthew are doing well after the night's excitement," Emily said with a smile.

"Oh, please, you must call me Jo. I should feel awkward standing on ceremony when I have barged into your home in such a fashion," Jo replied with flushed cheeks.

Emily grinned at her and opened the back door of the house. "Very well then, I shall call you Jo, and you will call me Emily. I apologize, but we felt it was safer to bring you in the back way in case there are any neighbors arriving home from the night's entertainments."

"No need to apologize. I appreciate the warm bed for myself and my son. I hope we won't be any trouble," Jo said softly as they all filed into the house.

"No trouble at all," Emily assured them. "Now, I assumed you'd feel best keeping Matthew with you tonight, so I have a trundle bed set up for him in your room."

"Thank you." Jo looked abashed as she realized she was empty-handed. "I'm afraid I failed to bring anything with us but a few pieces of jewelry shoved in my corset."

"I do hope they were cabochons and not faceted. I remember clearly how the faceted gems dig into the skin when crammed down a corset," Emily pressed on, without missing a step as Jo blinked at her in astonishment. "We weren't sure, so we assumed you were coming to us with the clothes on your back. I have a little of everything you both might need for the next day or so until we can make other arrangements." Emily walked them all into the chamber where Jo and her son would sleep.

Jo laughed as she followed. "I'm sorry, do you often carry your jewels stuffed down your corset?"

Emily smiled. "Not for a while now. But that is a story for another day."

Cooper stepped forward. "We have men patrolling the grounds and you are sleeping in a chamber next to Emily and myself. If you need anything, just yell out."

Jo's cheeks turned pink. "Thank you, my lord."

"Cooper, please. You are amongst friends." He put an arm around Emily and looked at Linc and Arthur. "Gentlemen, I'll wait for you downstairs in the study."

"Thank you, Cooper," they both murmured.

Finally, alone with Jo—or almost alone, anyway—Linc turned to look at her more carefully. "Are you well, Wood Sprite?"

Jo nodded, but moved into his arms. Linc wasn't sure, but he may have needed to hold her more than she needed to be held, just then.

"Come, Matthew, let me help you get settled." Arthur led the boy—who was watching them with fascination—away.

Linc cupped her face in his shaking hands and kissed her gently on the lips. She responded, melting into him. He quickly pulled back before things got out of hand. "I was so worried when I saw Matthew perched in that window."

"Dear God, I was terrified they would catch us." Jo whispered, dropping a kiss on his lips. "But then you two were there for me, just as you said you would be."

"Always, Wood Sprite." Linc let go of her. "I'm sure Arthur needs a moment with you as well. Let me finish up with Matthew." He smiled softly at her and walked over to where Arthur was helping the boy finish changing his clothes. "Go on, I've got this."

Arthur nodded and stepped over to hold Jo in his arms.

Matthew yawned mightily as his head poked through his borrowed nightshirt. "Can we climb down a rope again tomorrow night?"

Linc laughed. "I hope that won't be required two nights in a row."

"But it was great fun once I saw you and Uncle Arthur there. At first, it was awfully scary. But then you two appeared, and I knew you wouldn't let anything bad happen." The boy grinned up at him as he climbed into the trundle bed that rode low to the ground.

Linc's heart gave a slow thud at the boy's faith in them. "Of course we wouldn't. But maybe still, we can find some other adventure to get up to tomorrow?"

"Very well." He yawned once again. "I'll sleep on it."

The boy promptly fell asleep.

Linc stepped over to where Arthur and Jo were still huddled together. "He is quite enamored with the night's fun. But I suspect he'll sleep the night through. He seems worn out."

"No doubt." Jo smiled at them. "I was disappointed we would not be staying with you two, but I see the sense of staying here."

"Good," Arthur murmured. "We'll be by tomorrow morning to see you both, and we can sort out what comes next. We'll also introduce you to everyone."

"Very well." Jo yawned herself.

"I wish we could sleep with you in our arms tonight, but it will be enough to know that you are safe here." Arthur caressed her cheek and pressed a kiss to her lips.

Linc embraced her once more. "We'll see if we can arrange some time for just the adults soon."

"Please." She smiled softly at them. "A lady must reward her heroes."

They slipped from her room and left her to prepare for bed.

Chapter Twenty-Nine

A rthur stood in his study and stared at the fire. He knew what he wanted to do, what he needed to do. But he was worried about Linc.

There was a short, sharp knock on the door, then it opened. "There you are."

Arthur turned and found Linc standing just inside the door. "Yes, I've been here brooding." He couldn't help but offer a sardonic smile.

"I can see that. The question is, what precisely are you brooding about now?" Linc strolled toward him.

He sighed. "You."

That pulled Linc up short. "Me? Why?"

"Yes, you." Arthur felt the love he had for him well up inside. "I think about you often, you know."

Linc sauntered forward and pressed up against him. Chest to chest, he cupped his face. "Only the best thoughts, I hope." Linc winked at him in a saucy manner.

Arthur couldn't help but chuckle. "Almost always." He drew in a deep breath and found Linc's gaze. "One of us needs to marry Jo to protect her."

Linc nodded solemnly. "I agree. The protection of one of our names would be very helpful, under the current circumstances, though I must say that would only be the icing on the cake. The real treat is, of course, having Jo in our lives forever."

"Very much agreed but that does beg the question. Who should marry her?" Arthur winced as he posed the ultimate question. "Legally, I mean."

"I understand what you mean. I should think the answer would be obvious." Linc stepped back, letting his hand drop from Arthur's face.

Arthur huffed, annoyance nipping at him as he tried to read Linc's reactions. "If it was obvious, I wouldn't have been sitting in here brooding about it."

Linc chuckled softly. "I beg to differ. You are a bit of a brooder. Obviously you should be the one to marry her, legally."

"What makes you say that? Why am I the obvious choice?" Arthur knew Linc was a good choice to be Jo's husband. He was kind and patient, but he also made her laugh, and he'd be wonderful with Matthew.

"Don't be ridiculous. You are far more disciplined than I am, which is good for both her and the boy. You love her deeply. And you need an heir to carry on the family title. She could give you that." Linc shrugged.

"You need an heir as well." Arthur couldn't help but point out the obvious.

"I have other male family members who can carry on the title—and mine is a minor title. Your more elevated title will offer her and the boy more protection and, most important- ly, you need an heir, or the Dunmere title is passed on to some distant relative."

Arthur bit his lip and hesitated, but he could not remain silent. He needed to voice his concerns. "But...but won't you feel left out?"

Linc stepped back into his embrace and wrapped a hand around the back of his neck as he pressed his forehead to his. "Do you love me?"

"You know I do." Arthur rasped the words out as emotion bubbled up from within.

"And I love you. And I love Jo, who I believe loves me. That is all that matters," Linc said, low and with such fervor that Arthur wanted to believe him.

And yet he could not ignore the doubt.

"That is all that matters," Arthur agreed and reached up to grab Linc's lapels to bring their lips together, plunging past his lips to seek out the heat and warmth he knew he'd find within.

Their tongues dueled as each one fought for dominance in the kiss. Finally, Arthur rotated them until Linc's back was pressed against the side of the fireplace. Heat seared their sides from the fire as the heat of their passion burned between them.

As his own cock took notice, Arthur drew back from the kiss. "You know the hard part of all this is going to be convincing Jo we should wed."

Linc panted as he tried to recover from their kiss. "No doubt our little Wood Sprite will fight this tooth and nail—but together we can overcome any objections and help her see the wisdom of this course of action."

"I hope you have the right of it." Arthur said and kissed him once more.

Jo was wearing a borrowed day gown that was a lovely shade of soft green. It was a trifle tight across her bust and hips and came up a bit short, but with her own petticoat underneath, she made it work. She was in the nursery with Matthew, ensuring he was doing well. He had barely been fazed by their late-night adventure and sat playing happily with Emily's two children.

A maid entered and curtsied. "My lady, Lords Dunmere and Lincolnshire are here to see you."

Pleasure wove through her as Jo fought the urge to jump up and run downstairs. "Thank you. Please tell them I shall be down momentarily."

She stood up and went to her borrowed bedchamber. There she took a moment to compose herself and ensure her coiffure remained in place. Then she made her way down to the front salon. Jo stepped inside the room and found Arthur, Linc, Emily, and Cooper all together. "Good morning."

Arthur stepped forward and swept her into his arms for an embrace and a kiss. Then he passed her to Linc, who followed suit. Jo's cheeks heated as she stepped away to find Emily and Cooper serenely ignoring the entire exchange as though it were an everyday occurrence.

"I must thank you all once again for everything you've done for Matthew and I." Jo smiled at all of them.

"It is nothing we wouldn't do or haven't done for any of our friends." Emily smiled back.

"Speaking of our friends," Arthur said, drawing her attention to him. "The rest of them will be here to greet you later this afternoon."

"I would be pleased to meet them."

"In the meantime, there is a matter Linc and I need to discuss with you." For some inexplicable reason, Arthur looked nervous. "Perhaps we should discuss this privately."

Emily and Cooper stood. "Of course. We just wanted to be sure you didn't need anything else," Cooper said.

"I do not, and thank you," Jo assured them.

"Then we shall see you all later when the others arrive." Emily smiled and followed her husband from the room.

Jo's heart raced as she waited to hear whatever it was Arthur and Linc wished to discuss. Perhaps they planned to wash their hands of her after all the recent excitement? They'd helped her escape, but she certainly couldn't blame them if that was where they wished to leave it. Bernard would clearly go to any lengths to control her—even violence.

She shook herself mentally; that kind of thinking was such tripe. They were obviously good men, and she knew in her very bones that they would move heaven and earth for her.

"Jo," Arthur started, drawing her out of her thoughts. "Under the current circumstances, Linc and I both feel it is important that you marry. Doing so would offer you and Matthew the protection of my name, as well as assuring us all that we can be together for the rest of our lives."

Jo flinched and looked at the man who sat across from her, before darting a glance at Linc, who sighed and shook his head.

"Bloody hell, Arthur. You certainly cocked that up."

Jo's breath rushed back into her lungs as she laughed. *Linc was not wrong.* Good heavens, Arthur was excellent at many things. Kissing, making her come, and definitely dirty talk. But the man had no idea how to propose to a woman—not that she was going to say yes.

She was done allowing her circumstances—her age, her family's financial status, her family's need to climb the social ranks, her need to protect her sister—to dictate her relationship status. The question was, would Arthur and Linc understand that? Or would they be like every other man in her life and try to control her?

Her gut clenched at the thought and her resolve was strengthened. "My answer is thank you, but no."

Arthur shot a glare at Linc, then turned back to her. "What do you mean, your answer is no?"

"I mean, I shall not marry you merely for expedience nor for the protection of your name. I have been married twice now. Twice I have been in less than satisfactory marriages for mercenary reasons, because of circumstances I often did not have control over. Each time I have paid a price in the end. If I marry again, it will be for love and it will not be one sided."

Arthur tipped his head back and pinched the bridge of his nose. "Linc's right. I've completely botched this."

"Arthur, I am not rejecting you, or Linc, for that matter. I am simply rejecting marriage as an instrument for achieving one's goals in life. I care for you both deeply but I have no intention of marrying anyone simply for protection." Jo's heart squeezed in her chest. *She cared for them?* Dear heavens she loved them both, but she wouldn't make such an admission now. Not in the face of such a proposal.

She glanced back and forth from one to the other, trying to decipher their reaction.

"Jo, we care for you as well or we would never have suggested marriage." Linc looked at her with a tenderness in his eyes that spoke volumes.

"Yes, we care for you—no, I love you, and I'm sure Linc does as well. We want to spend the rest of our lives with you," Arthur said earnestly as he slanted a frustrated look at Linc.

"I believe we can do so without the construct of marriage." Jo clutched her hands in front of her. Doubts warred with her fear of making another mistake when it came to marriage. What if she married him and something terrible happened? The feeling of being cursed in marriage—if not love—haunted her.

"We could live as bohemians and flaunt all of society's strictures, certainly. But what we cannot do is protect you from men like Lord Downs without that construct. We cannot avoid the censure of Society without the construct of marriage. It would shield us, the three of us, from the majority of scrutiny. We want to be with you, but we do not wish to damage Matthew's prospects nor your reputation," Arthur tried to reason.

Jo took a deep breath. "My answer is still no. I've never cared what Society thought and I still do not. I refuse to live my life in fear. If Lord Downs should try to force me to marry him—and I have serious doubts he would try such a thing, despite his threats—I shall take action, but until that comes to pass, I shall live life on my terms. I'm done with men dictating the circumstances of my life, even you." Tears welled in her eyes. "I'm sorry." Jo turned and fled the room, unable to remain there a moment longer.

"Well, that didn't go at all well," Linc said as they stood alone.

"No, it didn't. In fact, I'm not sure it could have gone any worse," Arthur growled in frustration and shoved his hands in his hair before dropping into a chair.

"It wasn't a no forever. I think our poor Jo has had her hand forced so many times by the men in her life, she wants to go into a marriage knowing she chose it. And really, we did not give her much in the way of declarations of love." Linc shrugged a shoulder.

Arthur's heart ached in his chest. Linc was right. He'd cocked up the whole thing. He should have waited; should have dropped to one knee with flowers and a ring and poured out his heart...not just declared their marriage as a tactical objective in their battle plan to defeat Lord Downs. He sighed and closed his eyes. He was a bloody arse.

Linc knelt before him, wedging himself between Arthur's legs as he cupped his face. "Arthur, look at me."

Clearly wishing to wallow in his despair for a few moments longer, he refused to look at his lover.

"Arthur." Linc's tone was commanding, so much so, that Arthur cracked his lids open. "You love Jo. We need to focus on protecting her for now. Then we can make things right with her."

This man humbled him. Arthur nodded and sucked in a deep breath before he leaned forward and pressed his lips to Linc's. The kiss was nearly chaste, just a perfectly firm pressure until he slid his tongue along the seam of Linc's lips before pulling back. "The question is, how do we protect her?

Despite her inability to understand how determined Lord Downs is to reclaim the family title and fortune, we shall have to find a way to protect her outside of marriage."

"Very true. Well, I suppose we shall start by having one of us following her at all times. If you should like to take the first shift, I shall send around to the Lustful Lords and organize some sort of schedule to ensure she is protected at all times." Linc jerked on the lapels of his coat to ensure it lay correctly after their reverential kiss.

"Very well. I shall remain here to start—send someone as soon as you can and I shall help you where I can."

Together, they walked out of Brougham's house. On the street, Linc climbed into the carriage they had arrived in and rode away and Arthur headed down the street a bit in search of a shadowed doorway he could lurk in for a bit. He'd have to find a better location later, but for now, whatever he could find would do.

The most important thing was protecting Jo.

Chapter Thirty

J o looked down at her son and smiled. It felt good to be out of confinement—even well-meant confinement. The sun was actually shining as they strolled down Bond Street on a beautiful spring day. Emily had kindly allowed her to use their carriage, which now lurked behind them despite all the traffic. With her son's hand in hers, she appreciated the sense of normalcy and hoped it was a hallmark of her life returning to normal.

"Mother, where are we going?" Matthew asked as he looked up at her.

"I have to go by the linen shop and the dressmakers." Jo stopped and tapped her chin with her index finger. "There is one more stop, and I can't quite remember it..."

Matthew grinned, hope shining in his big brown eyes. "The sweet shop?"

Jo shook her head. "No, that wasn't it." She paused. "What was it?"

Her son bounced up and down, yanking on her arm. "The toy shop! It was the toy shop!"

She laughed and squatted down. "That was it! See how helpful you are? I'd completely forgotten."

He threw his arms around her neck. "I love you, Mother!"

Jo hugged him back. "I love you too, sweet boy. Now we have to get going if we are going to complete all our errands."

She stood up and took hold of his hand once more. They walked to the corner, looked both ways, and then Jo stepped off the curb. With her skirts in one hand and her son's hand in the other, she hastened across the street. That was why she was about halfway across the cobblestone street when she heard the thunder of hooves and the clatter of wheels bearing down on them. Someone shoved her from behind and sent her and Matthew careening across the road and out of the path of the vehicle. Stumbling forward, nearly to the other sidewalk, Jo managed to keep her feet as she yanked her son protectively into her arms.

Heart hammering, chest tight, lungs working hard, Jo turned in time to see a man rolling out of the way of the horses' hooves towards them. When he stopped on his back, she gasped. "Linc!"

One of the men she loved groaned as he sat up. "Are you and Matthew unhurt?"

"We're fine. Are you injured beyond the obvious?" Jo knelt down and cupped his face, probing a scratch she could see on his cheekbone.

"I'm well, as long as you two are." He moved to stand up, but groaned as he half sat, half fell back down. "Perhaps I should sit here a moment more."

One of the footmen from Lord Brougham's carriage came over. "My lord, are you hurt?"

"I am perhaps a little worse for the wear. If you wouldn't mind helping me up?" Linc's lips quirked up on one side.

Jo and the footman helped Linc to his feet as Matthew clung to her skirts. With the man's help, Linc made his way over to the waiting carriage. Once they had him sitting inside, the footman lifted Matthew up then helped her into the carriage where she settled next to her quivering son.

Taking him into her arms once more so she could assure herself he was well, Jo turned her focus to Linc. "You saved my life. Our lives." She swallowed the lump in her throat. "Thank you, Linc. I don't know if I can ever repay you."

He leaned back against the cushioned seat of the carriage. "There is nothing to thank me for. I would never let harm come to you or Matthew if I could help it."

"Still, thank you." Her heart continued to pound in her chest, but her breathing had evened out.

"You're welcome."

"If you hadn't been there..." Jo's voice trailed off as images of Matthew's broken and bloody body assaulted her. She felt a fool for having missed the carriage in the street. She swore she had looked and it had been clear. Taking a breath, she gathered her thoughts and asked the one question that was burning in her mind at the moment. "How did you happen to be there?"

Linc's cheeks turned ruddy as he cleared his throat. "I...well. I was following you."

"Following me? Why?" She tipped her head to the side, curiosity rising within. Why in the world would he have been following her?

Linc grunted. "Jo, we tried to tell you yesterday—you aren't safe just because you escaped your home. Lord Downs is determined to keep the title and the fortune in his family's hands. If he can't do that by legal means, we believe he will do it through more...nefarious methods. Since we left you yesterday, we've had someone watching you at all times. Today, it was me."

Jo sucked in a sharp breath and hugged her son closer, pressing her hands over his ears. "He was trying to *kill me?*" Her voice came out as a whisper from both shock and a need to protect her son from the truth.

Linc's blue gaze bore into her, serious and weighty in a way she'd never experienced from him. "We strongly suspect so, and...not just you." He let his gaze drop to her son.

Fear ripped through Jo in an unexpected stab that stole her breath. "No!" She shook her head in denial, though whether it was a denial of Linc's words or merely a refusal to allow anyone to harm her son, she couldn't say. In either case, she knew she would do whatever was required to protect her child.

"I'm sorry, Jo. Perhaps we should have been clearer about what we wanted to protect you from when we—when Arthur asked you to marry him in such spectacular fashion."

"I'm afraid I understood to some degree. I just never imagined that it might come to an attempt on my life, or..." Jo looked down at her son. "But clearly I have underestimated Bernard at every turn." Her laugh was bitterly. Frustration and anger slid through her veins, a thick and sludge-like sensation. "You'd think after all that has happened to me in my life that I would learn to believe the worst of men right from the start." She looked down at her son. "But I refuse to raise a cynical boy, and if I had been such a bitter, cynical woman, I would never have met you and Arthur."

"And that would have been an absolute shame." Linc smiled. "But now is not the time for looking backward. We need to look ahead and determine what comes next." The carriage lurched to a stop, causing him to wince. "Perhaps we can start by ensuring that you and Matthew are unharmed, and have a physician take a look at me."

The door of the carriage opened. "An excellent starting point," Jo said as she released Matthew into the care of the footman, who helped him exit. "Then I think I should meet all of my guards so I know who they are. Arthur should come, so we can talk."

Arthur walked into the drawing room where she and Linc waited for both him and the physician who had been delayed. Her heart skipped a beat in defiance of her head cautioning her. Arthur stopped short before rushing over to drop to his knees before both her and Linc. He grabbed each of their hands. "Thank God you both are safe!"

"We are well enough." Linc darted a glance her way, as if to ask if she would contradict him.

"Yes, most of us came out unscathed," Jo said sardonically. "We are glad you came, Arthur."

"Of course I came! But who is not unscathed?" he asked as he looked around the room as though they were hiding someone from him.

"I got a tad banged up when I rolled out of the way of the carriage that tried to run Jo and Matthew over," Linc offered with a sheepish smile.

Arthur took his face in his hands and turned it from side to side, wincing as he spotted the scrape high on his cheek. "Where else are you hurt? This cannot be your only injury."

"My side hurts as well, though I am fairly certain I missed the horses' hooves." Linc's eyes twinkled with merriment and a little pain.

"Bloody fool." Arthur leaned in and kissed him.

"It was worth it, to ensure Jo and Matthew were safe," Linc said, his gaze locking with Arthur's.

For a moment Jo felt uncomfortable as the men shared a moment.

Arthur looked over at her. "I am grateful you and Matthew were not harmed."

"As am I." She reached out and swept her fingertips over his right brow, nudging a stray lock of hair back into place.

A knock at the door sounded, and it opened as Arthur stood up and turned around.

"The doctor, my lady. My lords," Peters said as he allowed the physician to enter the room.

Jo rose. "Doctor, thank you for coming."

"Of course, my lady. I apologize for the delay." The doctor bowed over her hand and then to each of the men now standing. "And who is the patient I need to see?"

"I believe you are here to see me." Linc eased back into his seat. "I attempted to wrestle with a team of horses today."

"I should hope you don't do such things regularly." The doctor's reply came as he bent to set his bag on the side table closest to Linc.

Arthur and Jo moved out of the way to let the doctor have unfettered access to Linc, though Arthur helped him remove his shirt so the doctor could see his torso. Linc groaned softly as the doctor poked and prodded him.

A short while later, he stood up from where he'd been stooped over his patient. "I believe you are a bit bruised up, but nothing appears broken. I suspect you shall not be feeling tip-top for the next few days. You'll need rest, and laudanum as needed for the pain. You should see steady improvement over a couple of weeks. You can increase activity as your body permits."

"Thank you, doctor." Jo showed him the way out as Linc and Arthur tried to put his shirt back on. By the time she returned, Linc was covered again. "Linc, Arthur should take you home and put you to bed so you can rest, as the doctor has indicated."

"All in good time, Wood Sprite." Linc shifted in his seat and winced.

Jo picked up the laudanum and held it out to him. "You need to take this."

"Not quite yet," Linc refused stubbornly.

"Why not?" Jo wanted to slap the back of the man's head.

"Because we need to speak to you while he has a clear head," Arthur said and took the bottle from her before setting it down. "Now sit." He angled her toward the seat that sat next to the settee Linc currently occupied.

"Very well." She did as he asked, having some idea of what would come next.

She was not wrong.

"Jo, I love you. Linc loves you. Neither of us is willing to see you harmed, nor are we willing to lose you once again." Arthur stopped and swallowed, his throat bobbing. "We were devastated the first time. We nearly lost each other in the wake of losing you and frankly, I don't think we could survive it if we lost you again."

"I love you both as well," Jo assured them, feeling her heart swell in her chest as if it might burst. She truly loved them, and they had only ever tried to protect her, right from the first.

"In that case, Lady Josephine Marie Downs, would you do me the honor of becoming my wife? Of becoming our wife?" Arthur tipped his head to the side to indicate Linc as well. "We can't both legally marry you, but we would like to have a second, private ceremony to acknowledge that we are both committing to each other, and ourselves to you, and you to the both of us."

Jo's hands shook as she sat there, trying to shape her answer. It was unequivocally a yes; she had been a fool in thinking these men would try to control her. They were not her father, nor were they either of her previous husbands. They loved her. They wanted her to be happy. So much so, they allowed her to make her own choices, even when they feared for her safety—and loved her enough to still take steps to ensure her safety.

What else could she say?

"Yes. Yes, I shall marry you both. And not for protection, but because I love you both and I want nothing more than to be with you forever. I...I'm sorry I allowed my past to cloud my view of the present, my view of you two, who have done nothing but try to protect me, to protect my freedom of choice at every turn. I shall love you both until the seasons cease to pass."

Arthur hauled her into his arms and kissed her until he stole the breath from her lungs. Then he handed her to Linc, who kissed her thoroughly, if less rapaciously, but to no less devastating effect. When the kiss ended and Jo stood up on wobbly knees, she smiled at the two men who shared a passionate kiss. "Now I believe you need to get our patient home and into bed, and I have a wedding to plan."

"As you command, my love." Arthur nodded with a smile. "I shall ensure Emily sends for the ladies to lend you a hand with the arrangements."

"Very well. I suspect assistance will be both welcome and necessary." Jo smiled as Arthur helped Linc off the settee and down the hall.

She had much to accomplish if they were to marry soon, and soon it would need to be. Though she had forgotten to ask about guards, she suspected her protection would continue, whether or not it was discussed.

Chapter Thirty-One
The Next Day

J o sat in Emily's drawing room as she met all of Linc and Arthur's friends. They were legion.

At least it felt that way to Jo, after having so few friends in her life.

Honestly, Arthur and Linc were her first real friends. Growing up she had her sister, of course, but they were friends primarily because they had no one else. There were girls in the village, but they so rarely went to the village as her father felt it was inappropriate for them to socialize with those he deemed to be of a lower class. All of her very best friends were discovered in books.

As she looked about the room and tried to follow all the introductions, her head spun. Obviously, there were Lord and Lady Brougham, her hosts—Cooper and Emily had been so gracious to her. Then there was Lord and Lady Stonemere, Lord and Lady Wolfington, Lord and Lady Flintshire, Lord and Lady Portridge, Lady Carlisle, and Lady Hartfield.

Fortunately Emily had ordered tea, so everyone was getting settled as Jo furiously tried to commit names and faces to memory.

Lady Stonemere smiled at her as she sipped her tea. "I want to apologize to you, Lady Whitestone. I'm sure we are an overwhelming lot."

Jo chuckled. "I must say, when Arthur and Linc said he would have the ladies come by, I was not aware they had an army of you at their disposal. And please, all of you, call me Jo."

Lady Stonemere grinned. "Please call me, Theo."

The rest of the ladies chimed in with leave for her to call them by their various preferred names.

"And while I would expect Linc to be so mischievous as to surprise you in such a way, I have come to expect better from my brother." Emily lifted one eyebrow as she let her gaze drift over to the two culprits.

"Well, we were rather focused on securing a yes from her this time. I suppose the details got lost in all the excitement." Arthur shrugged.

Emily and Theo both snorted.

"Well, regardless, it sounds as if we have a wedding to plan," Theo said through her laughter.

"Indeed, and while you might think I'd be an old hand at this after two husbands, I honestly left each of my weddings for my mother to arrange. They were not of my choosing, and so I had little interest—but not this time. I wish very much to put my stamp on this one, and I can't do that with her involved. I shall gladly take any assistance you have to offer."

Jo's cheeks warmed as she pushed aside her worries about a third marriage. The feeling of being cursed wouldn't leave her, though she was working on pushing past the idea. She was deeply in love with both Arthur and Linc, and they loved her, so marrying them—or at least, legally marrying Arthur—made complete sense.

"Before we delve into fripperies and decorations, we need to discuss a few other concerns." Arthur broke into the conversation before the ladies could get started.

"Concerns? What other concerns?" Jo looked at him, curiosity overriding her joy.

He set his teacup down on the mantle of the fireplace where he stood. "You and Matthew are still at risk. If yesterday proved nothing else, it is the lengths Lord Downs will go to—and I believe Matthew is the greater target."

Jo's stomach flipped as his words took root. "I thought our wedding would solve that issue?"

"It will prove to him you are not unprotected, that Matthew is not unprotected, and it will most certainly make things more difficult for him to get to you—but the truth is, Matthew is the key to his goals. I want to be certain he understands the lengths we are willing to go to ensure you are both safe." Arthur paused, taking a breath, then looked at each of the men in the room. "To that end, I am asking everyone here to continue to help with their protection."

The men chorused a round of agreement and Jo flushed with delight. To have such friends!

"I'm certainly happy to contribute however I can," Lady Portridge—Amelia—spoke up as she patted her hip.

Jo was a little confused about that, or even why she might offer to help with protection.

"Don't leave me out," Lady Flintshire, or Ros, chimed in.

Her husband growled softly, "Absolutely not."

"I'm not suggesting I take a formal shift, but I can certainly wield a whip well enough to help offer her additional protection when needed." Ros glared at her husband.

"Exactly, Ros." Amelia nodded. "Her skills are excellent. I should know, since I trained her." She winked at Jo.

That certainly explained her earlier comment and motion. She must carry a whip with her regularly. Jo attempted to smile, though fear for her son made that challenging. "Thank you all. I appreciate that you all are being so generous with your time."

"It's nothing that many of us haven't needed on our own journeys to love," Julia, or Lady Wolfington, said as she waved a hand around the group of ladies.

"Still, thank you, all of you. It is critical, Jo, that you not make yourself or Matthew vulnerable by being alone outside of this house." Arthur glanced at everyone. "I think the gentlemen can retire to my study to review the plans once more, while the ladies work on the wedding arrangements."

"God yes!" Lucifer set his tea down. "I need a whisky."

Everyone chuckled as the men departed the room though Jo noted that Linc still moved gingerly. He should be in bed resting, but she had no doubt an argument would have ensued had she raised her concern when they had arrived earlier. There was no arguing with that man.

Free of the gentlemen now, Jo looked at the ladies. "So, where do we begin?"

Theo grinned. "We should make a list of all the things we need to cover."

Lizzy, Lady Carlisle, pulled out a small notepad and pencil. "I'm ready to take notes."

"Very well then," Julia grinned at them all. "We should start with where the wedding will take place. A church, or at someone's home? Perhaps Arthur or Linc's home?"

"Not a church." Jo refused to marry in a church for a third time. "I think Linc's home would be perfect if he'll agree. I want him to feel as much a part of this union as he is, even if he won't be on paper."

"I want to offer our home as an alternative," Theo spoke up. "I merely offer it for a few reasons. First, it is large enough to accommodate all of your guests easily. Second, and I speak from experience, if you have it somewhere other than your own house, it is far easier to escape when the time comes. And finally, Stone and I can take Matthew for a few days while you three...honeymoon." She winked at Jo with a smile.

"Thank you, Theo. I am certain you offer sage advice, so I shall take you up on your offer as long as Arthur and Linc agree, though I suspect we shall keep the wedding to a few guests."

"Excellent, now we should discuss the guest list," Julia pressed on. "You can have as many guests attend the main ceremony as you wish. Then I would advise that you can be more selective about who joins you all for the second ceremony and wedding breakfast."

Jo considered her suggestion. It made sense, as many would be unaware of the second ceremony, including the priest who would marry them. "I suppose I should invite my family to the main ceremony. Other than that, I would look to you all for guidance on who I should invite."

Theo tapped her lower lip for a moment. "Julia, perhaps you and I should make a proposed guest list for Jo. She's rather new to Society proper, so we want to be careful about who we include. It needs to be a few of our set who are of an unimpeachable reputation so Lord Downs can't claim the marriage isn't legal, but not so many that it doesn't feel ex-

clusive. That will make having you and Arthur attend any social functions a boon while you are establishing yourselves."

"Agreed," Julia said.

"I appreciate all this help, ladies. I honestly do not have a
clue who to include and who not to." Jo sipped her tea and
shrugged a nervous shoulder.

"Then we can reduce the list for breakfast and the second
ceremony, as we said." Julia picked up a scone and plopped
a dollop of cream on it.

"I would choose to limit the guest list of both to those
of you in this room. Perhaps my family as well, since not
including them would be an absolute snub that my father
would never let pass. But I'm worried about what he might
say—or do during the second ceremony." Jo cringed inside.
If she was honest, she was worried about what he would do
or say at either ceremony, but to deny him might well lead
to him causing a greater scene if—no, when—he found out
about it.

Which option was the least painful to bear, in the end?

Marie, Lady Heartfield, cleared her throat. "This is your
third marriage. Considering he forced you into the previous two, I'd say excluding him and your mother is a reasonable choice. Things are happening quickly—one might
even think too quickly for them to arrive in time to attend.
Perhaps you'd like to include your sister, who I assume is in
town, to keep that sense of family without sacrificing your
joy?"

Jo couldn't help but smile. It was a marvelous suggestion.
"That's a brilliant suggestion, Marie!" After all, her sister was
happily married now, and while this third marriage might
be unconventional she believed Becca would support her.

"Not at all. I know a thing or two about being avantgarde and navigating interesting family members." A serene smile graced her face as she sat back and took a sip of tea.

Julia clapped her hands. "Wonderful! Ladies, you are invaluable with your guidance and suggestions. Now on to the easier topics. We need to decide flowers, what our beautiful bride will wear and, of course, a menu."

Jo sat back in awe as the ladies continued to run through the gamut of decisions which needed to be made. All along they sought her input, and she was pleased with everything once they were done.

The wedding was planned.

Arthur looked at all the men in the room, one after another, as Linc stood beside him. "I cannot say how much I appreciate you all being here for Linc and I. That said, I am afraid that around the clock protection seems to be in order. When they are here with Cooper, I'm confident that will be enough, but should they absolutely need to leave, as limited as that may be, two of us should watch over them." He certainly hoped all of the wedding arrangements could be made by Jo and the ladies from the safety of Cooper's home.

"Agreed." Linc nodded, pleased with how his partner was handling the conversation. "We'll cover what we can, but will certainly need you all when we cannot." Linc shifted and winced. "Which for me is the next few days. I fear my adventures yesterday have left me in less than full health."

Everyone murmured agreement.

"I am concerned about Lord Downs. Have you considered approaching him to warn him off?" Stonemere asked.

"We intend to do just that, but feel it is best left until after the wedding," said Arthur firmly. "Until she bears my name he will be a problem, and I see no point in alerting him to our plans prematurely." He glanced at Linc for his concurrence. He nodded, in full accord on this point. After all, they'd discussed this at length the previous night.

"Very well." Stonemere gave a curt nod. "Then we shall have to be extra vigilant until the wedding."

"Thank you." Linc drew in a deep breath and clenched his teeth against the pain. "Fortunately, the wedding is only a few days away—unless the women have run away with wedding planning in the other room."

The men all chuckled. They all knew their women were a lot of things, but they were not socialites to the extent that the wedding would take weeks to pull together.

At least, Linc hoped not.

Chapter Thirty-Two
Two Weeks Later

L inc took another look at himself in the looking glass before turning to Arthur. "Nervous?"

"God, no. The planning took longer than I'd hoped—procuring that bloody special license was excruciating—though I am glad your injury had time to heal. Now I'm just ready for her to be ours." Arthur's grin stretched from ear to ear.

Linc felt a pit in his stomach. *Ours.* He loved both of them, but unwanted doubt crept in again. He'd willingly let Arthur marry her so his family line could continue, but it didn't stop the feeling of separateness from creeping in. Jealousy was an insidious thing, a craven thing. He squashed it down ruthlessly. "As am I."

"How do I look?" Arthur brushed his fingertips down the front of his morning coat.

"Handsome enough to sweep our Wood Sprite off her feet." Linc couldn't hide his smile.

Arthur pulled him in for a kiss. Their lips met as their tongues tangled in a fierce display of dominance. Linc liked to fight a little and make Arthur work for it. Finally, the man was pinned against his body, his growing erection pressing against his as he surrendered to Arthur's claim. The doubts and ugliness of moments before faded into obscurity.

A knock on the door broke their kiss.

"Come in." Arthur rasped out as they each fought to regain their breath.

Emily stuck her head in the room. "The guests have started to arrive. You should come down soon."

"I'll go." Linc reached up and cupped Arthur's face. "I'll give you two a moment." He slipped past Emily as she stepped into the room and closed the door.

Arthur couldn't believe the day had finally come. He was getting married, to the two people he loved most in the world. As he watched his sister move into the room, his heart swelled with affection for Jo, Linc, and, of course, his sister.

"Don't you look handsome in all your finery?" Emily smiled as her eyes filled with tears.

"Tears, Em?" Arthur's heart lurched. *She wasn't upset about his choice, was she?*

"Tears of joy." She dabbed at her eyes with her handkerchief. "I never thought this day would ever come. The way you kept dodging the marriage mart, I expected you to be a lonely old man—or I had thought that, until you found Linc. Now I'm just overjoyed for both of you that you found another person to add to your family."

Arthur opened his arms and she stepped into his embrace. It felt good to have his little sister there with him as he embarked on this new part of his life. "Thank you. None of it would have been possible without your prodding and bullying."

She chuckled wetly. "True. Someone had to see you didn't shirk your duty."

He hugged her tightly. "I love you Em."

"I love you too." His sister returned his embrace. "Now it's time to go downstairs so this can get started."

"Shall we?" Arthur gestured toward the door.

"Absolutely." She grinned at him as they walked out of the room. "By the way, your bride looks amazing."

"Don't spoil it for me," he said, aghast. "Besides, my bride always looks amazing."

Em shook her head. "You are utterly besotted."

"Indeed I am."

Jo paced from one end of her room to the other. Emily had just left to go see about her brother, but Theo was still with her as the other ladies were downstairs greeting guests. Emily and Linc were standing as witnesses for them, so Theo was there to help her stay calm.

She snorted at that thought. There was no keeping her calm.

"The ceremony should start soon," Theo said from where she sat.

"Not soon enough." Jo shook her hands out at her sides. "What is taking so bloody long?"

A knock sounded and Emily popped her head around the door. "It's time."

Jo's heart fluttered in her chest as Theo handed her the flowers she was going to carry. She looked down at the beautiful gown Emily had found for her to wear. It was cream with lace trim that had a soft green velvet ribbon woven through it around the hem, the sleeves, and the rather scandalous neckline.

This was it.

Theo smiled at her one last time and slipped out of the room.

Then Emily, her future sister-in-law, looked at her. "I know I've told you this already, but you look lovely. Arthur and Linc will be beside themselves."

"I can't wait to see them." Jo's heart swelled with the love that felt like it would spill over and escape her body.

"Then let's go." Emily smiled. Her soft green dress complemented Jo's gown. They walked downstairs and into the Stonemeres' ballroom where all the guests were waiting.

The music started, and Emily headed down the aisle, and then it was Jo's turn.

As she walked toward her future, she noted all the people who had come to stand witness. For the first time, butterflies danced in her stomach as she walked toward the man she would marry in the eyes of the law. Next she spotted her sister, who smiled at her with love in her eyes. Jo was glad she'd decided to invite her sister. As expected, Becca had been nothing but supportive of Jo's marriage. Hopefully, her father was still in the dark about what was truly happening. Then suddenly she had reached the top of the aisle and Arthur was looking at her as though she were his whole world. Just beside him stood Linc, Arthur's best man, who looked just as taken with her.

The butterflies in Jo's stomach dissipated only to be replaced by a warmth that spoke of the love she felt for both men.

The ceremony flew by in a whirl of words until the reverend said, "I now pronounce you husband and wife."

When Arthur kissed her long and deep, quite contrary to what the wedding service required, a chuckle rippled through most of the people present. Once they walked down the aisle together, everyone followed them out to wish them well. From there the guests not staying for the second ceremony filtered out, including the vicar who had married them and her son Matthew, who was bundled up and taken upstairs to the nursery to play with the other children.

Once the crowd had dwindled to the Lustful Lords, their wives, her sister and brother-in-law, Lord and Lady Carlisle, and Lord and Lady Hartfield, they were ready to hold the second ceremony.

Stone stood where the vicar had stood a short while before, and Jo stood between Linc and Arthur. "We are gathered here to stand witness as the three of you commit your hearts to one another. Do you, Arthur, swear your heart and soul to Linc and to Jo for all eternity?"

Arthur looked at each of them for a moment. "I do."

"Do you, Linc, swear your heart and soul to Arthur and to Jo for all eternity?"

He did the same, looking at each of them in turn. "I do."

"Do you, Jo, swear your heart and soul to Arthur and to Linc for all eternity?"

She looked at each of them as well. "Without a doubt, I do." She wanted to grab each of them and pull them close. She could never be close enough.

"Three hearts entwined to beat as one. Three souls merged to live as one," Stone intoned the words with warmth which reverberated through Jo's core.

Before another word could be spoken, a ruckus arose out-side of the ballroom and the door burst open.

"Where's my daughter?" Everyone turned as Jo's father stormed into the ballroom. "Get the bloody hell away from my daughter!"

Arthur stepped in front of her as Linc flanked him. "Mr. Marshall, you were not invited to this gathering. Please re-move yourself."

"The hell I shall!" the man blustered. "I'm here for my daughter."

Jo resisted the urge to roll her eyes at the man and his shenanigans.

This was everything she had feared would happen. How he could have forgotten her two dead husbands and her third—*and final!*—marriage, she could not fathom. But the man held no power over her. He had not for many years now.

Jo's sister stepped forward. "Papa, stop it."

"R-Rebecca? What are you doing here?" He sounded shocked that his other daughter was in attendance.

"I'm watching Jo get married. For the third time, but finally to someone—two someones—she actually loves." Rebecca looked at her father pointedly.

Mr. Marshall sputtered, trying to retort, but Jo stepped from around her husbands—they both belonged to her now.

"Father, you should go. I'm married again. You have no control over me, no say in what I do."

"You ungrateful little *tramp*! Two men!" His face turned red as his hands fisted uselessly at his sides.

Jo drew up to her full five feet five inches, standing with her men at her back. "That's Lady Dunmere to you. Now, I suggest you leave—before you are thrown out."

"I'll disown you, you hussy. No one in polite society will receive you!" her father bellowed as he strode a few steps forward.

But Flint and Wolf stepped in his path as Arthur and Linc drew her behind them. Two footmen appeared and with their help, her father was escorted from the room.

Disown her? Was the man mad? He was nobody in Society—possibly less than nobody, without the association of her or her sister. He'd never once in his life protected her. He'd merely used her as a bargaining chip over and over again.

As Jo watched him leave, she realized she had long since lost any love she may have once felt for him. That part of her life was over. It was time to start her new life.

As her father was dragged from the room, Arthur turned to her. "Are you well, Jo?"

At that same moment, her sister rushed up to them. "Jo, I'm so sorry. I swear I did not tell him about your wedding today."

Jo looked at her sister's stricken countenance and knew Becca would never have shared such information with him. Her younger sister was just as grateful to be free of his clutches as Jo was. "I know, Becca. There were no banns as Arthur secured a special license, but I'm sure word got around once the invitations went out." She looked at Arthur and Linc. "I fear, in our efforts to legitimize our union, we may have exposed ourselves to my father. We can but hope that word has gotten to Lord Downs as well."

Becca hugged her tightly before releasing her. "Please, don't let his disruption sour your special day. If there is more to the ceremony, you three should continue on."

"Only if Jo is in a calm enough state to do so." Arthur's gaze fixed on her, seeming to penetrate right to her very soul. She knew without a doubt they would stop things then and there if she wished it.

"Absolutely." Linc pressed a hand to her back as he leaned in. "This can wait if you need a moment, Wood Sprite."

She shook her head. "No, I'll not let that wretched man spoil one more moment of my life. Let's finish what we started."

Stone chuckled. "Did any of you have anything you would like to add?"

Arthur nodded. "I promise to love and protect you both, never taking either of you for granted. I shall give you both the shelter of my body and my home and promise to seek the same from you when I am in need. And Jo, I promise to love Matthew as if he were of my flesh and blood."

Jo's heart squeezed as a soft sigh escaped her. Beside her, she felt a small shudder run through Linc. "I love you Arthur and you Linc, and I shall for the rest of my days." She let the love that filled her burst through as she smiled at each man in turn.

Stone looked at the remaining partner with a silent eyebrow lift.

Linc cleared his throat. "I love you, Arthur, and you, Jo, and our boy Matthew. I promise to make all of you laugh and to ensure all of Jo's curiosity is slaked to the best of my ability. Whatever is mine is yours, including my heart."

"Then I pronounce you all bound for eternity." Stone grinned. "You may all kiss."

Arthur pushed Jo into Linc's arms first. The man kissed her as though they had no audience, her toes curling as he bent her backwards a bit. When he released her, Arthur was there to take over. He kissed her just as thoroughly, his tongue tangling with hers in an erotic kiss full of promise. Then he set her back from him and reached for Linc. Before everyone, he hauled the man in for an equally long kiss. Jo swore she would melt into a puddle just watching them. Behind her, a few of the women sighed softly as everyone watched.

Then Arthur released Linc and looked at their friends and family gathered there. "I believe breakfast is in order!"

Everyone pushed forward to congratulate the three of them as they made their way into the dining room, where a lavish breakfast awaited them. Jo tamped down her excitement as she staved off thoughts of the night to come, and tried to eat. She would need her strength.

Chapter Thirty-Three

A rthur looked around the dining room, pleased to see everyone enjoying themselves. The day had been everything he'd hoped for, with the exception of the one interruption. He still wanted to curse himself for a fool over having been so wrapped up about Lord Downs that they'd completely forgotten about her father who, while no real threat to Jo's physical safety, was absolutely a threat to her happiness.

He looked over at Linc, on the other side of Jo, and saw a look of relief and need etched on the man's face. Not unlike himself, he suspected Linc was glad to have Jo safely wed and was now done with the social part of the event.

Arthur stood. "Thank you all for attending our wedding. Linc, Jo, and I appreciate your love and support. But I believe that the three of us are ready to retire. I hope you all feel free to stay until Stone decides to toss you out on your arses."

Everyone laughed as Linc and Jo rose.

"Be careful you two, I hear brides can be testy on their wedding nights!" Cooper called out as they departed.

"Really, Cooper, has your bride ever ceased being testy?" Wolf could be heard ribbing their friend.

The laughter around the room continued as the three of them escaped. With Matthew safely ensconced in Stonemere's nursery for the night with his and Theo's children, they could focus on the night ahead.

A short while later, they walked into Arthur's home—well, their home now—and were greeted warmly by Harris.

"Good evening my lords, my lady. Congratulations to the three of you." The man bowed as he took their coats.

"Thank you, Harris." Arthur offered a relaxed smile now they were away from all the pressure of the wedding. "We are headed upstairs, likely for the rest of the day. We'll ring down when we are ready for food."

"Very good, my lord."

Arthur gave Jo a little nudge toward the stairs before she could start asking after Harris' family members. He didn't want to wait. Linc followed her up the stairs and he trailed behind.

In their bedchamber, Arthur walked in and found Linc was already kissing Jo. The two were meshed together, his legs lost in her skirts. Easing up behind her, Arthur unfastened the laces of her bodice as he pressed hot kisses down her neck. Linc reached up and helped him ease the top down her arms, even as they continued to kiss. Next Arthur untied her skirts, loosening her outer skirt and then the multiple layers of petticoats before releasing the mass of fabric to the floor. Linc released her lips and turned her to face Arthur, who sucked in a breath at the love shining in her beautiful green eyes as she looked up at him. Then he leaned in and captured her lips with his own.

Jo sighed softly as their tongues twined sinuously around each other. The feel of her in his arms paired with the taste of her and Linc on his lips had Arthur's cock growing harder by the minute. When he felt her corset loosen and drop between them, he hesitated a moment as Linc pulled her chemise off over her head.

He resumed their kiss as a low moan of pleasure ripped from her. He felt Linc's hands slip between his chest and her breasts, caressing them. Arthur continued to explore her mouth, relishing the heat and welcome he found there. As his hands found the soft skin of her stomach and hips, he enjoyed the silky feel of her under his fingertips. He deepened the kiss and pressed her back into Linc's chest, loving the way she had nowhere to escape him. Then her hands were pushing his coat off his shoulders, forcing him to drop his hands from her waist as she wrested control from him.

Lifting his mouth from hers, he glanced at Linc. "Strip."

Linc grinned. "Thought you'd never ask."

"That wasn't a request," Arthur growled as he tore at the cravat wrapped around his neck.

Jo eagerly helped him, pulling the flap of his trousers open and pushing them down his legs. Then she spun around and finished helping Linc before she removed her own pantaloons. Arthur noted that she left her stockings in place, just as he preferred.

Dropping to his knees, he began pressing kisses to her stomach. Linc eased up along her side, his cock hardening as he leaned over and sucked one nipple into his mouth. Arthur reached over and grabbed Linc's length, stroking it firmly, Linc groaning low as his hips pumped into Arthur's fist. Meanwhile, Arthur was dragging his tongue along the wetness he found between Jo's thighs.

"Good God, that is incredibly arousing," Jo whimpered as she threaded her fingers into his hair, pulling him closer to her pussy.

Unable to respond since his tongue was buried in her cunny, he simply swirled his tongue over her clit and stroked Linc's cock.

Reaching down, Arthur lifted one of her legs and eased it over his shoulder so he could have better access to all her silky pussy. Her sweetness flooded his mouth with each drag of his tongue as he let go of Linc's cock and feasted—feasted on their wife. Then Linc was there, pressing his cock into her soaked and dripping entrance from behind her as Arthur continued to lick and lap at her clit. Balanced between them, Jo shuddered as they worked her together. One of her hands gripped his hair and her other wrapped around Linc's neck.

All too soon Jo was moaning, "I'm coming!" She groaned, a long and low inarticulate sound of ultimate pleasure. Arthur continued to lick that sensitive bundle of nerves as Linc worked his cock in and out of her tight channel. "Yes! Don't stop."

And they didn't. They continued to love her as she crested on a loud wail of pleasure which Arthur was certain the servants could hear from their quarters.

As her orgasm eased, he let her leg slip from his shoulder and stood up. His cock ached as he pressed against her and they kissed.

Her tongue slicked over his before Jo drew back. "I can taste myself."

Behind her, Linc made a soft humming noise. "That sounds delicious." He reached around her to pull Arthur closer, and they kissed over Jo's shoulder. Their tongues dueled for dominance, but Arthur inevitably won.

There was something very different about kissing a man versus a woman. It was rougher, more elemental. Kissing a woman could be rough, but was often a sensual or gentle experience that one melted into.

As Linc pulled back, he licked his lips. "Mmmmm. I can taste you, Jo. You taste—"

"On the bed, you two," Arthur commanded, the need to be inside one of them riding him hard. He would have what he desired.

Linc helped Jo onto the bed before joining her. As Arthur came over toward them, his cock throbbed with need. He'd been inside Jo, but had pulled out after her orgasm. He was fine with waiting—the anticipation would make his release all the sweeter.

But Arthur was being rather bossy at the moment, and it was time someone else took control for a bit.

As Arthur moved to climb onto the bed, Linc pressed a hand to his stomach and stopped him from joining them on the bed. Bending over as he knelt on the bed, he took hold of Arthur's shaft and licked the tip. Arthur grunted and tried to push him back, but Linc resisted, instead pushing forward and taking nearly Arthur's entire length down his throat.

"Fuck," Arthur ground out as he sank a hand into Linc's hair.

Jo crawled over and kneeled on the bed so she could kiss Arthur as Linc continued to work his cock. At some point, she dropped to the floor on her knees and slipped between the bed and Arthur's legs, slightly under Linc to lick at Arthur's balls as he continued to suck his weighty cock.

"Oh fuck! Yes!" Arthur cried out and came hard.

Linc swallowed his cum as he took him deep while Jo continued to massage Arthur's sac with her tongue.

Panting heavily above them, Arthur looked at them both with love in his dark eyes. Linc's heart thumped in his chest as he sat back and caught his own breath.

Just as Linc flopped back on the bed, Jo clambered on top of him and kissed him. She pressed her breasts against his chest and slid her tongue into his mouth, ravaging his mouth, plundered it like a first-class rake. He resisted the urge to chuckle at her rapacious kiss.

Then she was straddling him and sliding down on his throbbing cock. As she rode him, Arthur crawled over and took the tip of one of her breasts in his mouth. She moaned as he and Arthur pleasured her once again.

Jo whimpered as she slid down on Linc's cock. He felt so good inside of her—the sensation heightened by Arthur sucking on one of her breasts and pinching the tip of the other. She laid her palms flat on Linc's chest and ground herself down on him as pleasure rolled through her.

"Yes!" The cry was pulled from deep within her as she slid up and down his length, reveling in the stretch of his cock. Linc grunted beneath her with each upward thrust of his hips to meet her.

Arthur kneeled up by his head and nudged his cock near his face. "Suck my cock, Linc. Get me wet and hard. I want to fuck her next."

Jo's pussy clenched at those words as she shifted to grind down on Linc's cock. She was so close, and the thought of taking Arthur next had her nearly over the edge. "Yes," she breathed her agreement. "I need to feel Arthur deep in my pussy. Suck his cock for me."

Both men groaned as Linc opened his mouth and took Arthur's semi-hard cock onto his willing tongue. She watched as Linc lay there in utter submission, having his mouth fucked by Arthur as she rode his cock. The man was at their mercy, and she loved it.

With yet another circle of her hips after a long, delicious slide on his cock, Jo's orgasm broke over her like a rogue wave. Her body flew apart into tiny bits and pieces as she shook.

Linc let out a muffled groan and his hips jerked as he joined her. Arthur withdrew from his lover's mouth, allowing Linc to grab her hips as he pumped up into her twice more before he lay boneless beneath her as Jo slumped over and tried to catch her breath.

As her senses returned to her body, Arthur pressed against her back and peppered her shoulder with kisses as he slid her disheveled hair off her shoulder. With gentle hands, he eased her to the side until she lay next to Linc who seemed to still be in a daze. Arthur moved over her, his hips nestled between her splayed thighs, and kissed her with a gentle, lingering kiss that was so sweet her heart squeezed.

"Wood Sprite, are you well? If I slide inside you, will it be too much?" Arthur murmured the words between nibbling kisses.

"Never," she replied as she kissed him back. "I need you inside me."

Arthur moaned softly. "You humble me."

He aligned his cock with her entrance and pressed inside her. As he seated himself inside her, Jo moaned softly at the overwhelming sensation that remained from her orgasms. Then he withdrew and slid inside of her again. She exhaled as pleasure sparked to life once more. As his strokes grew longer and stronger, a frisson of sensation cascaded through her body.

"Oh God, Arthur!" It felt so good having him inside her. So right—just as it had with Linc.

"That's it Jo, take me. Take all of me," Arthur moaned and continued to thrust inside her as he levered himself up so that he could pound harder into her.

Linc rolled over and watched for a moment before he leaned over and sucked on the nipple closest to him.

The tug of his mouth sent desire rippling down her body that entwined with all the pleasure Arthur was delivering. "I-I'm going to come." She arched her breast up into Linc's mouth as Arthur worked in and out of her body.

Arthur groaned. "Yes. Come for us. One more time, Wood Sprite." He gritted his teeth and surged into her again and again.

Her orgasm slid through her, a gentle wave of pleasure that seemed to buffet her as she lost all ability to speak. Linc's mouth continued to suck and pull on her nipple and Arthur pounded into her until he stiffened and sank inside her one last time as he cried out.

"Jo! Fuck."

The three of them lay there in a post-sex heap of erotic bliss, and Jo's heart swelled with all the love she felt in that moment for the two most wonderful men she'd ever met.

Chapter Thirty-Four

After a delightful three days of privacy, Jo declared she missed her son and wished to collect him from Stone and Theo. Arthur sent around a note so there would be time to get Matthew ready to leave while they dressed themselves. With all the wandering hands and eyes, it was a miracle of Jo's resolve to see her son that they were eventually presentable and ready to depart.

As they walked into the entrance hall of Stone's townhome, a not-so-small bundle of energy hurled itself into Jo's legs, nearly toppling her over. The happy tears she shed as she hugged her son had Arthur's throat closing as memories of his own parents—and ultimately their loss—bubbled to the surface in a most uncomfortable and unexpected fashion.

A hand squeezed his arm, causing him to glance over at Linc. The man who'd stolen part of his heart gave him a sympathetic look before he turned a sparkling smile to the boy, now wrapped around his legs.

Jo looked over at Arthur, concern dancing through her speckled green eyes. The dark flecks he could sometimes see always seemed to come out when she was upset. Determined not to ruin this moment for her or Matthew, Arthur reined in his memories and tried to find the peace he'd long ago grabbed a hold of. It served no one, least of all himself, when he allowed the sadness of his past to have control.

He summoned a smile for Jo that had her brow smooth out as Matthew latched on to his legs next.

With a peal of excitement, the boy asked, "Can we, Uncle Arthur? Can we go to the park?"

Arthur wasn't sure what he'd missed, so he shot a glance at Linc and Jo in turn.

Linc took pity on him. "I think we'd better save a trip to the park for another day. Your uncle and I have an errand to run after we deposit you two at home."

Arthur let out a breath on a whoosh. He hadn't been sure if either Linc or Jo had made the suggestion, and hadn't wanted to countermand one of them. But it simply wasn't safe for Matthew or Jo to be in such a public and wide-open space right now. Hopefully, after their errand, that would change.

Disappointed, the boy nodded. "I suppose so."

"I think perhaps there may be a treat for you when we get home. Cook has made a special treat for the new master of the house." Jo grinned as her son was instantly distracted by that exciting bit of news.

With a crisis averted for the moment, they managed to remove themselves from Theo and Stone's foyer.

Linc looked at Arthur as the carriage rumbled toward Jo's former home. Lord Downs had installed himself and his family there post-haste after her escape. It was easy to imagine the greedy couple occupying the Lord and Lady's chambers, congratulating themselves with smug faces.

When would they figure out just how much a house of that magnitude cost to maintain in London?

Soon, he suspected. Very soon.

The carriage rolled to a stop and the door was opened. They exited the vehicle and quickly climbed the steps to the front door.

Arthur reached up and firmly rapped the knocker against the door. As they waited, he looked at Linc, his brown eyes darkly intense. "Be prepared for anything."

"No question. The man is a loose cannon." Linc nodded, acknowledging that this conversation could go sideways far too quickly.

The door opened, and a man stood there. It was not Bell, the previous butler. Linc wondered if this was Jasper who Jo had fired.

"Good day, my lords." The butler bowed stiffly, just enough to be courteous.

"The Earl of Dunmere and Baron Lincolnshire, to see Lord Downs." Arthur stood ramrod straight next to him as he explained who they were.

"Just a moment, my lords." The man closed the door and left them standing on the front step.

A few minutes later, he returned and granted them entrance. "Lord Downs will see you in the study."

Neither spoke as they followed the servant into the house that had once been Jo's home, and down the hall. Normally they had visited Jo in the drawing room, so this was a part of the house they had not seen previously. The butler knocked on the door and announced them.

They entered to find Downs sitting at the desk in a dark, wood paneled room. He didn't bother to stand up as they walked in. "Lincolnshire. Dunmere, I hear congratulations are in order."

"That is why we came to see you." Arthur stared at the man from where they stood.

"Me? I can't imagine why your marriage would necessitate a visit with me." Downs leaned back in his chair, smugly casual.

"I am almost certain you can imagine why a visit with you is required now Jo and I are married," Arthur said flatly.

Linc listened and watched, hoping he wouldn't need to intercede. Downs was needling Arthur in a most unhealthy manner, and it could all change in a moment.

"I'm afraid I really don't. I'm pleased Josephine has found a...protector." The man clearly strove for an innocence which did not ring true, considering what they knew.

Linc smirked. "I'm sure you felt something at her recent nuptials, though pleasure is a bit of a stretch."

"I believe I am offended by your suggestion. I like Josephine. I wish her only the best." Downs spread his hands, as if that proved his sincerity.

Arthur snorted. "Regardless of your nonsense, I wanted to make it clear where things stand."

Linc's heart pounded in his chest. *This was where things would get dicey.*

Downs leaned forward and rested his forearms on the desk. "And where precisely do things stand, from your perspective?" The tone of the question was decidedly less friendly than the rest of the conversation had been, but that was to be expected. Things were about to escalate.

"Jo and Matthew are now under our protection." Arthur pointed at himself and Linc. "You will cease any attempts to contact them. You will cease any efforts to harm them."

As inappropriate as it was, Linc found himself aroused by the forcefulness Arthur displayed. He took a deep breath and willed his cock not to thicken, trying to refocus on the conversation at hand.

"I do not know of what you speak. I have never attempted to harm Jo or my nephew." Downs said flatly.

Linc couldn't contain the grunt of disbelief. "You deny that you held her captive in her rooms for three days?"

"Ha! I believe she misunderstood what was intended as a protective measure."

Another snort escaped Arthur. "Absolutely no one misunderstood your intentions in locking her and her son away. You will cease your pursuit or we shall end your activities ourselves. Permanently."

Linc repressed a groan. Fucking hell, the man was stimulating when he got all protective.

"I'm afraid I'm still baffled by this threat of violence," Downs reiterated with a wry smile.

"Regardless, know this is your first and last warning. My wife and son are not to be targets," Arthur growled.

"Very well." Downs said and slumped back in his chair once more. "And since I've done nothing up to now, I can assure you nothing will happen moving forward."

Linc looked at the man askance. He played innocent, but he just didn't believe him.

"Then we have an understanding." Arthur nodded sharply and turned to go.

Linc fell into step behind him until they reached the hallway.

As they made their way out, Arthur looked at him. "I have my doubts about him. But I believe we should take him at his word—" they stepped outside "—mostly."

They climbed back into the carriage. "Agreed. We should take him at his word for now, but that doesn't mean we ever leave them unprotected. They belong to us." Linc leaned over and turned Arthur's face toward him. "My God your fierceness in there was arousing as hell."

Arthur chuckled, instantly shedding the anger which had simmered while they'd been in there. He reached up, wrapped a hand around the back of Linc's neck, and kissed him. Their tongues met and tangled, slipping over each other as they took comfort in each other's touch. They separated, pressing their foreheads together as they each caught their breath.

They would face this situation shoulder to shoulder. Together, they would protect their woman and their son.

But it seemed the threat was over. Lord Downs understood Jo was no longer without protection. She nor her son would be easy prey.

Could this be the happily ever after they'd hoped for?

Chapter Thirty-Five

July 1867

Jo stood between Arthur and Linc as they greeted their guests. It had been blissfully quiet with no further attempts on her person, or against Matthew. His arm was even out of the cast now. She had gone shopping, run errands, taken tea with the ladies, and anything else that struck her fancy.

She felt gloriously and wonderfully free. No father controlling her movements or pestering her about where she'd been. No unwanted husband to answer to. No brother-in-law spending her money and controlling her staff.

Instead, she had two men in her life who loved her, protected her, and supported her. It had taken years to achieve this state, but here she was. Happy.

Arthur leaned in close so she could hear him over the din of voices in the ballroom. "You look lovely, if I haven't already told you tonight."

She laughed, delighted. "Only about ten times, husband."

She felt lovely. Her gown had been specially designed by Madame Le Fleur, a modiste Theo had recommended. The bodice was fitted with two layers of ruffles which came down into a vee over her decolletage in emerald green silk. An overskirt of the same emerald green silk wrapped around to each of her hipbones and created a train behind her which had a matching set of two ruffles around the hem.

The underskirt was a pale green skirt with the same ruffle detail as the train and bodice. There were also little gathers of fabric that looked like three rows of bunting across the skirt and above the ruffled hem. Her matching pale green fan was embroidered with leaves and vines in emerald green. She wore a simple emerald headband in her hair which had been gathered to the back of her head, where it dangled in perfect coils.

"But can a wife as lovely as you hear such things from either of her husbands too often?" Linc asked as he also leaned in. He'd clearly heard some part of their exchange.

Jo smiled coyly, bring her fan up to her face to hide her grin. "Perhaps not."

Linc laughed, as did Arthur, and her toes curled in her satin slippers as she thought about how they'd spent the morning together in bed. By the end, they'd been entwined and laying in each other's arms with her sandwiched between the two handsome men.

Theo and Stone approached in the receiving line, the rest of their friends trailing behind as though they'd all arrived together.

Theo smiled and gasped as she saw Jo's gown. "Oh, you look gorgeous, Jo." They kissed each other's cheeks and then she moved along after Stone greeted Linc and Arthur. Emily and Cooper were just behind, followed by Ros, Julia, Wolf, and Flint. They all hugged and kissed and moved along to keep the line flowing. Then came Amelia and Lucifer, Marie and Hartfield, and finally Lizzy and Carlisle. Jo was delighted they had all come. Along with Linc, Arthur, and Becca, they were her family now.

Before long all their guests had arrived, and they were free to move out into the ball. Arthur and Jo opened the festivities by leading the first dance. They'd decided it would be a waltz in lieu of a more traditional option, such as a quadrille or a march. After all, they were bucking the norms in so many ways. Why not the order of the dances?

As Arthur swept her into the opening waltz, he smiled down at her. The people on the edges of the ballroom swirled by, a kaleidoscope of colors that melded together then fractured apart.

Jo laughed, happiness bubbling up from deep inside her. "Thank you, Arthur. This is a lovely evening."

"You are most welcome. I would do anything to put that smile on your face, even get all dressed up and smile at a great deal of people I neither know nor care about." His low baritone rumbled through her since she was pressed so close to him. Scandalously close—even for a husband and wife.

"You do say the most outrageous things at times." Jo allowed her lashes to lower slightly. "But it's the outrageous things you do to me that I truly enjoy. Both of you."

Arthur threw his head back and laughed as he continued to spin her around. By the time the waltz ended, she needed a moment to set herself back to rights. He led her over to where Linc and the other Lustful Lords stood.

Jo exhaled with a grin. "Gentlemen, I need to visit the retiring room and then I am going to visit the nursery to check on Matthew."

Linc pressed a hand to her lower back. "I just checked on the boy. He and Nancy are doing well upstairs and a footman is standing guard in the hall as well. Stay down here, enjoy your evening."

Jo smiled up at him, tipping up on her toes to plant a chaste kiss on his cheek. "You are a wonderful husband. You know that, don't you?"

"I do try, my dear." He smiled smugly and winked at Arthur. "Though I believe I have more competition than most."

She laughed and stepped away from the group.

"Are you going to the retiring room?" Amelia asked.

"I am. Would you care to join me?"

"Absolutely. It's a bit warm in here for me." She smiled, looking a little green about the gills.

They walked toward their destination at a sedate stroll, arm in arm, as Jo asked, "Forgive my directness, but are you feeling well?"

"I have been feeling tired lately, no matter how much I sleep. I dare say certain smells are affecting me far more than I am accustomed to." Amelia pressed a hand to her stomach and drew in a shallow breath. "I've learned deep breaths are only for outdoor spaces or private ones."

Was Amelia with child? It certainly sounded that way. "Have...have you seen a doctor?"

"I plan to. I am trying to find a time to sneak away when Lucifer is occupied. The man is so very protective. If I say a word, he will worry himself into a frenzy."

Jo laughed. She could see both Arthur and Linc being the same way. "If you need someone to go with you, please don't hesitate to ask. We could call it a day of shopping and add an extra stop." She grinned conspiratorially.

"That sounds perfect!" Amelia smiled as they entered the retiring room.

Three hours full of dancing and laughter later, the sumptuous supper she had planned had been served and the dancing resumed. Everyone seemed to enjoy themselves, as was she. Jo continued to dance with each of her husbands, interspersed by their friends. She was just coming off the dance floor after a gallop with Stone when she saw a footman speaking in a low, hurried voice to Arthur and Linc.

As she walked over, she noted the tightness of their features, and her heart mirrored their tension. "What is wrong?"

Arthur and Linc led her out of the ballroom as Arthur spoke. "Jo, there is an issue upstairs."

"What is it? Has Matthew fallen ill?" She glanced from one face to the other, worry intruding on the happiness she'd been feeling all night.

They were in the hall now, and she was fighting the urge to run toward the stairs.

When Arthur spoke it was in a quiet, worried voice. "Matthew is missing."

Jo's knees abruptly gave out, but between the two men, they kept her upright. "Missing—missing? What do you mean, he is missing? When was he last seen?"

Linc's voice sounded like it came from a long way away. "I checked on him an hour or so ago and he was fine then, but when I checked just now he was gone—and Nancy is missing as well. The staff have been organized and are searching for him. We are keeping the guests confined to the ballroom for the moment." Linc's voice was calm, almost detached, until his voice cracked. "Oh God, Jo, I'm so sorry. All was well when I checked earlier. I swear it."

"Matthew." Jo whispered her son's name and broke into a run as she flew up the stairs. On the second floor, she tore down the gallery and into the nursery but found naught but an empty room. Arthur and Linc appeared just behind her as she cried out, "Does no one know where Nancy is?"

"There has been no sign of her according to Palmer, the footman who came to alert me." Arthur placed his hands on his hips as he looked helplessly around the room.

"Nancy didn't take him. I can't believe she would, she loves Matthew!" Jo let out a small cry of frustration as she ran around the room, opening all the doors to the various cupboards—was he hiding?—but she found nothing.

Halting her frantic search, Jo looked around the space and noticed his blocks were spread out on the floor. Kneeling, she touched one and tried to calm her spinning head. She drew in a deep breath. As her gaze focused on the blocks, she noticed something sparkling on the rug.

Jo reached down and plucked a diamond hair pin from beneath one of the blocks. "Arthur! Linc!"

They rushed over. "What is it?" Linc asked.

"I found a hairpin." She held up the trinket.

A footman burst into the room. "Nancy has been found. She was bound, gagged, and shoved in a cupboard near the servant's stairs. She says it was a woman who took Matthew."

"Which way did she go?" Arthur's cracked out a demand rather than a question.

"Out the back of the house." The man pointed in that general direction.

Jo's heart pounded wildly as she ran from the room, tearing down the stairs and out to the mews. Many of the guests' carriages were lined up as she ran down the line of vehicles. Arthur and Linc were right on her heels.

They came to the last carriage in the line and Arthur asked the driver, "Did a carriage just leave here?"

"Yes, my lord," the driver responded, instantly alert.

"Was it a woman with a boy?" Linc jumped in to ask.

"Aye, my lord, and the boy was pitching a fit about going."

"Did you see which way they went?" Arthur demanded.

"Aye, my lord."

Arthur threw open the door of the carriage and helped Jo climb up as her heart pounded. He and Linc followed her in as Arthur called out, "Follow that carriage!"

The man grunted, the reins snapped, and the carriage took off. Linc lifted the leather covering on the side of the door and leaned out to see if he could spot the other vehicle. It was the early hours of the morning, so there was far less traffic on the road, as many of the balls planned for that night had yet to end.

"I think I see them!" Linc cried as the carriage bounced and jounced down the road.

Jo could feel tears pooling in her eyes as she sat and waited, her chest tight as worry for her boy squeezed her. They continued following the carriage they suspected held Matthew, moving at a furious pace.

But then Linc informed them in a raw voice, "We may have lost it. It turned up ahead somewhere—I can't see where."

Arthur cursed, low and ugly, as the first tear slipped down Jo's face. Her heart broke as they clattered on, but suddenly the carriage jerked to a halt.

Linc leaned out the window once more. The driver said something and Linc replied, "Take a closer look, if you can." He ducked back inside the carriage. "He thinks he saw the carriage down a rear alley we just passed. He's going around the way to go down the other end of the alley and get a closer look."

Worry knotted Jo's stomach as she fought back, the tears now freely slipping free.

After a few minutes, she heard the driver exclaim, "It's the one, my lord. I recognize the fancy gold trim."

Jo bolted from the carriage, nearly ripping her train off as it caught on a part of the carriage, her men right behind her.

She only hoped they'd got there in time.

Chapter Thirty-Six

Linc raced up behind Jo and grabbed her arm, preventing her from entering the house. "Jo! Jo, you can't just barge in there!"

"The hell I can't! Some woman has my son in there. My. Son." Jo pounded on her chest with her small fist as she said the last two words in a low, fierce tone.

Linc pulled her into his arms, his heart aching for her. "Shhh. I know, love. I know, and we are going in there to retrieve him. We are going to save our son—but we need to be careful."

Arthur stepped hurriedly over to them. "I've sent the carriage we borrowed back for assistance, he'll lead help back here."

"I won't wait!" Jo grabbed Linc's lapels crushing them in her small fists.

Guilt threatened to double him over, but Linc pushed it down ruthlessly. There was no time for such sentiments. "No. We'll not wait. I won't make the same mistake I made with my sister," he reassured her.

Wait. Had he said that last part aloud?

"You have a sister?" Jo and Arthur asked simultaneously.

Linc wanted to curse himself. "I did, but there is no time for that story now. Later." He looked at Arthur. "We can't wait, Matthew needs us."

"I know, but we need to go in cautiously." Arthur turned to their beautiful, panicking wife. "I don't suppose there is any chance you'll wait out here."

"Hell no," she said emphatically.

Arthur sighed. "I thought not."

Neither had Linc. He hadn't even been so brave as to suggest it after her initial declaration, but perhaps Arthur hadn't heard it while dealing with the carriage driver.

"All right, let's go quietly in the back door." Linc took Jo's hand and drew her forward. The swishing of her skirts sounded so loud in the relative silence of the night—after all, it was London—that he stopped and turned to face her. "Jo, your skirts have to go if you are coming inside. They make too much noise. I'm sorry, I know it's a new gown—"

She looked over her shoulder at Arthur. "Loosen my skirts. Nothing is more important than my son."

One of Arthur's eyebrows drifted up in a mockery of surprise. The woman had always been too brazen for her own good, and Linc knew that Arthur had grown terribly protective of her. There was a beat of silence, and while Linc could not see Jo's face as she was twisted toward Arthur, he could easily imagine the silent argument the two were waging. Arthur would come to his senses on the matter any moment—or at the very least lose the war of wills.

"Very well," Arthur hissed, evidently having lost.

He partially lifted the bottom of her bodice up, as much as one could, and found the strings of Jo's skirts. It took a few moments to wrestle with all the various layers of overskirts, underskirts, and petticoats, but finally the entire mass of fabric sank to the ground, trapping Jo in a puddle of material.

Linc swiftly lifted her out of the mess, leaving her in her barely decent muslin drawers.

"Shall we?" Jo urged.

Frankly, her impatience was adorable, no matter how inappropriate the thought was at the moment. Linc turned back and once more led them into the house. The lower floors were well lit, suggesting someone was most certainly in residence at the moment.

Despite that, there were no servants about. The house was eerily quiet.

A noise sounded upstairs, a loud wail which sounded distinctly like a child's cry.

Jo bolted forward, but Linc caught her before she made it past him. "No. We shall get there in a moment. He's alive, that's an excellent thing," he whispered to her.

His beautiful wife bit her lip and nodded, tears welling in her eyes. Her obvious distress bothered Linc deeply, twanging against the heavy dose of guilt he felt for not having secured Matthew well enough.

It was all his fault.

Pushing the emotion aside for the moment as the hinderance it was, Linc crept forward through the kitchen, spotted the servants' stairs, and pointed as he looked back at Arthur.

His husband nodded in agreement. It seemed the back stairs would be safest at the moment, since there were no servants running about.

They slowly eased up the dimly lit, narrow stairs. It was a good thing they'd rid their bride of her cumbersome skirts. Linc highly doubted she would have fit up these stairs as voluminous as her layers had been.

They reached the first landing and paused to listen. Nothing.

They pressed on. At the second floor, they stopped and listened again. Everything was quiet, but well lit. Someone had been moving around up here recently. The hairs on the back of Linc's neck stood up, but he went left as he pointed Arthur to the right. Taking Jo with him, the pair of them continued down the hall, stopping to listen at each door. When they heard nothing, Linc eased the door open and peeked inside. Each time, they found nothing.

Soon Arthur joined them, having found nothing down the shorter right side. "Not a sign of—"

Voices—voices two doors down from the room they had just checked. They were muffled, but one was distinctly masculine and the other feminine. They crept closer until they reached the door and Linc could just make out the distinct words of an argument.

"What the hell have you done?" the man's voice ranted. "It's just a bloody title. We have enough money to survive on if you'd just stop spending like you were the Queen of England."

"You fool! That title belonged to you! It belongs to our son, not that misbegotten brat your brother sired on his broodmare," the woman hissed. "God, you have no spine at all."

Linc caught Jo and Arthur's gazes, nodded, then pointed at the door. He counted to three on his fingers then threw the door wide and rushed inside with Jo on his heels. He ran straight for Lord Downs who turned, eyes widening in shock as Linc crashed into him. Jo launched past them, a blur of muslin and green. Downs struggled, his shock clearly giving him a strength Linc was not prepared for. He couldn't hold him, he was going to fail them again—

Luckily Arthur was there in a flash and together they wrestled the man to the ground.

As Linc had rushed in the room, Jo spotted Bernard's wife, Agnes, standing beside a crouched and terrified Matthew.

Thought was not necessary. With a screech of rage, Jo launched herself at the woman. "How dare you—get away from my son!"

The woman sneered. "You common whore. You don't deserve the bloody money and your whelp doesn't deserve the damned title! It should be Bernard's!"

Before Jo could slow her hasty progress across the room, Agnes whipped out a small Derringer pistol and raised it toward her—but it was far too late for that to stop her.

With all of her weight and momentum pushing her forward, Jo collided with Agnes, the other woman's skirts tangled around their legs. They crashed to the ground with a muffled thud on the thick Aubusson carpet. A noise—the gun went off, and Jo felt a burning pain along her side.

Pain. Pain?

"Fuck!" Jo tried to pin the squirming Agnes down, but it was no use. "No—no—"

"Stop!" Arthur had come to her aid and restrained the out-of-control Lady Downs.

Relief flowing through her, along with a sharp agony, Jo crawled off to the side to where Matthew sat curled up in a ball. With tears running freely down her face, she wrapped her arms around her son and tried to bring him into her lap, but the searing pain in her side put that notion to rest almost immediately. Instead, she tucked her legs under her and levered up to her knees so she could cocoon Matthew. Her son wrapped his small arms around her side, and despite the fresh wave of pain that sent shimmering through her body, Jo said nothing. Holding her son was more important than anything else.

"Jo! Are you hurt?" Arthur crouched next to her once he tied up Lady Downs with a torn strip of her own gown. Linc was quickly there as well.

"I'm fine now I have my son back, though I...I do think the bullet hit me." Jo's words were muffled, her face buried in her son's hair.

Arthur reached down and tried to peel her arms away from her son, but she refused to let go, not just yet. "Jo, we need to see to your injury and we should look Matthew over."

She whimpered softly, "I'm not ready to let go of him just yet."

Linc leaned over and pressed his fingers against her side where her injury was. "Just for a few moments, love. Then you can hold him all night if you wish it. We're both here. No one is going to harm him."

Her heart cried out its objection, though Jo did as they asked. She was wildly afraid that if she let him go, she would never hold him again. It was an absolutely irrational fear yet having lost him once tonight, it was too hard to wrestle it into submission. Taking a harried breath, Jo acknowledged the pain of releasing him, and did it anyway.

Arthur quickly helped Matthew to his feet. "Are you well, my boy? Are you hurt anywhere?"

Matthew shook his head. "No, I'm not hurt like Mummy. The mean lady just pulled on my arm very hard when I tried to run away from her."

"Good boy, good lad," Arthur murmured as he ran his hands down each of his arms. Matthew winced a little when he touched the upper part of his right arm, but he seemed otherwise uninjured. "We'll have a doctor check you out just to be safe, but I think a brave boy like you will be just fine."

Jo released a breath she hadn't realized she'd been holding.

Linc tugged off his tie and pressed the white silk to her side. "You, on the other hand, shall likely require a surgeon and stitches, my lady."

She gritted her teeth, but refused to cry out for fear she'd worry her son. He had been through enough today, she was not going to add to his terror.

That was when a clatter of stomping feet sounded up the very same stairs they had ascended. Arthur stood up and faced the door as though he might launch himself at whoever was coming through that door—but instead of a new threat it was Stone, Cooper, and Wolf. A few moments later Flint, Lucifer, Ros, and Amelia all barreled into the room as well.

"We had to take the front entrance, since the obstinate ladies wouldn't fit up the servants' stairs," Lucifer drawled.

They were all crammed into what Jo assumed was the master bedchamber. "Did anyone see any staff about?"

"Not a one." Wolf looked about the room. "Which is quite odd in itself. The boy is fine?"

"Matthew is quite well," Arthur said in a low, calm voice with a pointed look at Jo. "We are all doing our best to remain calm."

"The servants must all be at the other townhouse." Jo looked over toward Agnes, who sat there looking furious.

"Is anyone injured?" Ros asked as she stepped farther into the room.

"Jo was shot." Linc spoke in a low voice, and Jo smiled to see how careful he was not to frighten their son. They both looked down at where he held his neck tie over her wound.

"Right, we should move Jo to another room where I can look at her wound." Ros took control, as she often did. The woman could put a field marshal to shame. "Has anyone sent for the magistrate?"

"I'll go fetch him now," Flint offered and quickly departed the room. "We've had dealings before."

Linc helped Jo to her feet, causing Amelia to chuckle.

"Oh, I do approve of your choice of attire for this event!"

Jo looked down at her drawers. "Well, as you yourself discovered, there was no way I was getting up those stairs in all those skirts, not to mention all the noise they would have made as we snuck in here."

"Imminently practical." Ros nodded approval as they left the room.

"This is all your bloody fault," Bernard hissed at his wife. Jo started. She had almost forgotten him.

"Oh, shut your gob! I should have been the bloody marchioness, not that scheming shrew." Agnes sneered back. "And I would have been if you hadn't interfered and seduced me."

Jo stopped and turned. Now that was an interesting remark to make. "What on earth do you mean by that?"

Agnes snorted. "During my come out I tried to make George jealous by paying more attention to Bernard—but George was bloody ignorant. Bernard wouldn't take no for an answer until he got under my skirts when he got me tipsy one night, and then...well. I had to marry the younger brother. He ruined everything." The woman sniffed and looked away from her husband.

Jo rolled her eyes heavenward and walked out of the room. Those two were a match made in heaven: both of them scheming for a title which did not belong to them.

"Come along Matthew, let's go have Aunty Ros look at your arm as well." Arthur urged him to stand and follow his mother out.

Jo was glad to keep the boy near for now, possibly even forever.

Well, at least for a very long time.

Exhaustion tugged at Arthur's eyes, but he ensured that Matthew followed Ros, Jo, and Linc into another bedchamber. There both patients were settled on the bed side by side, and Ros began barking her orders for supplies.

"I need fresh sheets, hot water, and the best bottle of whisky or brandy you can find."

Arthur and Linc quickly headed downstairs to fetch what she requested.

"You'd best boil the water. I'll go find the linens and booze," Arthur said to Linc.

"Why do I have to boil water?" Linc looked incredulous.

"Because you wouldn't know a good bottle of whisky from rotgut if it bit you, and I haven't a bloody clue how to boil damned water," Arthur shrugged with a mischievous grin.

"And I do?" Linc still looked both surprised and offended.

"You are far more resourceful than I am. You knew how to start a fire and make a bed...that's leagues above my domestic skills." Arthur smiled and winked before he peeled off to find the linen closet.

After acquiring both items Ros requested, and verifying the quality of the whisky he found, Arthur headed back upstairs and found Linc hadn't returned yet. Ros was already working on her patients with whatever she had in the black satchel she'd brought with her. "What is in your bag, Ros?"

"A field medical kit. I always keep one in the carriage since the lot of you seem to get into trouble rather often. I grabbed it before we rushed over here. First time I've had to treat one of the ladies, though." She snorted softly in disgust. "Rushing in there without us!"

Arthur shrugged and handed her his items. "We did what had to be done. Linc should be up any moment with the water."

"Excellent. I'll start with Matthew if you can hold on a few more moments for that hot water, Jo." Ros looked at the pale and now very subdued woman Arthur loved.

"Please do. I'd like to know he is well," Jo said in a whispered tone. She was clearly in a great deal of pain. Arthur went to her side as Ros took a closer look at Matthew.

Ros briskly checked the boy over. Then she took a square of sheet she'd torn off and made a sling for his arm. "You should have the doctor look at it again tomorrow to be sure, but I believe he'll just be tender for a day or two. I'm putting him in a sling until you see a doctor so he doesn't do little boy things and make it feel worse." She tapped his nose gently and smiled at him.

Matthew grinned back. "I won't. Probably."

"We shall see. Now, let me take a look at your brave mother." Ros moved around the bed as Linc walked in with the pot of hot water carefully balanced.

"Where should I put this?" He looked about the room for a suitable spot.

Ros moved some things on the bedside table. "Right here, please. I must say, I'm impressed you know how to boil water."

Linc set the pot down and stepped out of the way. "When I had just a few rooms as lodgings, there were a few things I took care of myself to conserve expenses. Making tea for myself was one of the things I figured out how to do on my small stove. So you were in luck."

"You are a man of hidden talents. Why don't you two take Matthew into another room while I take care of his mother?" Ros suggested meaningfully as she started tearing off strips of linen.

"I'll take him," Linc offered. "Arthur, you stay here in case Jo needs you." He reached out and took the boy's hand as he gingerly got off the bed with one arm incapacitated.

The pair left the bedroom, leaving Arthur and Ros to care for Jo. Ros set about slicing Jo's bodice off her body quickly and efficiently. Then she had Jo roll onto her left hip so she could see the injury more clearly.

She scrutinized it. "It was hard to tell what happened with your bodice still on, but I am happy to say Lady Downs was not a good shot. It seems you have just been grazed. Obviously, nothing vital was hit. But you are still at risk of it festering if any material got stuck in there. That's the good news."

Jo nodded as Arthur's jaw tightened. "And the bad?"

"The bad news is, this is going to hurt like bloody hell when I clean it out. Feel free to scream," Ros said grimly as she doused a piece of linen in hot water.

Arthur climbed on the bed and held Jo through the pain of her wound being tended. He wrapped his arms around her as she buried her face in his shoulder and screamed, the pain clearly beyond agony. He comforted her as her tears fell, and she refused Ros' offer to stop. He braced her as the burn of the whisky poured into the wound caused uncontrollable shivers of pain and he immobilized her as Ros pierced her skin with a needle and thread.

Before long, her sewing closed the gash. "That's a nice little scar you're going to have there," Ros said when she was done.

"Is it?" Jo asked listlessly as she lay there still shivering in Arthur's arms.

His heart ached for the pain Ros had caused her, but he knew it was necessary. The wound had to be cleaned and closed up to prevent infection. He was sure the doctor would agree with their choice.

Ros quietly slipped from the room, leaving the two of them alone.

"What can I do for you?" Arthur asked in a low murmur.

"Just hold me and tell me this nightmare is over." She sounded so small and fragile at that moment.

He gently pulled her even closer to his body. "It's over now, love. You and Matthew are safe."

Jo melted against him, clearly exhausted. As he held her, it was an almost perfect moment. Almost because one person was missing—their husband, Linc.

Chapter Thirty-Seven

Later That Night

They had returned home to find their guests gone and the staff well on their way to clearing the worst of the mess away. Linc carried a sleeping Matthew upstairs to the nursery while Arthur helped an exhausted Jo to bed. He settled the boy into a bed of his own and stared at the child's arm, back again in a sling.

Guilt punched him in the gut. Linc had been so busy chasing after him, rescuing him, caring for him he'd avoided the knot that had been in his stomach all night since they discovered the boy was missing. But here, alone in the darkened room, looking at Matthew's rounded face and long lashes laying against chubby cheeks, there was nowhere to run. Nowhere to hide.

Linc knew he hadn't done enough to protect the boy. There was no way around it. He had been responsible for seeing to his safety; he and Arthur had discussed it, and since Arthur was officially married to Jo and needed to play the host to her hostess, Linc was to see to Matthew's care throughout that night. He had thought it was working well...until it wasn't.

He was fond of Matthew, loved him as if he were his own son, which made it even more important that he not risk the boy's life with his carelessness. He needed to step away;

remove himself so Arthur could find someone who would be more effective. Linc would never risk Matthew's life again.

He left the nursery, moved down the hall, and found Arthur still shuffling around the dimly lit bedchamber, getting ready for bed as Jo slept. Linc watched as the muscles rippled over his lover's chest and wished he could caress him once more, but he knew if he did that—if he touched him—he wouldn't have the strength to do what was needed.

What he'd come here to do.

"There you are. I had begun to wonder if you were going to sleep in the nursery with Matthew," Arthur chuckled softly. "Come to bed, Linc."

"I can't." Linc stood there lurking in the dark shadows where the hall melted into the doorway and the light from the lamp didn't quite reach.

Arthur looked up, surprised. "Why ever not?"

Linc's chest felt tight, almost painfully so, but he forced the words out. "I just..." Arthur sat on the edge of the bed and stared at him in confusion. "I just can't. I can't take care of him, of our Wood Sprite. I'm sorry." He melted into the shadows, let the darkness swallow him as he pulled the door closed and left Arthur and Jo alone. As they should be.

The pain of walking away from everything he'd ever wanted was soul crushing, but Linc couldn't see another way. Jo and Arthur were good for each other. Jo was an excellent mother. Arthur was good for Matthew. But him? He was just the fun one, the one everyone liked to have around to entertain them. He certainly was no protector. Not a husband. Not a support.

Linc neared the door that separated their homes and hesitated as he heard footsteps coming behind him. Picking up his speed to evade the person he was sure would be Arthur, he approached the door and went through it one last time. On the other side—his side—he locked it.

It was late, so he supposed bed was the best choice. Linc walked into his cold, dark bedchamber. He hadn't slept there in years, though the room was kept up on the off chance appearances had to be upheld. Perhaps maintaining the space showed how separate he really felt from Arthur and now Jo.

Had this distance always been there? Linc wondered as he walked around the bedchamber, looking at the things he'd left in the room. A portrait of his mother and one of his father. A vase of fresh flowers and a brush for his hair. He looked over at the enormous bed and shuddered. The sheets would be cold and the bed so very empty if he crawled into it right now.

No, that was not something he could face.

Linc walked out of the room and headed downstairs to his study. This was a room he still occupied once in a while when he needed to take care of business or other correspondence. This room at least was laid ready for a fire.

He knelt down, got one started, and rose with a sigh as his gaze took in the decanter of whisky, quickly deciding a drink was in order. After pouring one, he sat down and sipped it as he stared into the fire.

Yes, this hurt, but not as bad as it would have had Matthew been killed or otherwise lost to them tonight. He was doing this for them.

Arthur rushed over to the door where Linc had just been, pulling it open and looking out into the hallway. Linc was just closing the door between their homes and he rushed after him, determined to figure out what the hell was going on—but when he got to the door, it was locked.

Locked! The bastard had bloody well locked him out!

Standing there, cold, hurt, and confused, Arthur banged on the door a bit in hopes Linc would come back but to no avail.

He returned to their bedchamber and found Jo awake and sitting up.

"Where's Linc?"

Arthur wasn't sure what to say as he looked down at the floor. "He went back to his townhouse to sleep. I...I think he didn't want to disturb you while you slept."

"What? Why?" Jo looked as confused as he felt.

He moved over to the bed and climbed in beside her. "I don't really know. He seemed upset, but he wouldn't say much."

"That's ridiculous. Go fetch him," she all but demanded.

"I tried, Jo. He locked the bloody door—he clearly wants to be alone. Let's give him a little space, and I'm sure he'll come to his senses," Arthur said as he urged her to lie back down.

"But I need him here with us." Her soft words pierced Arthur's heart, because he needed him there as well.

"I'll check on him tomorrow. Now get some rest," he urged her.

Arthur spent most of the night wide awake and worried. What was going on with Linc? Why had he pulled away so suddenly?

Why wasn't their husband with them?

Chapter Thirty-Eight

Three Days Later

J o found Matthew sitting in the nursery playing listlessly with his toy soldiers. The doctor had come the day after Matthew had been kidnapped and looked both of them over, declaring Matthew's arm but a minor injury and that the sling was no longer required. As for Jo, he admired Ros' handiwork and ordered bedrest for a couple of days. If any redness appeared or the pain increased along with fever, she was to call for him immediately.

That meant today Jo could abandon her bed and move about, however gingerly.

Sitting down in the rocking chair that she sometimes sat in and read to him, Jo sucked in a soft breath as the pain flared across her side. "Matthew, what's the matter?"

Her son looked up as if he'd just that moment noticed she was in the room. "Oh, hello Mother." He rose and came over to her listlessly.

"Hello, my son. You look sad. Do you want to tell mother what's wrong?" Jo held her arms open to him.

Matthew happily crawled into her lap, causing her to suck in another sharp breath as she winced at the pain. Perhaps inviting him into her lap had been a bad idea. She winced again as he wriggled around on her lap to get settled.

He plopped his little head on her shoulder and sighed. "I miss Uncle Linc."

She wasn't surprised he had noticed her wayward lover's absence; both Linc and Arthur spent a great deal of time with Matthew, but she hadn't expected that her son would have felt his absence so acutely. "You do?"

"Uh-huh." Matthew nodded his head decisively. "He used to come up every morning and say hello, and ask me what I was going to learn about today. Sometimes he would even play soldiers with me. But he hasn't been here since the night with the bad lady."

Jo drew in a slow, steady breath. This one was born of the emotional pain Linc had caused her son, not the physical pain that was currently simmering along her side. "I'm sorry he hasn't been to visit you. I know he has been very busy the last few days."

"I know. Grown-ups are always very busy." Matthew fell silent for a few moments, as though he was considering their conversation. Then he straightened up and looked at her with big, solemn eyes. "Did I do something to make him angry with me?"

Jo willed her tears back as she shook her head. "No, of course not. You have done nothing to upset anyone."

He looked uncertain for a moment. "Are you sure?"

"I am very, very certain that whatever is keeping Uncle Linc away has nothing to do with you or anything you did. I'm sure it is just adult things that he needs to take care of." Jo wanted to gnash her teeth. Instead, she managed a soft smile for her son.

"All right. If you're certain." Matthew sounded less convinced than she would like, but he also seemed less sad.

"Perhaps we should go to the park tomorrow. How does that sound?"

He perked up immediately. "May we?"

"Yes, I'll ask Cook to pack us a picnic and everything." Jo smiled as her son bounced up and down.

"Oh, boy!" Matthew chirped happily, his earlier sadness forgotten.

"Excellent. Well, I am going to go have some breakfast and I shall alert the staff to our plans for tomorrow. Perhaps I can even wrangle Arthur to join us." Jo smiled at her son, her heart in her throat.

She would absolutely drag Arthur along—and if she had her way, Linc, as well.

Jo was done being avoided.

Later that day, Jo went in search of Linc. The connecting door to his home remained locked, so she sailed out the front door, down the front steps of Arthur's home and up the front steps of Linc's. She knocked on the front door and waited for it to be opened.

When his butler appeared, she walked in the open door and right past the gaping man. "Good afternoon, Mr. Powel. Is Lord Lincolnshire in his study?"

The butler sputtered and followed her down the hallway, since she had yet to stop. "I... I... I believe so, my lady. But I don't think he wishes—" Jo would not be stopped and opened the door of the study "—to be disturbed."

She just caught the last part as she closed the door firmly behind her. There, across the room, slouched in a wing chair before the fireplace, was the very man she was looking for.

"There you are."

Linc looked up in confusion as she crossed the room to stop before him.

"Well, you certainly look and smell like a veritable mess." Jo sniffed delicately. "And just when was the last time you bathed?"

Linc blinked as though he was trying to determine if she was real or not. "Wha day isth it?"

His words were slurred and rather disjointed, but she got the gist of what he was saying. "It is Tuesday. I feel certain based on the smell in this room and your general state of drunkenness that you have not, in fact, bathed since the ball on Saturday."

"I can't rememememember." He continued to slur his words, but he at least attempted to sit up.

"Well, I think we need to rectify that situation immediately before we speak. Perhaps by then you will find yourself in a more sober state." Jo turned on her heel and marched out into the hall to find Powell hovering nearby. "Oh good, you're still here. Please have a bath drawn for Lord Lincolnshire, then return and help me get him upstairs."

Powell bowed smartly and disappeared with a grin on his face. Before long, he reappeared with a footman in tow. "I believe your stitches are still healing, my lady, so I suggest Burns should help me get his lordship upstairs."

"Very well, that's probably for the best." Jo followed them upstairs where a steaming hot bath awaited Linc.

Once there, the men stripped him down and then guided him into the bathtub. Jo stood by directing servants to bring soap and towels. Once the man was finally in the bath and there was just her and Powell, who acted as Linc's valet, she looked at the man and smiled. "Be a dear, and please dump one of the remaining pails of water over his head."

Linc was lolling in the bathtub as if every bone in his body had been liquified. He was still not coherent enough to hear her message. He might not be until he sobered up a great deal more, but she had to get through to the man.

His valet picked up the pail with steaming water in it.

"Not that one. I think the cold pail will do nicely." Jo wanted to cause him a little discomfort, considering all the discomfort he had caused herself, Arthur, and most of all Matthew the last few days.

"My lady!" The valet seemed shocked.

"Do it," Jo said sternly, unwilling to relent.

"Very good, my lady." The man did not look pleased, but then he had not seen Linc when she'd found him. Clearly Powell agreed with her directions since he had seen to it everything was prepared.

The butler/valet dumped the cold water over his master's head.

A soaked and sputtering Linc shot up halfway out of the bathtub. "What the bloody hell Powell!" He exclaimed before spotting her and sinking back down in the tub. "Oh, I see. Wood Sprite."

"Don't you Wood Sprite me, you unfeeling ogre," Jo all but snarled at him. Turning to Powell, she smiled sweetly. "Please put a bit of the hot water in the tub now, if you please. I don't want my husband catching his death of cold."

Powell nodded and then added some hot water to the tub, at which point Linc sank down into the water until just his head poked out.

"That will be all, Powell. I shall let you know when he requires your assistance." She dismissed him with a nod and he left the chamber.

"What is the meaning of all this?" Linc asked as he glared balefully.

"This is what happens when you disappear from my life, from our lives, like a ghost," Jo glared back at him.

"Disappeared? I was right here, next door, as I have always been." He tried to sound innocent, but she knew his nonsense for what it was.

"You hurt my son, Linc," she breathed, and he stilled in the tub.

"I am sorry. I didn't mean to." An anguished look crossed Linc's face, one far more pained than she thought appropriate. "You are right, it's my fault he was injured once more."

Confusion rolled through her. *What was he blathering on about?* "What? I'm not speaking of the kidnapping, that was certainly not your fault. How could anyone blame you for that? I meant your choice to retreat from our lives."

Linc snorted. "I didn't think I'd be missed in the midst of all the connubial bliss."

"Of course you were missed! We love you, Linc." Jo paused and looked for a reaction from him, but his face was shuttered. Frustration rose inside her as she realized she may not be getting through to him. Desperate she tried a tactic her mother had often used: a command performance. "Well, I expect to see you at dinner this evening." This was not a negotiation. He would come or she would drag him over.

"No. I am unavailable for dinner tonight." Linc's words were a shock to her.

"What do you mean, no?" Jo demanded, frustration flaring into white-hot anger.

"You said it yourself. I hurt all of you—let you down. I shall not compound my transgressions by adding to them as I inevitably will. This..." he dragged in a breath. "This game, adventure, experiment, whatever you want to call it, is over. Now if you will leave me to my bath, I would appreciate some privacy."

Shocked, hurt, and wildly confused, Jo stood and stared at him. "Why would you think you will compound your supposed transgressions with your presence? What you are saying makes little sense—it is your absence that is the offense."

"Jo, I let your son be taken. I failed him and I failed you in the worst possible way. It is better for all of you if I remove myself from the situation."

"Are you daft? We just discussed this, it wasn't your fault." Jo leaned over, wincing at the pain in her side once more, and pressed her fingers to his temple. "Did you fall and hit your head while you were pickled?"

Her love swatted her hands away. "I did not hit my head. I am in my right mind for possibly the first time in months. I do not wish to discuss this any further—please leave."

"We are married, Linc. Are you calling our wedding a mistake? Are you saying you were not in your right mind when you pledged your heart and soul to Arthur and me?"

His lips pressed together for a long silent moment as though Linc struggled to say the words that came from his mouth next. "Yes. I never should have married you. Either of you."

She growled, "You bloody fucking fool! I cannot believe you are doing this. Do not think this is the last of this discussion."

Jo turned on her heel and left him in his bathtub. As she breezed through his bedchamber, she saw Powell. "Linc will likely need your assistance with bathing—hell, with breathing. The man is incompetent, as far as I can tell."

Only then did she storm out of his room and out of his house—choosing not to walk around outside but instead unlocking the connecting door. He could lock it again later, if he thought to check it.

Furious, Jo went in search of Arthur to share the story of her confrontation. He would know what to do to make their husband understand—the man was entirely off kilter at the moment. Someone had to make him see reason.

Chapter Thirty-Nine

The Next Day

L inc sat in his study just as he had the day before, but today he was sober as a judge. After Jo's sneak attack the day before, aided and abetted by his own damned servants, he had cleaned himself up and gone straight to bed.

This morning, he'd woken up with a hangover that seemed painfully fitting for a three-day bender. His head pounded and his stomach rolled as though he were on a carousel, but he was determined to get himself back together—after all, he could only remember a few bits and pieces of his conversation with Jo. He'd already focused on forcing down some breakfast. Now he sat in his study, trying desperately to review his latest correspondence, but the words on the page were not cooperating. They insisted on dancing around on the page as though they were not anchored. Clearly, his head was still spinning from all the drink.

Then a vision in cobalt blue twill floated into his study. He blinked once and then once more. Did it have wings? No, it couldn't have been wings. He sighed and rubbed his forehead.

A full round laugh that could only belong to one woman pealed through the room and his head. He looked up again and blinked to clear the fuzziness.

It was Theo, standing in his study. "Has Stone lost you once again?"

She laughed again. "Stone knows exactly where I am and with whom." She strolled into the room and sat down in the chair across from his desk. "In fact, he was going to come over here and, I believe, 'beat some bloody sense' into you. I suggested a different approach would be in order. Come for a drive with me. I assumed since you've been drinking for three days that riding would be far too painful for you, but I think a drive and some fresh air will be just the thing to set you to rights."

Linc looked at her and let all the skepticism he felt for her suggestion show on his face. "I think a drive with my ninety-year-old aunt might be helpful. A drive with a dervish such as yourself might be utterly catastrophic for my well-being, let alone my state of mind."

Theo harumphed and shot him a disgruntled look that was adorable, but not at all convincing. "Well, I hate to tell you that your choices are a ride with me through the park or rounds at Gentleman Jack's with Stone and Flint." She sighed dramatically. "I really thought I had offered the lesser of the two evils, but you never know, I might be wrong."

Linc snorted. "Unfortunately, it sounds as though your assessment is accurate. A drive with you would be the least painful of the two options." He stood up. "I don't suppose you would consider allowing me to drive?"

Theo laughed long and loud as she slapped her thigh and bent over double. After a long and head splitting moment, she straightened up and smiled. "Nice try, but nobody drives my phaeton but me."

Linc groaned again. "You couldn't have brought a barouche or carriage?"

Theo snorted. "Only the best and fastest vehicle for me, my good sir."

"Of course." He rolled his eyes heavenward in a prayer for strength. This was going to be one hell of a ride.

A short while later he was settled on the bench next to Theo, who had a firm grip on the reins of her two horses pulling her phaeton. As they clopped along the street, he found the fresh air was clearing his head and helping to shake off the dregs of the last few days. He was just feeling more himself when Theo broke in to his contemplations on his health.

"So, I understand you are under the impression that what happened at the ball is your fault." She lifted one eyebrow and cocked her head at him while keeping her other eye on the road.

"News does travel fast." Linc darted a glance at her from the corner of his eye.

"Indeed, it does. Oh, bloody hell!" Theo cursed roundly as she hauled back on the reins to avoid trampling a dog that shot out into the street.

Linc's heart now pounded in his chest, and he was honestly feeling a little green with that abrupt stop.

"As I was saying, Matthew being taken is absolutely not your fault," Theo said the statement as if it were fact.

Her utter confidence in her knowledge was shocking—mostly because he knew with the same certainty that it *was* his fault. "I'm afraid it is my fault. I was the one responsible for ensuring he remained safe during the ball. I was the one who went up there to check on him throughout the night. I was the one who promised Jo her son would be safe after Arthur and I visited the brute of a brother-in-law. Who else is responsible?"

"How about Lady Downs? She is, after all, the one who slipped up there and took Matthew," Theo said archly.

"But had I done a better job of securing Matthew, she would not have been able to take him," Linc pointed out in what he felt was a perfectly reasonable tone.

"Possibly, but you and Arthur laid out the plan for Matthew's safety together, did you not?"

Linc sighed inwardly. *She had a point.* "Yes, but I handled the execution of the plan."

"Yet Arthur had a hand in designing it, believing it to be sufficient. Correct?"

"Well, yes." Linc couldn't deny that fact.

"And you do not blame Arthur for what happened?" she asked gently.

"I do not. You know I do not." Linc sighed, feeling her point being driven home.

"Then why on earth do you hold yourself responsible?" Theo's exasperation leaked out as she sedately nudged the horses on.

"Because..." Linc huffed out a breath of frustration. "Because once again I let someone I love down—and I won't do it again. I can't stand the gut wrenching feeling of disappointing people I care about. In the end, when they push me away because it has happened one too many times, it...it will destroy me." He wouldn't look at her as he heaved in a breath and tried to calm his racing heart. He couldn't bear it.

"Who was it, Linc? Who did you fail?" Theo asked quietly as they turned into Hyde Park.

It wasn't the popular hour for promenading, so they were relatively alone as Linc stared at the trees slipping by while images of his past crept up out of the darkness. "It was...it was my little sister." The words ripped free from him, scratching his throat.

Theo gasped in surprise. "You had a sister?"

"I don't talk about her because she died, and it is my fault. She's dead because I failed her." Linc's chest felt like Theo had reached over and sliced him open from neck to navel and reached in to grab a hold of his heart.

"What happened?" She nudged the horses off the path and pulled them to a stop to allow other vehicles to go by before turning to face him on the bench and press a hand over the one that lay fisted on his thigh.

"She was so pretty. All golden hair and big blue eyes, like a little doll. She was five, I was ten. She would follow me everywhere." Linc chuckled grimly, the pain of discussing this stabbing at his insides. "I hated that she tried to come with me. Most days I let her, of course, but that day...that day I was determined to leave her at home. I was meeting my friends to go exploring, and they had all said not to come if Melanie came along. The servants were accustomed to her following me, so no one was concerned at first when they couldn't see her."

Theo squeezed his hand in silent encouragement.

"By the time I got home from a day of exploring, everyone was worried. When I showed up without Melanie, everyone panicked. I swore to them she was home when I left that morning. At first, they didn't believe me. They swore I was playing a dirty trick on them. But I wasn't." A tear slipped down Linc's cheek as the pain of that day returned. "They organized search parties, looked everywhere for her. Finally, I went down to the river we often swam in and hoped I would not find her there. I...I found her floating in the water. Her hair was caught in the brush by the water's edge, holding her there. It took me a moment to realize she wasn't alive and...and she had on nothing but her chemise."

"Oh God!" Theo choked out the words as tears ran freely down her cheeks.

Linc saw the horror he'd felt that day reflected in her eyes. He'd known, even then, that something terrible had happened to his sweet, sweet little sister. Later, of course, he understood the true magnitude of it all, but when he'd called out to the searchers and the first adults had arrived, he'd known immediately that it was bad. He had waded into the water to pull her out, but she was too heavy for him so he'd pulled off his coat and draped it over her floating form to hide the sheerness of her wet chemise from everyone that came.

Linc's mother had arrived as one of the footmen carried her child out of the water, and the woman had collapsed in tears.

"As my mother lay weeping over Melanie's body, my father looked at me where I still stood, knee deep in the water. He pointed his finger at me and bellowed that it was my fault—that if I had taken her with me that day, this wouldn't have happened, that...that his baby girl would still be alive. And I knew it was true. If I hadn't left her at home, she wouldn't have tried to go swimming on her own. It was all my fault, because I hadn't done what I knew I should have. Just like with Matthew." Linc shrugged, his shoulders tight with tension.

"No! No, your father was wrong to say that. Wrong to blame you, Linc. Melanie's death was nobody's fault but the man who attacked her." Theo's words came out urgent but gentle.

"Regardless, my father held me responsible and shipped me off to boarding school in the autumn. It was the last time I was home until I became an adult. Even decades later I rarely go home and I certainly have no interest in carrying on the title." Linc sighed. "But I did fail her. Just as I failed Matthew. And it will happen again. I refuse to inflict that on either Matthew or Jo. It is best if I pull away now."

"No. You are absolutely wrong, Linc. They need you—all of them need you. More importantly, they miss you." Theo turned and took the reins back into her hands. With a quick shake of the reins and click of the tongue, they lurched forward. "I'll show you."

A few moments later, as Linc collected himself, Theo pulled up near one of the ponds in Hyde Park. There he spotted Arthur and Jo sitting close together on a picnic blanket as Matthew ran about chasing the ducks.

"What do you see, Linc?" Theo asked, waiting for him to answer.

He grunted. A pain shot across his chest as he watched the cozy scene, a scene that felt so distant, so out of reach. "I see a man and a woman sharing an intimate moment as their son plays nearby."

"Look again. What I see is a man consoling a woman because one of the men she loves, that they love, is not there. He is willfully absent from them. I see a boy who is chasing the ducks, but with a fraction of the gusto he is capable of because he misses his Uncle Linc, who is usually the one chasing the ducks with him." Theo looked at him pointedly.

Linc watched them and he could see the sadness which hung over the little outing like a pall. But it changed nothing. He would do more harm than good if he were there.

"Linc, you were a boy. You were not responsible for Melanie's death. That was a horrible thing your father said in a moment of grief—and what happened to Matthew the other night lies solely at the feet of Lady Downs. No one else is responsible, except perhaps her husband who pursued the issue to begin with. I would wager that if you walked over there, the three of them would welcome you with open arms. They love and miss you as much as you love and miss them. But I believe you owe Jo and Arthur an explanation for why you pulled away. Without that, they will never fully understand why—and who you are."

Theo's words settled in Linc's gut and curled around his heart.

Perhaps...she was right? Intellectually, he knew there was little he could have done to stop what happened to his sister. He had been a boy who wanted to go off and be a boy. He hadn't done anything more than be a child.

Could he just walk over there and apologize?

He wouldn't know if he didn't try.

Without a word, Linc climbed down out of the carriage and started over to where his family waited for him.

Chapter Forty

Arthur looked up and stared for a moment. Then he blinked—but no, he was still there walking across the lawn in Hyde Park toward them.

Linc was there.

He leaned over to Jo. "He's coming."

She gasped softly and turned to look at him. Then she tugged on his arm to demand, "Help me up."

Arthur did as she bade, rising to his feet and helping her to hers as Linc approached.

Before they could do more than wave tentatively, Matthew launched himself at Linc's legs. "Uncle Linc! You came!"

Linc smiled softly at their boy, but there was a tinge of sadness to it and that sadness worried Arthur. Linc knelt down to talk to Matthew, though they could not hear what he said. Then he hugged the boy and sent him off. A delighted Matthew went back to chasing the ducks with a vigor which had been missing earlier.

Linc approached them with a curt nod. "Arthur, Jo."

"Hello, Linc." Jo smiled. "Please, sit down, join us."

Linc nodded and lowered himself to the blanket they sat on. Arthur helped Jo sit so she wouldn't put any strain on her side. It was healing well, but she was a few weeks away from being back to her normal, active self.

"Would you care for a glass of lemonade, or perhaps some wine?" Jo offered, gesturing to the picnic basket.

"Lemonade would be fine."

From what Arthur could see, Linc looked contrite. He must be nursing quite the hangover, based on what Jo had related to him the night before. She'd been beside herself with worry, so he'd invited Stone and Theo over for dinner to discuss the situation. Of course, Stone had been all for pounding some sense into Linc. But Theo had insisted on another course of action: this course of action. Talking to him in the clear light of day and out in the fresh air. They'd planned to take Matthew to the park anyway, so it was quite easy to arrange everything else from there. The only risk was Linc refusing to take the drive, but Theo had assured them she could get him in the vehicle. How, Arthur hadn't wanted to know.

Jo handed him a cup of lemonade then waited. Linc was the one who needed to speak first.

"I'm sorry. I'm sorry for the last few days and I am sorry for not sharing more openly with you both before now." Linc stared at the cup of lemonade in his hand.

"What have you not shared?" Arthur asked, curiosity getting the best of him. He and Linc were so close, he found it hard to believe there was much he didn't know about this man; about the man that he loved.

"I had a sister," Linc started with a deep exhale.

Shock and a spark of a memory from the night Matthew was taken slammed into Arthur, hard and brutal. "A sister? How? You've never spoken of her." He inhaled sharply. "That's not quite right. You mentioned her that night outside of the Downs' home."

"Yes. I haven't spoken of her in years," Linc agreed.

Arthur looked over at Jo, who looked terribly pale at this point, but he didn't want to interrupt Linc's story. Linc went on to explain how his sister died and what happened afterward with his parents.

"Oh, my poor Linc. You do know it was not your fault, don't you?" Jo asked as she leaned across and took his hands in hers.

Linc had long since finished the drink and set the glass aside. "Yes, and no. As an adult, I understand I was not responsible for what happened, any more than Matthew was responsible for what happened to him. But that little boy still lives inside me and at times I still *feel* responsible. It makes little sense, but it's not something I can seem to control." He shrugged. "So when Matthew was taken that little boy reared his head, and I felt responsible once again when...when perhaps I shouldn't have."

"If anyone was responsible, of the three of us, it was me," Jo said firmly. "I was the one who married Lord Whitestone, I was the one who allowed the situation to get so out of control. But truly, in the end, it was all Lady Downs. She is the one who chose to take Matthew. She couldn't let the title go, even once they had the unentailed portion of the money."

Linc nodded. "I am sorry I didn't tell you of Melanie before now. Perhaps the last few days could have been avoided had I been more open with you both."

"Perhaps, but perhaps not. You may have had the same reaction—the only thing which might have changed was how we dealt with it," Arthur offered with a smile. "I certainly wouldn't have let you sod off on your own like I did."

Linc chuckled. "I probably would have fought you on it, but either way, I am sorry."

"So are we." Jo squeezed his hand. "We should have realized there was something more going on with you, not just left you to get blazingly drunk alone."

"Apology accepted." Linc smiled at them.

"It's getting late, but Linc, we'd like you to be in our home for dinner tonight, the home of all three of us—and back in our room, where you belong." Jo looked at Linc, and then over at Arthur. Her heart shone in her eyes as she looked for his agreement.

"Absolutely, Linc. Come home. We miss you." Arthur leaned over to slap Linc on the shoulder.

"That would be wonderful," he said with almost a shy smile. "Assuming I can get a ride with you. Otherwise it may be a long walk home from here, and missing dinner is a very real possibility."

They all laughed.

"Of course we have room for you. Unlike Theo, we brought a very practical landau." Arthur grinned and they began packing up the picnic.

That night, after a lovely dinner, Jo waited for Linc and Arthur to join her in the drawing room. She had been busy finding as many candles as she could after they got home. Every surface was covered in candles and a pair of maids had been lighting them since halfway through dinner. There were only a few left to light by the time she came in after excusing herself. Once Linc and Arthur joined her all was ready, and she waited for them alone.

Linc came in first. "What's all this?"

Behind him, Arthur smiled, because he'd known Jo had been up to something. "This is what you were doing instead of resting, as you should have been after the picnic."

"It was." She smiled lovingly at both of them: her men, her hearts. "I wanted us to renew our vows to each other. I think it's important, after all that we've been through, all we've learned."

Linc nodded and took Arthur's hand and walked him over to where she stood. Then he took Jo's hand, and held them both in one hand. "I swear to love, honor, and cherish you both. To never hold secrets that aren't wonderful surprises. To never pull away from you without talking to you both first. And I promise to love our son and any future children, and protect them as fiercely as I shall love and protect you both."

Arthur said the same thing. "I swear to love, honor, and cherish you both. To never hold secrets that aren't wonderful surprises. To never pull away from you without talking to you both first. And I promise to love our son and any future children, and protect them as fiercely as I shall love and protect you both."

Jo smiled through the happy tears that slipped down her cheeks. "I swear to love, honor, and cherish you both. To never hold secrets that aren't wonderful surprises. To never pull away from you without talking to you both first. And I promise to love our son and protect him as fiercely as I shall love and protect you both." She took a breath and then continued on. "Three hearts entwined to beat as one. Three souls merged to live as one."

Linc and Arthur repeated the phrase to finish the vow from their original ceremony. Then Linc pulled Jo into his arms and kissed her until she felt like she was floating three inches off the floor. After he released her, he kissed Arthur just as passionately, then Arthur kissed her.

It was a perfect moment, just the three of them. And Jo knew it was true, and forever.

As Arthur plundered her mouth, she felt Linc move in behind her. Her wound was still healing, but she wanted this—wanted them, especially with Linc having returned to them. Her bodice slowly opened as Linc undid each small button down her back, then he tackled her skirts. All the while, Arthur distracted her with a deep, rapacious kiss. She loved it when these men allowed their passions to roam free. It inevitably led to great pleasure.

Once her skirts finally dropped to the floor, Arthur broke their kiss, and she turned to face Linc. She needed more of him. He welcomed her into his arms, though careful of her side, and captured her mouth in a searing kiss once more. Her heart skipped a beat as Arthur loosened her corset.

Leaving Jo in her chemise and pantaloons, Linc pulled back from their kiss. "How is your side feeling?"

"Better every day."

Linc narrowed his gaze at her. "But it still pains you?"

"It does, but I don't care—I need you both." Worry that they would end things here and now had her stomach knotting for all the wrong reasons.

"I need you two as well." Link's words were a husky caress as he leaned in to kiss her again.

"I think we can do this gently," Arthur offered.

They were both still fully clothed which absolutely could not continue, so Jo reached up and pushed Linc's coat off his shoulders. The candlelight bathed the room in a warm glow, and she was curious to see the way the light flickered over their bodies. She refused to be deterred. Fortunately, they both seemed willing enough so Linc aided her efforts to remove his clothing. Behind her, she could hear the rustle of Arthur's as he also disrobed.

By the time both men were nude, Jo's body ached with need. Linc wrapped her in his arms and leaned down to capture one nipple in his mouth. As he sucked gently on her already sensitive tip through the soft cotton of her chemise, she heard Arthur move around behind them before Linc released her puckered nub and scooped her into his arms before he knelt down and gently deposited her on a bed of blankets.

"Where on earth did these come from?" Linc asked in obvious wonder.

Arthur smiled. "You are not the only one who can plan ahead. I figured we would eventually wind up making love in here, so I had some thick blankets stashed in the old trunk under the window."

Jo smiled and readied herself for whatever came next. Linc kissed his way down her body, pushing her chemise up as he went. He tugged her pantaloons down and off her legs while Arthur reached helped her remove her chemise. Fully naked, she watched contentedly as Linc nudged her thighs wide and nestled between them. As his tongue speared through her slick folds, Arthur leaned over and sucked on one of her nipples as he plucked and strummed the other.

Her body arched up gently, her side only allowing so much movement—but the pain of her movement melded with the pleasure Linc was delivering between her legs and the desire Arthur stirred higher up.

She truly was a lucky woman.

As Jo edged toward her first orgasm, Linc withdrew from between her legs. "I want to feel you come wrapped around my cock."

"Yes, please." Jo was a little surprised to hear the words out loud. She hadn't meant to say it aloud, though she knew her men would welcome such agreement. She looked at Arthur. "Grab a pillow from the couch so I can suck your cock while he fucks me."

Arthur growled, low and hungry. "Yes."

After a moment, her head was propped up and Linc was in position between her legs. As he slid inside of her, Arthur pressed the tip of his cock against her lips, then traced it along the seam. "Open for me."

His commanding tone had her doing as he bid. Jo wanted this, gladly taking him in as Linc filled her up. The pair of them possessing her felt right, good, everything she'd ever wanted.

As Linc slid in and out of her pussy, Arthur worked his cock in and out of her mouth, pushing deep into her throat. Jo loved it, reveled in the way she could please both her men.

When Linc reached down and strummed her clit with a finger, she found herself once more on the precipice of orgasm.

"That's it Jo. Take his cock in your sweet cunny while I fuck your pretty mouth." Arthur's dirty words pushed her over the edge and she moaned as the men fucked her good.

Linc stroked into her once more and then a final time before he came. He arched back a bit as he buried himself deep inside her pussy. She loved how it felt to have him inside her. Arthur withdrew from her mouth and waited for Linc to finish. Once Linc had pulled free of her body and fallen to the side, Arthur slid into place between her knees, and thrust inside of her.

Oh, Jo loved it, loved the feeling of needing more and knowing it was coming.

As Arthur sank inside her, Linc reached over and plucked at her hard nipples while Arthur shuttled in and out of her body at a steady yet gentle pace. Just like Linc, her second husband was taking care not to jostle her too much.

Arthur sank into her over and over. "God, you feel good, Jo. I can feel Linc's seed inside you, making you so slippery for me." He pumped inside her and then slid out. "Can you feel me? Feel the way I fill your sweet pussy up?"

"Yes," she moaned as a new orgasm built inside of her. Need had her hips thrusting up to meet his, but always the protector, Arthur pinned her down and refused to let her injure herself further. It was a tantalizing tease.

"Hold still, Jo." Arthur pumped into her a little harder.

Linc sat up and reached down to where Arthur met her opening. He ran his fingers around where they were joined and gathered more moisture. "Hold still Wood Sprite." He stroked over her swollen clit and her body became taught like a bow.

Jo panted as Linc stroked that little bundle of nerves while Arthur pumped into her, pouring more and more pleasure into her until finally, she shattered. Her body flew apart as wave after wave of pleasure buffeted her. Linc worked her clit as Arthur thrust and she couldn't control herself. As they continued to work her body together, her orgasm ebbed, but another built right behind it.

"That's it, love. Come again for us," Arthur commanded as he fucked her slowly but firmly.

"Let go, Jo." Linc leaned over, sucking on her nipple as he stroked her clit once more.

Jo's orgasm burst over her and she lost all sense of the here and now as a roar of pleasure sounded, breaking through her haze. Arthur was coming as well. He pumped into her as her release eased to gentle pulses of pleasure.

Beside her, Linc snuggled close until Arthur collapsed on her other side. Together they kissed her, one on each cheek, as they caught their breath. Jo lay there, knowing all was finally right in her world. Their world.

Three hearts entwined to beat as one. Three souls merged to live as one.

The End

Author's Note

I imagine you have some questions – and yes, I have answers!

As of 1861 buggery was no longer a capital offense, the penalty having been reduced to life in prison with the implementation of the offences Against the Person Act of 1861[1]. The last men to be hung for buggery were James Pratt and John Smith in 1835. "Until 1818 sodomites and their accomplices could also be sentenced to stand in the pillory."[2]It wasn't until 1885 that the Labouchere Amendment was passed which made "gross indecency" between men a crime. That would have made any relationship between two men impossible. It was dubbed the Blackmailer's Charter, since it created a situation where any whiff of homosexuality was a punishable offense. This is the famous law under which Oscar Wilde and Alan Turing were respectively convicted. The Sexual Offences Act of 1967 finally decriminalized consensual homosexual acts between persons aged 21 and over.

The years covered in this book are from 1861 through 1867. For the period covered in this book, while technically illegal, the relationship between Linc and Arthur if kept quiet could have gone unremarked. This was the purpose of a number of constructs established in the book. Two separate homes with a private door between. Well paid and loyal servants to ensure their secret does not come out, and the public marriage of Arthur and Josephine. The reality is that many individuals who were born with a natural attraction to the same sex were forced to either hide their preferences through subterfuge and at the risk of punishment or to remain alone resulting in a less full and open existence. Thankfully, things have changed in most places, though the LGBTQ+ community is still fighting to exist as they choose to be and not as the moral majority of the world believes they should.

Love means love.

1.   (n.d.). *A History of LGBT Criminalisation: Over 500 years of outlawing lesbian, gay, bisexual and transgender people.* Human Dignity Trust.https://www.humandignitytrust.org/lgbt-the-law/a-history-of-criminalisation/

2.   (n.d.).   *Law   and   Oppression.*Historic England.https://historicengland.org.uk/research/inclusive-heritage/lgbtq-heritage-project/law-and-oppression/

Love Revealed

Start Reading the Series that Started it All...

Heath's shoulders ached as though the weight of the world rested upon them. Well, the weight of Christine's future anyway. His niece needed a husband. As her guardian, he had to ensure she made the best possible match. His brother would have expected nothing less. He ran his finger along the collar of his shirt to relieve the sensation of slow strangulation.

It was hard to say which was more choking—delving back into society in order to marry off his ward, his shirt and cravat, or the duty of filling in for his dead brother.

Absorbed in watching the young buck escorting Christine into the next dance, he missed his opportunity to avoid the pack of women bearing down on him. Lady Albright and her winsome daughter lead the charge, followed smartly by Ladies Winthorp and Rollings, widows of dubious reputation.

Gritting his teeth Heath bowed as the gaggle came to a full stop before him. The pungent mélange of their perfumes punched him in the face. "Good evening Ladies, Mademoiselle."

"Good evening Lord Heathington." They chorused back to him and curtsied. The two widows dipped so low he thought they might not make it back up. There was also the very real possibility one of them might dislodge a precariously perched breast. Heath struggled to control the curl of his upper lip.

Clearing her throat, Lady Albright shoved her daughter forward. "You remember my daughter Clarisse? You met her in the spring at your cousin's house party."

Repressing a long suffering sigh, he nodded. "Of course. How do you fare, Miss Albright?" A stealthy glance around the room held no salvation.

"My lord, I am well." Her limpid smile and shy darting glances were off-putting under the best of circumstances.

Elbowing the poor girl out of the way, the wicked widows pressed their bosoms against each of his arms. "Lord Heathington, we missed you at the Hampton house party last month," Lady Winthrop purred and pressed closer. Lady and Miss Albright stood by, mouths agape. Not unlike the trout he sometimes fished for at his country estate.

"I'm afraid I had another engagement that required my attention." He stepped back and attempted to disengage from the slavering pack of women. "I believe I see my cousin, please excuse me." He made his escape.

How much was one man expected to contend with?

He was at cross purposes with every matchmaking mama and horny widow in the immediate vicinity. Marriage was of no interest, and dalliances too risky. No, he'd continue to manage his sexual needs at The Market, with a woman who could handle his baser desires. It worked better that way. No chance of miscalculated expectations ruining things, or of terrifying an unsuspecting lady, and no chance Christine could be tainted.

"Heath." The soft voice of his cousin's wife intruded on his brood. "You look upset. Is anything wrong?" Cassandra asked, a worried furrow forming between her eyes.

"Not at all. I was just mulling over a few things after a quick escape from a gaggle of enterprising ladies. I am pleased to see you here. I take it Dorian is with you?"

"Here I am, Heath." Dorian joined them. "I see my wife has found you again. I wonder if I ought to be jealous." They all laughed at that silly idea. Heath and Cassandra attempted making a match of it years ago, before he recognized his darker sexual needs. Then she met Dorian and fell in love.

"No, I am just glad to see you here. You know how much I enjoy these occasions." He flashed a wry smile and clapped his cousin on the back. "Shall we go find ourselves and the lady a drink? I believe Christine will be busy for the next few dances."

They proceeded to the main ballroom and looked around at the swirling mix of gowns. The wave of heat slapped Heath in the face, followed in rapid succession by the less appetizing odor of bodies and perfume. A sudden burning need gripped him, the need to inhale the scent of Kat. Her smell always lingered on him for hours after they were together at The Market.

Tonight she would be his, nobody else's.

His jaw clamped shut as the idea of her in the arms of another man annoyed him. Shaking off the foolish notion he excused himself and edged around the ballroom. Fresh air might be in order.

As he neared the potted plants in the corner, Heath spotted Lady Drummond. Rather plain, with her simple bun, pale cheeks, and brown eyes. Forever alone in the corner, it was rare that she danced. In fact, he wasn't sure he had ever seen her dance. Doomed to be left withering on the fringe of society, she was too old to be among the girls vying for husbands, and too young to be welcomed by the matrons who eyed her with suspicion. Not to mention the general scandal of her husband's death. He pitied her, often spent time discussing plants with her so she might feel less alone. It was time well spent in kindness to her and to himself.

He sidled up next to her and dropped to the bench she occupied. "Lady Drummond, I see you're taking a break from the crush." He nodded toward the dancers whirling past. A faint but familiar scent teased his nose. Sweet and soft. Carnations. Kat. His fixation with the mysterious woman was starting to bleed into every aspect of his life. He gave himself a mental shake and focused on the isolated widow at his side.

"Lord Heathington. Yes, I needed to catch my breath."

She lied. Her very calm even breathing and dry brow indicated the truth. Being a gentleman, he let her keep her dignity by accepting her statement in silence. "Did you attend the last lecture at the Botanical Society? Dr. Luden holds some interesting views on the hybridization of roses."

Dorian and Cassandra drew his eye as they weaved past to join the other dancers. The starched woman next to him recaptured his attention as her crisp accents broke through his distraction.

"I did. I was most disappointed in his lack of interest of splicing plants together to make the most of their strengths. Why wouldn't you want a rose that could grow in cooler climes and resist pests? Why must everything always be about superficial wants? Why not make a better quality flower? A stronger one? Not just a pretty thing to look at."

Heath noticed a sparkle in her eye as her passion for plants broke through her reserve. She bordered on pretty. That was not how he saw her under normal circumstances. "I completely agree. Strength is more useful than beauty alone. It is very short sighted of Luden." *And men in general.*

Lady Drummond nodded in agreement and they fell into a comfortable silence as they observed the dancers go by. The music ended and he rose.

"It was lovely to chat with you, as always, Lord Heathington."

"I do enjoy our botanical discussions. Perhaps you would be inclined to continue them on the dance floor?" To be honest, he could not explain why he asked Lady Drummond to dance. Maybe he was intrigued to feel her in his arms? Curiosity got the better of him. Would she light up while dancing as she did when discussing plants? He wanted to know.

Surprise flitted across her features. "You want to dance? With me?"

"I don't bite, my Lady," he assured her as he stood with his hand out.

Her brow creased in confusion before her manners re-asserted themselves. "Of course not. Thank you." A blush turned her face a rosy shade of pink, which made her look rather pretty. Again, his perceptions of her were challenged.

A waltz was starting as they walked toward the floor. A gentle tug on his arm indicated her hesitation. Ignoring her reticence, he shifted them on to the floor and swept her into his arms. Her lips parted, cheeks still a bit flushed. *Might she look similar in the throes of passion?* Her soft scent of carnations teased him again as the music began. He reminded himself he was heading to The Market later to see Kat. Perchance he needed an extra visit this month, without a doubt he was in need of some release.

Katherine looked up into the soft gray eyes of the Earl of Heathington and tried to imagine what was running through the man's head asking her to dance. What could he possibly want with her? Then he spun them into the lilting flow of the waltz. He swept them around the floor with effortless ease despite her awkwardness. She had not waltzed with a man since her dead husband had courted her, normally she was lucky to dance a Quadrille on occasion. Wary of her partner's motives, she held herself away from his body with an unnatural stiffness.

"Do you enjoy the waltz, Lady Drummond?" His warm baritone caused her heart to skip a beat.

"I do, my lord, but I am afraid I neither dance often nor with a partner as capable as you." Where had those words come from? The flames of mortification licked at her cheeks. Tucking her head down, she caught notes of lime and sandalwood. She breathed deep, absorbing the entrancing scent.

"Thank you. I find few women are capable of truly giving up control of the dance to their partner. Without trust, the waltz is but a battle of wills instead of the beautiful exchange it is meant to be."

Peeking up, her breath caught at his sensual smile. It was not the one she'd seen—always from across the room behind the plants—bestowed on countless ladies. This one held a warmth, an honesty, his usual grin lacked. Yet, it was too brash to believe he might intend anything but friendship. The rigidity eased as he continued to sweep her around the floor. "I appreciate the chance to experience such mastery of the dance."

"I always find you are full of excellent conversation, which only enhances an excellent waltz."

The heat sweeping across her cheeks had little to do with the exertion of dancing and everything to do with the kindness paid her by her dance partner. And still, she waited for the criticism or backhanded comment that inevitably came from her peers. Nothing. No rude comment or dry observation about how solid she was, stony. Instead they returned to their previous discussion of hybridization.

They made one last sweep around the floor before the music ended with a flourish, followed by a handsome bow from the Earl. Katherine dipped a curtsey, resting her fan over her breasts shielding them from view. Holding her body rigid in an attempt to hide her ridiculous thoughts, she rested her hand on his arm as he led her back to her bench in the bushes.

"Thank you for an exquisite waltz." She could not look up at Lord Heathington from her seat. Her gaze stayed glued to her hands in her lap. A flood of awareness and angst caused her to shrink back within her shell.

"You are welcome. I hope you enjoy the rest of your evening." Then he was gone.

Enjoy the rest of her evening? Not a probable scenario as the remainder of it would be split between the bench she occupied at present and the retiring room. His departure was for the best. She had no desire to forfeit control of her life to a husband ever again, not even to have someone to wake up next to in the morning. Men were not to be trusted. They wooed you, charmed you, lured you in and then like a Venus

Flytrap devoured you. Regardless, it was a non-issue when the lone man who spoke to her was Lord Heathington, and he was nothing but an acquaintance.

He danced with her. He talked plants with her. He didn't court her. He showed no interest in courting anyone for that matter. So the chances of her ever rolling over to look into his soft gray eyes in the pink haze of dawn was somewhere south of her becoming Queen.

An independent widow, her life was filled by books and research. When her physical needs became too great, she would sneak off to The Market to find release. The shame she experienced her first time had come close to paralyzing her. She had lain like limp cloth as the masked man above her rutted until he came.

Fortune smiled when she stumbled across The Hall of Windows.

Behind each pane of glass a set of curtains could be opened allowing the occupants to display themselves. Transfixed by the first couple, she had stared until her eyes burned with the need to blink. The woman writhed beneath the man as he pumped his cock into her body. Then suddenly they shifted, and she was straddling his hips bouncing up and down as her breasts followed.

It was erotic to watch.

With cheeks flaming she had fled, but soon after returned with the desire to experience the kind of pleasure that couple had shared. The Market had become her secret shame and greatest pleasure. Nobody would believe the retiring Lady Drummond enjoyed the pleasures of the flesh, and she intended to keep it that way.

A glance around the ballroom reminded her there was no reason for her to stay. She was invited out of some strange loyalty to her dead parents, or perchance morbid curiosity. Attending the few events she was invited to, gave her a chance to be out. However, over the years it seemed she was more tolerated than welcome. Maybe it was time to cease the charade and skip society all together? Well, except for the Clarendon's dinner. She'd at least attend their small gathering since they were such close friends of her parents.

The exit of the ballroom was in sight when she collided with a gentleman.

"Excuse me, Madame." As he turned to look at whom he had bumped into, recognition flashed before his face drew blank.

"No, it was—" before she could finish her mumbled words, he turned his back on her and walked away. No pleasantries, it was a simple and succinct cut once he recognized who she was.

Lord Drummond's proclivities were not precisely a secret, but his failing health had been impossible to hide. That he had contracted syphilis became the best-known secret in London. Of course, it was assumed she had the disease, too. Her apparent health was no deterrent to a juicy bit of speculation by the Ton. As though they expected her to suddenly leap off a balcony and wrench her hair out raving like a lunatic. She was aware of the truth. The visions appeared at the end when the victim was too weak to do much of anything but mumble in their delirium.

Resigned, she forged ahead gaining the foyer of the house where one matron, standing near the ladies retiring room, whispered to another. The damning words husband and syphilis floated on the fetid air of too many bodies packed into too small a space. It was cloying. Suffocating. More so than the truth of what she had known but refused to acknowledge. Katherine needed to escape more than ever as the horrid suspicions of her peers nipped at her heels.

Outside, she gained the cool night air and drew in a fresh, cleansing breath. As the burst of oxygen hit her lungs, all she wanted was to forget. Forget society, forget her dead husband, and forget who she was. The Market was where she turned to do that, and she was due there tonight. She tried not to be a frequent visitor. It would be easy to become addicted to forgetting, and that was something she could not afford to do for long. Remembering was important if she were to avoid making the same mistakes again.

Thankfully her carriage appeared, allowing her to escape into its dark confines. She would be more careful in considering which events she attended in the future. Indeed, it was quite obvious her invitations stemmed from morbid curiosity.

The coach rolled on as she allowed her depressing notions to float around her. She was alone in the world, her parents dead before her husband. For five years she'd had no one to turn to but herself. Independence was easy when there was no other choice.

Finish the rest of the story...

Love Revealed (The Market Series, Book 1)

Read the Whole Series

His Wanton Marchioness
A Lustful Lords Novella

She waited her entire life to be married, and she refuses to let anyone interfere with her happiness...not even her new husband.

Elizabeth Grafton, the Marchioness of Carlisle just married the man of her dreams. Or he was. Now, he barely spends time with her. But most disturbing, he comes to her bed under the cloak of darkness—the man won't even light a candle!—and insists she keep her nightgown on until he leaves.

Alexander Grafton, the Marquess of Carlisle is deeply, madly in love with his wife. But, he wants to do things to her that a man could only do to his mistress. He's struggling to keep his baser instincts in check, and that was before his wife decided to seduce him. If she knew what he really wanted...she'd run away.

Armed with "professional" advice, Elizabeth sets out to thwart all of her husband's best intentions and show him just how shameless she can be. Can her wanton nature tempt her husband, or will he win their battle of wills?

His Hand-Me-Down Countess
Lustful Lords, Book 1
His brother's untimely death leaves him with an Earldom and a fiancée. Too bad he wants neither of them...

Theodora Lawton has no need of a husband. As an independent woman, she wants to own property, make investments and be the master of her destiny. Unfortunately, her father signed her life away in a marriage contract to the future Earl of Stonemere. But then the cad upped and died, leaving her fate in the hands of his brother, one of the renowned Lustful Lords.

Achilles Denton, the Earl of Stonemere, is far more prepared to be a soldier than a peer. Deeply scarred by his last tour of duty, he knows he will never be a proper, upstanding pillar of the empire. Balanced on the edge of madness, he finds respite by keeping a tight rein on his life, both in and out of the bedroom. His brother's death has left him with responsibilities he never wanted and isn't prepared to handle in the respectable manner expected of a peer.

Further complicating his new life is an unwanted fiancée who comes with his equally unwanted title. Saddled with a hand-me-down countess, he soon discovers the woman is a force unto herself. As he grapples with the burden of his new responsibilities, he discovers someone wants him dead. The question is, can he stay alive long enough to figure out who's trying to kill him while he tries to tame his headstrong wife?

His Hellion Countess

Lustful Lords, Book 2

A duty bound earl and a jewel thief might find forever if he can steal her heart...

Robert Cooper, the Earl of Brougham must marry in order to fulfill his duty to the title. He's decided on a rather mild mannered, biddable woman who most considered firmly on the shelf. But, her family is on solid financial ground and has no scandals attached to their name.

Lady Emily Winterburn, sister of the Earl of Dunmere, is not what she seems. With a heart as big as her wild streak she finds herself prepared to protect her brother from his bad choices, even if it means committing highway robbery. But marrying their way out of trouble is simply out of the question. What woman in her right mind would shackle herself to a man, let alone one of the notorious Lustful Lords?

Cooper's carefully laid plans are ruined once he must decide between courting his unwilling bride-to-be and taming the wild woman who tried to rob him—until he discovers they are one and the same. And when love sinks its relentless talons into his heart? He'll do anything to possess the wanton who fires his blood and touches his soul.

His Scandalous Viscountess

Lustful Lords, Book 3

Once upon a time, a boy and a girl fell in love...but prestige, power, and a shameful secret drove them apart.

Julia fled abroad after the death of her husband, Lord Wallthorpe. She has finally returned to England, but little has changed.

Except for her.

As a dowager marchioness, Julia lives and loves where she pleases. And the obnoxious son of her dead husband does not please. But what can an independent woman do? Why, create a scandal, of course!

Viscount Wolfington is no stranger to the wagging tongues of the ton. Between being a Lustful Lord and the scandal of his birth, he learned long ago that society had little use for him. So when he walks into The Market and finds the woman who once stole his heart being auctioned for a night of debauchery, he jumps at another chance to hold her—even for just a single night.

As Julia and Wolf unravel their pasts, will villainy win again, or will love finally conquer all?

His Not-So-Sweet Marchioness
Lustful Lords, Book 4
He's shrouded in shame, fighting with his demons in the shadows. Until she sets her sights on him...

Mrs. Rosalind Smith once followed her heart and love to the battlefield and left a widow. Spending the remainder of her life alone is enough... until she meets a man who's need for pain sparks an answering flame deep within her soul.

Matthew Derby, the Marquess of Flintshire is a fighter, it is all he's known since childhood. Throwing his fists is the only way to keep his need for pain at bay, and a certain gentle woman off his mind. She deserves a better man than him—Lord or not. Though when faced with the prospect of losing Ros, Flint realizes he has found something to fight for...something to live for.

To Ros' dismay, everyone around her believes her demeanor too sweet for someone like Flint. When his world begins to unravel and his dockside violence bleeds into the drawing room, a shocking family secret won't be the key to all the answers. Questions remain, can he solve the mystery, tame his dark needs, and still win Ros' heart?

His Reluctant Marchioness
Lustful Lords, Book 5

A notorious woman must rely on the devil himself for help. Too bad she learned long ago never to trust anyone...

Frank Lucifer is having one hell of a week. His gambling hell is short staffed after firing his floor manager, and his half-brother has offered him a title—one he doesn't need or want. Then the woman he's obsessed with dismisses him from her bed, and the problem is he doesn't know who the hell she is.

Mistress Lash has her hands full. Her apprentice is missing under sinister circumstances, and Scotland Yard refuses to lift a finger. A liaison with Frank Lucifer—however attractive she finds him—is something she no longer has time for.

Besides, someone should take the arrogant rake down a peg or two.

She sets out to find her apprentice on her own, but everywhere she turns, up pops Lucifer. He's following her, and she's growing suspicious about why that is. When he suggests they join forces, she reluctantly agrees. After all, one should keep their friends close and their enemies closer... she's just not sure which he is. Yet.

Working together to find her missing apprentice, she worries about her ability to protect both her heart and her own secrets from the perceptive man. And as events play out, she must decide if Lucifer is the villain she is searching for... or just the devil who haunts her scorching hot dreams?

Other Books by Sorcha

The Market Series
Discover the series that started it all...
In this sizzling series The Market becomes the setting for Londoners of all walks of life to discover pleasure, lust, and even love. But can they do what is required to claim the ones they've fallen for?
Love Revealed (The Market, Book 1)
Love Redeemed (The Market, Book 2)
Love Reclaimed (The Market, Book 3)
The Market Series Books 1-3 (Boxed Set)
Love Requited (The Market, A Short Story)

The Lustful Lords
The Lustful Lords, a steamy historical romance series, focuses on a group of Victorian London lords who regularly gather at The Market, a notorious brothel, to indulge in hedonistic delights. As the series progresses, each lord will discover a woman who is his match both in and out of the bedroom.
Start the series now with a FREE copy of the first book in this historical romance series with His Hand-Me-Down Countess

His Wanton Marchioness (A Lustful Lords Novella)
His Hand-Me-Down Countess (Lustful Lords, Book 1)
His Hellion Countess (Lustful Lords, Book 2)
His Scandalous Viscountess (Lustful Lords, Book 3)
His Not-So-Sweet Marchioness (Lustful Lords, Book 4)
His Reluctant Marchioness (Lustful Lords, Book 5)
Their Brazen Countess (Lustful Lords, Book 6)

One Night With A Cowboy

The One Night With A Cowboy series is a set of short stories linked by cowboys and Soul Mates Dating Service, a dating service with an uncanny ability to match up soul mates. These sizzling little treats are perfect for a quick hot read.

One Night With A Cowboy Books 1-5 (Boxed Set)
Claiming His Cowgirl (Book 1)
Taking Her Chance (Book 2)
A Cowboy's Christmas Wish (Book 3)
Roping His Cowboy (Book 4)
Stealing His Cowgirl's Heart (Book 5)

About the Author

Sorcha Mowbray is a mild mannered office worker by day...okay, so she is actually a mouthy, opinionated, take charge kind of gal who bosses everyone around; but she definitely works in an office. At night she writes romance so hot she sets the sheets on fire! Just ask her slightly singed husband.

She is a longtime lover of historical romance, having grown up reading Johanna Lindsey and Judith McNaught. Then she discovered Thea Devine and Susan Johnson. Holy cow! Heroes and heroines could do THAT? From there, things devolved into trying her hand at writing a little smexy. Needless to say, she liked it and she hopes you do too!

Find all of Sorcha's social media links at
link.sorchamowbray.com/bio

~

or scan the QR Code

Made in the USA
Columbia, SC
10 September 2024